LADDERS TO THE MOON

RUTH GARRETT

This story is dedicated to all those seeking to live their lives in authenticity while sharing the gifts they brought to the feast of life!

✦

Also by Ruth Garrett

Nonfiction

Who Says You Have To Be Nice?

Resilience – Are You a Carrot, an Egg or Coffee Beans?

Journeying Back Toward Your Essential Self

Pack Light & Move Forwards – Your Ideal Life

For Children

The Adventures of Suzie: Ups and Downs and Helping Hands

(illustrated by darci-que™)

Acknowledgements

To all the wonderful individuals (whether they have brought chaos or calm) who have and continue to support me while I journey toward becoming the best version of myself, moment to moment.

Dr. Michael Potterton, Professor of History at Maynooth University, who helped considerably with the research on the historical elements of Trim. He's the author of *Medieval Trim: History and Archaeology* (2005) and editor of *Uncovering Medieval Trim: Archaeological Excavations in and Around Trim, Co. Meath,* as well as *The Hill of Tara* (2007).

To my wonderful friend Kerri. The constancy of your support has made such a difference to my life. I am both humbled and grateful.

Ladder to the Moon is the name of a 1958 Georgia O'Keeffe painting, conveying a powerful vision of the infinite possibilities of life.

"I've been absolutely terrified every moment of my life—and I've never let it keep me from doing a single thing I wanted to do."

–Georgia O'Keeffe

FOREWORD

It is with a mixture of sadness, gratitude, and admiration that we present to the world this final work by Ruth Garrett—a woman whose intellect, resilience, and spirit touched so many. Ruth, a trailblazer in the field of Human Resource Management, a writer of self-help books, and a tireless advocate for the empowerment of women, has left behind a legacy that will continue to inspire future generations. This book, however, is something entirely different—her first foray into fiction, a powerful feminist fantasy that encapsulates her unwavering belief in the strength and resilience of women.

Ruth entrusted us—her family—with the manuscript for this book. It was a dream of hers to see it published, and we took on the responsibility of ensuring her final words would be shared with the world. In a way, this book is more than just a work of fiction; it is a reflection of her life and her struggles, a poignant culmination of her journey as a woman who fought to overcome adversities both personal and professional. She faced many challenges throughout her life, but her final and most difficult battle was with ovarian cancer—a battle she fought with the same grace, strength, and determination that defined her.

Through her decades of writing, Ruth offered women the tools to find their voices, to stand up for themselves, and to reclaim their power in a world that often sought to silence them. This book continues that mission, but it does so in a different way. In this tale, readers are taken on a time-traveling journey, witnessing the lives of three women who, despite the oppressive weight of a misogynistic patriarchy, fight to retain their spirits, minds, and bodies. It is a story that speaks to the heart of Ruth's lifelong commitment to ensuring women's voices are heard, no matter the cost.

As we publish this book posthumously, we do so with deep reverence for Ruth's memory, and with the hope that her children, grandchildren, and the generations to come will find in these pages a reflection of the strength, wisdom, and fierce independence that defined her life. This has truly been a labour of love, and we are honored to bring her final work to life.

This book is her gift to all those who continue the fight for freedom, equality, and the empowerment of women everywhere.

With love and respect,
Phil Garrett and Brenda Martin

INTRODUCTION

Dear Reader,

Welcome to the pages of *Ladders to the Moon*, a profound and evocative journey that intertwines the threads of past and present, reality and imagination, into a tapestry of resilience, self-discovery, and hope. This novel, a labor of love dedicated to those who seek to live authentically and share their unique gifts with the world, invites you to step into the life of Tara O'Connell—a woman whose story resonates with the echoes of countless souls who have faced adversity and emerged transformed.

From the shadowed corners of a troubled childhood in Toronto to the windswept hills of Ireland and the vibrant shores of Marseille, Tara's odyssey is one of courage and awakening. Her encounters with the enigmatic Mamó, the spirited Dana, and the steadfast Cado are more than mere chance; they are mirrors reflecting the inner strength she has yet to fully embrace. Through her, we explore the extraordinary lives of ordinary women across the ages—women like Clarice and Ama—whose struggles and triumphs ripple through time, challenging the illusion of linear existence.

This story is enriched by the wisdom of history and the arts, drawing inspiration from the likes of Georgia O'Keeffe and the historical insights of Dr. Michael Potterton. It is a testament to the power of intuition, as illuminated by the documentary Innsaei, and a celebration of the Celtic heritage that pulses beneath Tara's journey. Yet, at its heart, Ladders to the Moon is a personal narrative—a call to recognize the divine within ourselves and to take responsibility for the paths we choose.

As you turn these pages, I encourage you to listen to the whispers of your own soul. Tara's story is not just hers; it is a reflection of the universal quest for meaning, the courage to break free from the bindings of others' expectations, and the joy of crafting a life that sings with authenticity. May this book inspire you to climb your own ladder to the moon—to reach for the infinite possibilities that await when you dare to be your truest self.

With gratitude and hope,
Ruth Garrett, PhD

CHAPTER ONE

Toronto, Canada, 1988

THE MAN LAY slumped in his recliner. Empty cans of beer cluttered the floor. An Export A cigarette teetered precariously between his fingers.

In Tara's mind, a vision flashed of her father being consumed in the combustible union of smoldering ash and orange shag carpet. She debated whether to act. But this image, like the others she'd known so far in her brief life, compelled her to act. She tiptoed to him, bent over his slumbering expanse of flesh, and attempted to remove the danger from his hand.

He jolted awake. His face registered a childlike, fallible confusion. For a moment, father and daughter met as equals. Two people with no idea how to navigate this adventure called "life." Two souls attempting to figure out who they were. As quickly as that sense of knowing came, it evaporated.

His left hand smashed down on the lever of the chair, bringing him to an abrupt sitting position. He catapulted himself to an upright stance, mere inches away from her tense body.

"Bloody hell, you little idiot. What do you think you're doing? You scared the Jaysus out of me!"

Tara's eyes focused on his brown slippers planted on the orange rug. "Sorry. I thought the cigarette was falling from your fingers and was trying to put it in the ashtray."

"What, you think your old man can't handle his own bloody cigarette? Who the Christ do you think you are, my savior or something?"

Her father's frame obliterated the scant light that penetrated the curtains and dust-streaked windowpanes. He was so close she could smell his acrid breath.

"Or did little madam have another one of her visions?" He searched his daughter's face for a sign of confirmation. "I knew it! What, you saw your dear old dad being fried to a crisp? Did you envision my flesh being seared from my bones, like a stuffed pig on a spit? Oh," he said in a taunting voice, "you did, didn't you? And you were trying to save me. How damned noble of you!" A gleam appeared in the dead blackness of her father's eyes. "Ever wonder what it feels like to be that pig?"

"No, Dadaí, I haven't." The sweat on her brow betrayed the calmness in her voice.

Her father glanced with calculated intention at the embers of the cigarette still clamped between his fingers. Before Tara could move, he had her right hand in a vice-like grip. Without hesitation, he stubbed the glowing end of his cigarette into the freckled innocence of her flesh.

She was eight years old and already knew not to cry out. It would only prolong the manic fury of his assault.

The ferocity of his attack vanquished the embers. Once his rage was quenched, her father stared as if seeing Tara for the first time.

"You make me so mad," he said, his voice thick and weary. "You have no gift of 'sight.' Why do you insist on such flights of fancy? You are like the rest of us, girl. You are not special."

Tara trembled with fear and rage. She perceived her parents were treating her wrong, but she wasn't sure how or why.

"I'm sorry, Dadaí," she stammered. "I will—"

"Child, I don't want you to be sorry," he said as the full force of his open hand connected with her cheek. "I asked when you're going to stop doing things that force me to punish you. When will you do as you're told?"

When the black dots receded from her vision, she hesitated for fear of offering the wrong response. "I will do whatever you want me to do, Dadaí. I promise."

Her father's expression softened a little. The veins on the side of his head stopped pulsating.

"Well, for starters, fetch me some tablets. You have given me a flaming headache!"

She ran to the bathroom to get the tablets for her father, her disfigured hand stinging with searing pain.

As she lay in bed that night, Tara peered into the darkness of her bedroom closet. Two things she believed in her heart: One, her actual parents must be somewhere beyond the recesses of that closet. It was the only explanation for the pitiful nature of her life. And two, although these "fake" parents mistreated her, she was powerless to do anything about it. She was convinced that God didn't know or wasn't bothered by her circumstances. What horrible thing had she done that even God didn't care?

Tara dug her nails deep into the soft flesh of her hands, feeling helpless and alone. The flush of rage grew hot on her face. In that moment, she believed no one would save her. She rolled onto her side, trying to eradicate her mounting fury. Her father's words jangled like the unwelcome chime of the bells before Sunday mass. Each word stung, fueling the inferno within, like gasoline.

He yelled repeatedly, always casting blame on her. "You could show some gratitude for all the things I do for you."

Unsure what all those "things" he did might be, Tara had to concede that perhaps she was wrong and those "things" were being done. Restless and somewhat repentant, she flipped onto her stomach. No wonder she got the treatment she did. It was clear she wasn't a very grateful daughter! She must try harder to please others. But still, her anger raged! Tears coursed down her cheeks and dripped from her chin. She vowed to never share her visions with anyone.

She sensed a familiar presence, one which often lit the dour darkness of her young life, reminding her she was never alone. As far back as she could remember, her two nocturnal friends came to visit. As time passed, they became her closest companions. She didn't know their names. It didn't seem to matter. They spent their time together exploring one another's lives, playing, and giggling. Fat tears of joy rolled down her face when they came. Their visits helped her forget the grimness of her reality for a little while.

Sometimes their visits were challenging. One friend was quick to anger and would fight about who won whatever game they played. Tara would become angry, too, annoyed that the little girl had to win at all costs. When she didn't, she always lashed out. Tara suspected that the other friend also suffered a surge of anger at the cruelty of the other girl but somehow managed to keep calm, smile, and move the game along.

Tara had never told her parents about these friends who came to her when she needed them. They would have laughed, called her stupid or crazy, or they would have battered her to beat the madness out of her.

Tara swore never to reveal her secret. Besides, it felt good to have something and someone all to herself.

CHAPTER TWO

Chiswick, London, December 2015

WITH MONET-LIKE SOFTNESS, the morning light radiated through the stained glass adorning the top of the curved bow of the bedroom window. The sun's fluorescent glow illuminated Tara's volcanic shock of red hair as it spilled over the pillow beside her.

The anonymity of sleep attempted to drag her back to her nocturnal wanderings while reassuring smells of familiarity came from the kitchen, just beyond the boundary of her current sanctuary. She opened her eyes to the dawn of a new day, her lips curled up with contented happiness.

After a languid, luxurious stretch, Tara gazed at the finished manuscript on the antique night table to her left while an eclectic chorus of birds camouflaged the drone of city traffic outside.

Her smile broadened.

So much for my critics and disbelievers, she mused.

She had landed a deal with one of the largest publishing houses in the UK. Well, Guy wouldn't agree with that, of course. He would say it was all his doing. And if she were honest, she realized it *had* been his extensive connections that brought about the deal of a lifetime.

Of course, she appreciated all that he'd done for her. No one in her life before Guy had stepped in and taken every opportunity to support and cater to her needs, although she drew the line at his constant offer to buy the clothes that would correct her severe "wardrobe malfunction." Guy always accompanied the comment with impish laughter, but she knew he meant it.

Yawning and without hurry, she extended her arms above her head until her hands clasped in unity. Life was so deliciously wonderful she wanted to pinch herself to ensure this wasn't a dream.

She harkened back to when it all began. She had walked into Guy's office twelve months earlier and brazenly asked what it would take for her to become a published author, dropping the first draft of her novel, *Beyond the Rim,* on his desk.

"Are you insane? Who do you think you are bursting into my office? Do you know who I am?"

"Yes, I do." Her words carried more bravado than she felt. "You're the man who is going to help me get my book published."

Cool, brooding, metallic-gray eyes stared at her, incredulous. Sweat crept over her shaking body. After several agonizing minutes, Guy looked from her face to the manuscript and back. He started to howl with laughter.

Tara was surprised and dazzled by the brilliant whiteness of his teeth. It was in that moment she fell in love.

"All right-y, then." He rose from his leather chair, well-honed muscles rippling beneath his shirt. "We'd better go to lunch and discuss your masterpiece."

As Tara reveled in the memory of their first encounter, Guy popped his head around the door jamb. "Come on, love,' up and at 'em. Breakfast isn't going to eat itself. And we have a big day today."

She kneeled seductively on the edge of the bed. "Join me, and it'll be an even bigger day."

"Well, that is a deliciously tempting offer, but have you forgotten we meet with BBC4 in two hours? Not everyone gets the chance to turn their book into a miniseries. Now hustle up, buttercup, and get your arse out of bed." Guy did a one-eighty and turned to the kitchen.

Tara couldn't help yelling after him. "Has anyone told you lately you have an arse to die for?"

"You, my dear, every day!"

As she bounced out of bed, Guy rushed back into the room. "Change your mind?"

"Don't be tiresome, pet. Just wanted to remind you to let me do the talking today. You're a brilliant writer but a crap negotiator. It will go much better if I handle it."

Tara let out a sigh to acknowledge his estimation of her bargaining skills. "All right! You know best."

Guy's lips curled upward into a smile. He pivoted and strode away.

CHAPTER THREE

Chiswick, London, December 2015

GUY WAS SILENT on the ride back from their meeting. Tara's unmerciful stomach churned as they stepped from the taxi. The graceful golden dance of autumnal leaves floating to the ground on their tree-lined street was usually enough to warm her heart and lift her spirits. But not today!

She glanced sideways to gauge Guy's mood but couldn't read his expression. She clasped her bag tighter and watched him as they entered the flat.

The moment he closed the door, Guy turned on her. "Why did you interrupt me? I could have negotiated at least ten percent more if you'd just kept quiet!"

Shocked by this sudden explosion of anger, she stared at his contorted face. "Sorry, my love, but I didn't like the direction they wanted to take with my book."

"Don't 'my love' me!"

Tara had caught glimpses of Guy's temper. He would detonate if he didn't get his way or someone didn't do as he requested, but until this moment, his wrath was never directed at her.

She tried to placate him by saying something to dampen the flame. "I'm sorry, Guy, I should have trusted your judgment. You're better at this game. I should have left the negotiations to you."

That was enough to burst the boil of his rage. He grabbed hold of both her wrists with unnecessary force. "I just care about looking after you. You understand I only want what's best for you?"

For the first time in their relationship, she hesitated before speaking. "I love you, Guy, and I'm so grateful for all that you do for me. Honestly, I am!"

He exhaled and released his grip on her wrists. "Go on, make us a cuppa."

Like a dutiful child, Tara went to the kitchen, eager to bring swift and peaceful closure to what had transpired. As the kettle hissed and gurgled, it occurred to her she would need to use caution before she spoke. In the space of an hour, she had become far less confident about their relationship. Did she actually know who Guy was? Had she misjudged him?

CHAPTER FOUR

Chiswick, London, December 2015

NAKED FROM THE waist up, Guy wiped steam from the bathroom mirror. Sex usually relieved his pent-up frustration and anger, but not tonight. He was still pissed at Tara. She had no right to direct the meeting earlier with BBC4. For the first time in their relationship, she attempted to usurp his authority over her literary career, and he didn't appreciate it.

His hands shook violently, as they always did when he experienced stress or felt a loss of control. The open tube of toothpaste he was holding slipped from his grasp.

The tremors were a constant reminder of his vulnerability. They started when he was eight, just after they shipped him off to boarding school. Guy clenched his fists and tried to control the barrage of images and feelings surrounding the kaleidoscope of abuse that he'd endured at the hands of those older and stronger than him.

He yanked at his pajama bottoms. How dare she undermine his role in their relationship? From now on, he vowed to keep a much firmer grasp on Tara's thoughts and actions.

CHAPTER FIVE

Chiswick, London, May 2016

IT WAS SIX months since Guy sealed the latest deal with BBC4. Tara was less free with how she expressed herself and much more conscious of her interactions with Guy. She went out of her way to placate his desires. It seemed to work. Their life together, on the surface, was back to "normal." He returned to being his attentive, agreeable self while she worked on her second manuscript.

Guy envisioned a precise structure, direction, and content for the book. The challenge Tara faced was that she wasn't enamored with any of it. As he hovered to make sure she followed his advice, she felt like she was falling into a dark abyss, a space where words failed to form meaningful sentences, never mind paragraphs or pages.

That day was no different. After three hours, the only illumination came from the screen of her computer, its blinking cursor taunting her from the empty page.

The intention was to write an intriguing narrative about the journey of the Celts from the sixth century BC to the sixth century AD. She tried to discuss her challenges with Guy many times, but he refused to listen. He insisted that conquering writer's block was part of the process.

He popped his head around the corner of the den. "How goes the battle?"

Tara let her guard down, confiding, "I'm losing the will to create, not to mention any belief that I might ever write something others will find interesting again. To be honest, researching and writing an account of the Celts' migration doesn't spark my curiosity."

He stood as close to her as the back of the chair would allow, massaging her shoulders to exorcise the kinks. "Tara, stop being so dramatic. You know that the deal with the BBC4 rests on you coming up with an intriguing storyline. Stop whining and start writing."

"But, Guy, I have written nothing plausible for at least two weeks. I need a break to allow the creative juices to flow again. And being cooped up with you checking on me every two seconds doesn't help." Even before she turned, Tara knew she'd upset the delicate balance that risked fueling his temper. She tried to claw back the peace between them. "Not that I don't appreciate your attention, I meant…"

The veins in his neck began to jackhammer. "Bollocks, don't use writer's block as a 'get-out-of-jail-free' card! You're trying to avoid the daily slog the writing process demands."

"But —"

"What is it? Has your earlier success gone to your head? Well, the money from that won't last forever. You need to create and create now. Our agreement with BBC4 is the ticket to a veritable pot of gold."

Tara struggled to find the right words. "I am not afraid of hard work. It's the subject I'm not feeling. It's like I'm being pulled between my desire to create and the fear that my lack of interest will bring nothing but blank pages."

Face crimson, Guy glared at her. "You've been fighting me ever since I agreed to the deal. Why the hell can't you just do what I ask? Is that so hard?"

"I'm not fighting you, Guy. I am trying to express my truth."

"Your truth! Oh, for God's sake! What a load of crap. Well, listen up. The truth of the matter is that whatever you think of the subject, you signed a contract with BBC4 and me to deliver a quality product within nine months, of which you have wasted almost two-thirds. So, get busy and write."

"But—"

"No more buts. Now get to work. I have to go out."

"Where?"

"I have to meet with Charlotte to go over some promotional details. Don't wait up. This could take a while."

After Guy exploded from the den, the exhaustion she held at bay for the last few months crept over her, sinking into every tendon, ligament, fiber, and muscle of her body, evolving into a cold, gray numbness.

She wished she could crawl into the safety of her bed and never leave it. A vague and distant vision of a peace she'd never experienced in her day-to-day life flitted across her consciousness, filling her heart with longing and desire. She tried to cling to its warming comfort, but it slipped from her grasp and sank like a dead weight into the abyss that was her relationship with Guy.

What had seemed like an ideal life with him at the start was disintegrating into ever-increasing periods of petty arguments, sulking, the silent treatment, and less-than-tender make-up sex.

And then there was Charlotte, a personal assistant Guy hired three months earlier. Their promotional meetings were growing longer and more frequent as time passed.

Tara learned that before they met, Guy was a well-known womanizer. At get-togethers with his friends, someone inevitably quipped, "Wow, Tara must be one hell of a lover for you to take on the monotony of monogamy!"

It was all too overwhelming. Guy was right about one thing. She signed a contract and pledged to complete the manuscript on time. To do that, she knew she must get away.

Tara turned back to her laptop. But instead of working on her manuscript, she typed the words "cottage for rent, isolated" and for a reason she couldn't fathom, she added "Ireland."

Two days later, over breakfast, Tara announced with trepidation that she had leased a cottage in Ireland.

"Good God! I apologized for losing it the other day. You can't just up and leave! You have a deadline to meet."

She sucked in her breath. "Guy, I can't write with you watching me like a hawk. I need to get away, clear my head, and write from a fresh perspective."

Her heart banged in her chest as Guy's face turned bright red, and his ice-cold, silent stare accelerated the pounding pressure in her chest. The warmth of the love she thought they'd shared a few months ago seemed like a fantasy.

"And where in Ireland is this cottage?"

Tara's resolve was in danger of evaporating, but her need to escape outweighed her need to pacify. "I'd rather not say." The tremor in her voice betrayed her confident words. "I'll call you when I'm settled."

"You can't just take off! I will not permit it. Do you hear me?"

The scrape of her chair across the black and white ceramic tiles was her response. She felt the molten heat of Guy's piercing stare follow her as she headed to the door and freedom.

CHAPTER SIX

Countryside near Dunsany, Ireland, early May 2016

TARA RUBBED HER right hand. The childhood wound always flared up on days when rain was forecast. She grimaced at the mottled, pitted ridges etched in the crescent between her thumb and index finger, one of the many telltale remnants of her father's tough love.

Crazed, chaotic rainfall had pulverized the parched earth into a mass of pureed mud ever since Tara's arrival in Ireland the previous week. The gusting vortices and diagonal sheets of slashing precipitation pummeled everything in sight, saturating the landscape.

Despite the weather, a brisk walk seemed like the best way to escape the dreariness of the rented cottage near Dunsany. Closing the ancient latch on the front door, Tara paused under the overhang of the slanting roof and peered at the rain-drenched day. She wondered if the purpose of rain might be to wash away the futility of life, heaven's attempt to cleanse the relentless tedium of day-to-day routine.

"Okay," she shouted, "I am going bonkers. Five euros and more thoughts like that will find me grabbing a coffee at Starbucks!"

Despite the weather, she'd fallen in love at first sight with the snug place, which crouched in the wild abandon of the untamed grassy knoll. Guy and her friends back in London wouldn't call it luxurious by any stretch of the imagination.

Hmm, Guy. Thinking about their relationship would have to keep for another day. A faint but clear voice whispered in her head, "Haven't you been saying that for a while now?"

"Oh, for God's sake, be quiet!" Tara fumed. "I can't deal with that right now!"

The voice was persistent. "So, when?"

"Not bloody now, all right?"

Eager to disembark from that train of thought, she shifted her focus to the cottage. The wooden window sash was flaking from years of neglect. Water pooled on its peeling ledge. The four tiny, rectangular, notebook-sized windowpanes were thick with filth and overrun by vine-like tendrils when she arrived. Her half-hearted attempts to clear them were slipshod.

The cottage offered many challenges. Tara had a constant battle with the ancient hearth when she tried to light a fire. Not one piece of clothing she owned was dry, and she had abandoned any effort to tame the havoc the damp created in her hair. Fortunately, other features of the place more than compensated.

Even though her home away from home was in the middle of nowhere and was costing her a small fortune in roaming charges, she loved that the only access was via a single, now-muddy track. This kept most two-legged visitors at bay and gave her the space to be in her own company.

Tara shivered as a wave of gloomy despair washed over her. To shake loose from its dark grasp, she examined the exterior of the cottage. Its slate roof shone like twinkling stars in the lukewarm heat of the spring day. The constant rain had transformed the stone of the exterior walls from gray into a kaleidoscope of glistening greens, browns, and blues.

She tilted her head to listen to the symphonic cornucopia of music being performed by her neighbors nesting in the copse of trees a short distance away. She was quite proud that in one short week she was able to distinguish between the strong, fluty "cherry dew, cherry dew, cherry dew" and "knee-deep, knee-deep" of a brown-bodied, black-spotted song thrush and the loud, bubbly string of notes, which resembled wolf whistles, offered by a chaffinch, or the rapid series of demure twitters by siskins, or the "teacher, teacher" of the great tit. A gray-collared dove flying overhead toward the wooded area beyond drew her attention to the sky. The shimmering black feathers of its outer wings did little to diminish the blandness of its pale body.

With these noisy neighbors, no one could say she was alone.

Tara watched the dove get smaller and smaller. She wished it were possible to transform into the likes of her winged friends. To cut through the air with wild abandon. To be whisked aloft on undulating gusts of wind. What joy, what freedom, to morph into a feathery adventurer, skimming the surface of land, sea, and sky, even for the briefest of moments.

A thought resurfaced: *If only.* If only she could leave life's absurdity behind, sweep away the introspective self-doubt and unrealistic expectations of others. If only she could let her need-to-do lists evaporate and replace them with the desires of her heart. These "if only" thoughts were draining her energy. Thirty-six years on this planet and she had yet to discover an escape from the drone of existence. She longed to experience the release of being sprung from her earthly shackles. She would rather be anywhere else than living this life. But here she was!

The choice to stay in Ireland was an unexplainable, spontaneous reaction to her desire to extricate herself from daily distractions and from Guy. To finish researching and writing her current book, she was convinced she needed a fresh perspective.

Why was she in this part of the world? Perhaps being in the land of the Celts might stimulate her creativity. So far, nothing had changed. The submission date for the first draft was fast approaching, and she'd written diddly squat.

It was the central theme of the story that eluded her. Every brilliant concept, idea, line, or paragraph that woke her up at night vanished by the time she turned on the bedside lamp and revved up her laptop, leaving her staring at a naked screen. The clarity of thought in her semi-conscious state faded to black when she was awake.

CHAPTER SEVEN

Countryside near Dunsany, Ireland, early May 2016

TARA STOOPED TO admire the profusion of yellow, white, and violet-blue wild pansies that covered the surrounding landscape. There was a heaviness in the air as she strolled along the now-familiar path, which ran parallel to a stream framed by reeds and shaded by oaks. As she stopped to catch her breath, she reflected that all forms of flowing water, whether streams, creeks, or rivers, were the liquid soul of their surroundings.

She laughed out loud. *Oh, my God! Why the hell can't I write like that?*

The sun peeked through the gray-black monotony of cloud cover in intermittent attempts to make its presence felt. When it succeeded, soft light pierced the shallow water, bathing it with glimmering, golden sparks. Tara's heart leaped each time as thousands of diamond orbs danced over the stream's surface.

Her spirit soared as she spied a carpet of fleshy, dark green, heart-shaped celandine leaves clinging to the banks. She wracked her brain to remember what Wordsworth had written about this narrow-petalled flower over two hundred years earlier. When his words came to her, she let them run over her tongue, hungry for their sweetness, not caring if anyone heard.

There is a Flower, the Lesser Celandine,
That shrinks, like many more,
from cold and rain;
And, at the first moment that the sun may shine,
Bright as the sun itself, 'tis out again!
Such simplicity, such beauty.

If only she could write like that!

To avoid falling into another pit of self-depreciation, she shifted her focus to a vast profusion of small pinkish-red flowers clustered along the hollow upright spikes of the butterbur. This little gem was native to Ireland and got its name from the now-defunct practice of wrapping churned butter in the expanse of its round leaves. Also known as the "plague flower," it contained properties that helped to remedy that affliction. She paused, wondering how she knew such things. It wasn't the first time that insights had sprung from nowhere and then receded in haste into the shadows.

The clouds were gearing up to deliver another serving of merciless and torrential outpourings. The oak to her left moaned as the wind whipped itself into a sudden frenzied state. Tara stooped to touch a delicate, pale, yellow primrose that flailed with the intensity of the growing breeze and matched the ferocity of her own internal chatter.

The persistent shrill ring of the phone lodged in her back pocket added to the chaos, and Tara braced herself against the storms growing around her.

CHAPTER EIGHT

TWO WOMEN SAT leaning against the creviced bark of an ancient oak in a grove a short distance from Dunsany. A massive gray wolf with piercing, ever-vigilant eyes lay next to the elder of the two.

For more years than they could count, these three had gathered on this spot. Sometimes to talk or to experience night transition into day. Or to sit in silence and contemplate. But on this day, the younger of the two had requested counsel.

The older woman watched as the younger attempted to relieve her frustration by scooping handfuls of hardened acorn shells and propelling them into the air. Before addressing the concerns of her angry companion, she stroked the softness of the canine's fur.

"Ah, Cado, it is a fine new day, is it not?"

She straightened and turned to the young woman who sulked beside her. "You must go, my child. Meet our new neighbor."

"But why me, Mamó? You're much better at this type of thing than I."

"Appealing to my vanity will not advance your cause, Dana. You have much to learn, and this young woman needs our help."

"Our help! But she has everything I do not. She has her freedom, opportunities to explore fresh places and enjoy wonderful experiences, while I am forever stuck here."

"May I remind you, dear one, that you chose this life. You agreed to live a life of service."

"I know, and most of the time, I am happy with that choice. But when I see people who cannot appreciate all they have and all that they are, I get a little crazy."

"That, dear one, is part of the process and an important aspect of your learning. Now go!"

CHAPTER NINE

HEAD DOWN, TARA ran full tilt while attempting to avoid the largest of the water-filled crevices. As she reached the cottage, without warning, she rammed into an intruder peering through one of the cottage windows and was knocked backward onto the sodden ground.

"What the frig!"

"Oh my, I am sorry." A woman extended her hand to help Tara to her feet.

Tara ignored the gesture of kindness, instead blurting out words in embarrassment and frustration. "Who are you, and what are you doing here snooping around?"

"Of course, you need an explanation. My name is Dana. Dana Pereiri. I live just down the track."

Tara's gaze swept over the small parking area just beyond the derelict garden to her left. She wanted to find out if this interloper had arrived by car, but she saw no signs of one.

Attempting to brush away the mud that clung to every shred of her clothing, Tara took in the measure of her unwanted guest.

Conspicuously tall and most likely in her mid-thirties, Dana had attempted to restrain thick, luscious waves of black hair with a length of hemp-like ribbon, without success. The creamy simplicity of her retro tunic accentuated her porcelain complexion and the thinness of her waist as it hugged the curve of her hips. But it was the ethereal grace of her face that was most striking. It reminded Tara of the angels in a Botticelli painting.

Mesmerized, Tara realized her casual observations had intensified into a full-blown stare. She shifted her gaze down and realized the woman wasn't wearing shoes. The complete picture took the edge off Tara's frustration. Her mood softened into a state bordering on welcome.

"Well, Dana Pereiri, what brings you to this neck of the woods?"

Dana's facial features relaxed. The soft vulnerability of her lips stretched into a smile, illuminating her eyes.

"Ah, my ma was forever telling me my curiosity would get the better of me! This property has been in our family for centuries, handed down from mother to daughter for eons past. There's a saying in my family that all the tears of pain and joy of the women who have gone before seeped into the soil of this, our ancestral home, and forever calls us to return to our roots. I'm visiting the neighborhood for a while and thought I would have a look-see about the place for old times' sake. Sorry if I put your heart crossways," Dana said, taking a breath. "And do you mind me asking who you might be? I didn't realize anyone was stopping here."

Stretching out a dirt-spattered hand, she answered, "My name is Tara. Tara O'Connell. I've rented the place for a couple of months while I write a book."

"O'Connell, you say. Did you know your last name means 'strong as a wolf'?"

"No, I didn't. I must admit to knowing very little about my heritage. My mother and father immigrated to Canada from Ireland before I was born and cut all ties to their past."

"Well, that's a fret. We should know where we have come from so that we know where we are going. I am sorry you do not have a sense of who walked before you in your family." Dana's words struck a chord for Tara, who had spent her life trying to hide her true self.

She struggled to preserve an air of nonchalance, but the corners of her lips threatened to come crashing down, and her eyes welled with unexpected tears.

Dana seemed to sense her discomfort and switched gears. "So, tell me, if you don't mind, what's your book about?"

Tara was grateful for the diversion, but her response lacked excitement or enthusiasm. "It's a book about the journey of the Celts between the sixth century BC and sixth century AD."

Dana's face filled with impish glee. "Well, you will need me to visit you more times than not. I'm a veritable encyclopedia on all things Celtic."

"Thanks." Tara had no interest in discussing her book, or lack of one, with a complete stranger. She edged closer to the door. "Well, I must do something about this 'new look' I've acquired." She hesitated, not wanting to appear rude. "You can come in out of the rain if you like, while I clean up."

Dana's smile broadened even wider at the invitation. "Thank you all the same, but it's fiercely wet out, so I'm gonna head on. But if it's all right with you, I'll call round for a *céilí* or two."

Seeing Tara's confused expression, she said, "Translation: The rain will not let up any time soon, so I am going to head back. But if it is all right with you, I will call round to yours for a chat and a cup of tea occasionally. Would that be okay with you?"

"Yes, yes, of course it is." Tara was surprised to realize she meant it. "Do you have to go far?"

"Not at all! Just across the meadow, through the copse of oak trees, over the hill, and I am there. A *ra* jaunt and no *bodhraigh*. I could do it with me eyes closed!"

Tara half-teased, "I can see I'm going to need a Gaelic-Irish-English dictionary for when we meet next time."

Dana laughed. "I will be off so you can get cleaned up! Good luck with your book."

"Thanks."

As Tara watched her new neighbor dash across the garden's mud-soaked earth, something made her call out. "I might take you up on the offer to pick your brain about all things Celtic."

Dana turned. A sweet smile illuminated her face. "It would be my honor. Until next time."

"How will I contact you?"

"No bother. I will come this way again soon. Oh, I should warn you, if you see a female elder adorned with a garland of posies carrying an ancient walking stick, do not fret. That will be Mamó. She comes this way often. She loves the garden!"

Before Tara had time to respond, Dana waved, turned her back, and seemed to vanish, quite literally, into thin air!

Tara's head ached. A quote from Neale Donald Walsch played over in her mind: "Without knowing who you are and why you are here, life has no meaning. Seek, then, to study the questions. Work to experience the grandest answers. Who You Are is an individuation of Divinity. Why you are here is to demonstrate that."

CHAPTER TEN

DANA CONSIDERED HER first encounter with Tara as she made her way back to her grandmother. She paused for a moment on the windswept mound of earth before entering the copse of oak trees. A smile danced across her lips. She raised her slender hands to secure her hair, which always showed flagrant disrespect for the confines of ribbon despite valiant attempts to keep it bound.

Dana realized she did not know what to expect from this first interaction. One thing she had not bargained for was that her initial jealousy would be abated by the discovery that Tara did not appear to be the self-absorbed brat Dana thought she would be. Tara's vulnerability reminded Dana of her own lack of self-love.

In a swift movement, she wrenched the ribbon from her hair, allowing the wind to whip the jet-black tresses wherever it pleased. She and Tara had a long road to travel, together and alone.

CHAPTER ELEVEN

GUY STEPPED THROUGH the art deco exit of the exclusive Mayfair casino into the gray pre-dawn air. He grimaced at his disheveled state reflected in the blue-tinged glare of the windows as he attempted to dig his car keys from his pocket.

It wasn't the first time he'd lost big, and now he was into Max, a brute of a loan shark, for another twenty thousand pounds.

Guy winced at the memory of his last encounter with Max, who drove a fist into his midriff as a reminder to pay up. The promise to extract, in Shylock fashion, more than a pound of flesh if payment wasn't forthcoming accompanied the blow. Max's parting shot was anything but music to his ears. "Believe me, you guttersnipe, I'd much rather rid the planet of your sniffling snobbery, even if you paid me three times what you owe, but my reputation is at stake. After all, I'm a businessman."

Guy bent to retrieve the keys that had fallen to the sidewalk. He longed for the days when gambling and winning had delivered an intense high, a sense of joy, of adrenaline. Those days were long gone, but the desire for them to return left him forever hooked to the electric mainlines of possibility, desire, and hope.

The pale hint of a smile crept to his lips. He had concealed this addiction from most who knew him for over twenty years. Even his closest friends believed in the innocence of his occasional "slip."

If Tara found out, she'd be off so fast he'd choke on the dust she stirred up. No, she must never know. Her writing was his meal ticket. He'd do whatever it took to keep it and her under control. He pulled out his cell phone and texted her again.

Chapter Twelve

IT HAD BEEN a couple of days since their first mud-soaked encounter. Dana returned just as Tara received another frantic text from Guy demanding to know her whereabouts and how the book was coming along. She hadn't responded.

The women lounged under the gnarled limbs of the sweet-smelling hawthorn, which had blossomed into a white mass of flowers. Fifty feet above their upturned heads, its dense crown of leaves pierced the imperceptible movement of the clouds. A small flock of male kestrels with blue-gray heads hovered, fanned-tailed, scanning the earth below for any telltale signs of small mammals.

The two women sat in convivial silence. Tara wasn't fond of the sound of silence. But as she sat with Dana, the quiet enveloped her like the warmth of winter fire, soothing her soul, taking away the jaggedness of the self-loathing that lingered below the surface. Of course, she knew the source of her latest bout of self-flagellation. She hadn't written a word since coming to Dunsany.

Dana let out a slow sigh. Without preamble, she patted the bark of the hawthorn and turned her attention to Tara. "Never break its branches or dig up any portion of it," she said. "If you do, a hex of misfortune will be cast on ye."

Tara stared at her guest with a healthy skepticism but from the far reaches of her memory, she recalled reading a poem that suggested the hawthorn could bring bad luck.

"Did you know that folk believe this remarkable tree is a place where the *aos sí* live?"

"*A-os shi?*"

Dana's voice dropped to a whisper. "Faeries. Hereabouts, we tend not to mention them by name for fear of angering or insulting the *beag* folk. Out of respect, we call them our 'good neighbors,' the 'fair folk,' or simply 'the folk.'" Dana continued in a hushed tone. "This tree is a trysting or meeting place for your good neighbors. I know this to be true."

"But surely you don't believe—"

Dana interrupted Tara, and her eyes grew serious. "You should know this is a sacred oasis. It is where the fair folk can access the otherworld at dawn or dusk. It is where the unbelievable becomes real."

Tara pursed her lips. Her mouth became parched, yet her palms dripped with sweat. The talk of faeries, trysting places, and hexes was unhinging her well-rehearsed veneer of calm. To shift the conversation, she said, "Yes, and I hear that the berries, leaves, and flowers of the hawthorn are good for the heart and circulation."

Dana's expression morphed into quizzical inquiry. "And how do you know that? Are you studied in the art of healing with herbs, plants, and trees?"

"No. I don't know where that came from." Tara felt a mounting discomfort at the direction their conversation was heading and was thankful when Dana shifted focus.

"So, have you visited your namesake hill?"

"You mean the Hill of Tara?"

"Ay, that is the one."

"Not yet. But the proximity of this cottage to the hill was a deciding factor in renting it."

Dana chuckled. It was a delightful sound, merry like a babbling brook flowing over rocky obstacles. "Well, if you do, you must not forget to touch the *Lia Fáil*."

"The *Lia* what?"

"The *Lia Fáil*, more commonly known as the Stone of Destiny. Legend has it that a godly people known as the Tuatha Dé Danaans brought it here. It is said the stone roars when touched by the rightful king of Tara. Others claim to have seen their future when touching the stone. I believe that might be a great place for you to start your book!

Tara was exhausted. Maybe it was all the talk of faeries, otherworlds, and destinies. But it might also be the realization that she hadn't a bloody clue who she was or what in God's name she was doing there. She yawned, making no effort to conceal it.

Dana took the cue, stood, smoothed the creases in her tunic, and bade Tara farewell.

CHAPTER THIRTEEN

TARA ROSE EARLY the next day. Armed with directions and a map of the Hill of Tara, she set off. Besides exploring the hill, she hoped the hike might kick-start her creative juices. Maybe she'd learn some of the secrets lying beneath its soil.

As she trekked across five kilometers of soggy fields, woodland, and inclines to get to the hill, her mind was lit with what she'd learned the prior evening.

While reading Michael Slavin's description of the hill, Tara learned that another O'Connell was a prominent character in shaping the history of Ireland. Daniel O'Connell was thought to be the "Liberator of Ireland" because of his relentless pursuit to have his homeland represented in the English parliament.

Oh, to be that clear about your purpose in life, Tara mused. Standing in the middle of God knows whose country, philosophizing, wouldn't get her to where the hell she was going, would it? She continued her journey into the unknown.

After twenty minutes, she arrived at a scantily dressed oak woodland. Glancing back at the dew-clad meadow she'd just traversed, Tara realized her footprints had left their mark. She thought she'd walked in a straight line, but the impression of her footsteps was decidedly ragged and bent.

"A bit like my life," she said to the woods.

Her focus was drawn to the free-for-all cacophony of color vibrating in waves as wildflowers swayed gently in the breeze. Shepherd's purse, so named because the white of its flat seed pouches resembled an old-fashioned leather purse, co-mingled with the purple-pink beauty of coltsfoot.

"You're not just beautiful, are you?" Tara spoke directly to the splendid array of colors on show. "All of you have a purpose, don't you?"

This knowledge made her shiver. She wondered how she knew that tea made from coltsfoot was good for asthma and troubles of the throat or that when dried, tea from shepherd's purse would stop a hemorrhage.

Tara raised her voice to the sun-steeped sky. "For the love of God, what's happening to me?"

Not expecting an answer, she swiftly turned her back on the beauty of the meadow and tramped through the cool woodland, humming with the vibrancy of new life.

Halfway through, she sensed a pair of eyes, or was it two, boring on her back.

Fear sizzled in her solar plexus, threatening to explode into full-blown hysteria. She whirled around to scan the terrain again and again. Darting her eyes in all directions, she saw nothing to support her sudden terror. Her pace quickened to double time, eager to leave the woods and the unwelcome sensations behind.

Eventually, she emerged from the woodland, which was infused with a white blanket of clustering wild garlic, the pale yellow and purple of primrose, the pale bark of the birch, the tight black buds of the ash, and the skeletal branches of the mighty oak.

Tara spotted her destination on the horizon. As she drew nearer, she rubbed her eyes in disbelief. In the honeycombed yellow of the early morning sun, the Hill of Tara glowed. It was dazzling, almost fluorescent. *So much so, it hurt her eyes.*

She stood, mesmerized by the gleaming waves of light that bounced from its apex. A kind of electric charge started to emanate from the ground where she stood. The intensity increased the closer she was to the hill. It became overwhelming. To stop the spinning in her head, Tara slumped to the earth on the verge of the hill.

Unable to shake her mounting uneasiness, Tara continued, concluding it would be crazy not to investigate more closely. She climbed the grass-covered ridge, avoiding a skittish flock of sheep and their droppings, pausing briefly to read what Slavin had written.

He asked his readers to keep three things in mind: One, this hill was a place of royalty where 142 Irish kings had been crowned and reigned. Each one was purported to have been blessed by the Earth's Mother Goddess Maeve. Two, this area had been, and was still, revered as a most powerful, sacred place where the gods dwelled. It was considered an entrance to the "otherworld" of eternal joy and plenty. And three, according to Slavin, the Celts had chosen to settle here because, for them, it was a site of significance. As a result, it became a location for one of the largest complexes of Celtic monuments in all of Europe. For over 500 years, from the first through the fifth centuries, the hill had been the ceremonial center for the high kings of Ireland.

After refolding her notes, Tara trudged upward. While she caught her breath at its apex, she surveyed the surrounding landscape. On the eastern side of the hilltop stood a plaque marking where the ancient Tara and the Tara of Christianity had once met. The only surviving remnant was a deconsecrated church dedicated to Saint Patrick.

She had no desire to visit the church. Instead, her feet led her to the north of the grass-covered summit to an Iron Age compound. It was an expansive area encircled by an internal ditch and external bank known as *Ráith na Ríogh*—The Fort of the Kings or Royal Enclosure.

The most prominent earthworks within Ráith na Ríogh appeared to be two linked enclosures. The first was a double-ditched ring fort and a ring burial barrow known as *Teach Chormaic* or Cormac's House. The second was the *Forradh* or Royal Seat. Its centerpiece was the standing stone Dana had told her about, the Lia Fáil or Stone of Destiny. Tara had read that where it now stood wasn't its original home. It had been moved from the Mound of the Hostages more than one hundred years ago.

Well, I guess that means our destiny is indeed a moveable feast, she mused.

She scanned the terrain and immediately located the stone. It reminded Tara more of a well-endowed, erect phallic symbol than a place where people saw their futures by touching it, as Dana suggested.

She glanced at her watch, then to the north of the ring forts. She spied what appeared to be a small, ancient passage tomb. Tracing the lines of the map, she saw that her assumption was correct. Known as *Dumha na nGiall,* or the Mound of the Hostages, archaeological wisdom estimated it was close to five thousand years old. Its name derived from the high kings' practice of holding persons of importance from subject kingdoms captive, which ensured the submission and allegiance of those lands.

Tara jumped as her phone vibrated in the confines of her back pocket. Wriggling it free, she glanced down at the message.

I demand to know where you are and how the book is coming. Call me!

Her right eye twitched. She wasn't up to engaging with Guy. As she crammed the phone back into her pocket, a ten-course serving of electrically charged rage erupted and threatened to consume her. The veins in her temples felt ready to explode.

Overwhelmed by fury, she screamed at the sky, "Why the hell does anyone feel they have the right to usurp, commandeer, and control the lives of others? And why in God's name does Guy think he has the bloody right to demand anything from me?" The venomous ferocity of her words was bitter to the taste. She closed her eyes, trying to curb the unexpected fierceness of her feelings.

The earth beneath her feet erupted into a vibrational force of electrifying intensity. Fear choked her throat. A reactionary cry for help lay frozen on her tongue. Terror forbade the movement of a single muscle. She stood rooted to the spot as if she had become one of the hill's stone monuments.

Her pulse banged in her ears, and she was chilled by the sweat that dripped down her spine. The air had become strangely dense. One thing she knew for certain: she no longer stood on a hillside in the middle of County Meath.

Tara slumped against the coldness of a stone wall. She waited for her eyes to adjust to the darkness, rubbing the scar on her right hand.

"Fuck!" Tara screamed as she came to realize she was no longer herself but had somehow become a child with thoughts and feelings different from her own. And, in that moment, this child, whose name she somehow knew was Clarice, was gathering some comfort from knowing that she shared the mark on her hand with her mother.

Tara lost complete sense of who she was and who she had ever been.

Chapter Fourteen

Marseille, 1423

HER ANGRY STOMACH grumbled as she pushed ebony tendrils behind her ears in a well-rehearsed motion. Crouched in the frigid, musty gloom of her family home, she swallowed a deep breath and let the air escape in a long, slow exhale.

As she swiped at her tear-stained face, the image of her mother appeared beside her. "Now, now, Clarice," she heard her mama whisper. "Don't wipe away your tears, my love. Tears are like words your heart has yet to find a way to express. Sit with them and the words will come."

That memory was from a happier time. A time when her mother would cradle her until she could find those words. The hairs on the back of her neck bristled as distant but distinct screams of terror and triumphant shouts pierced the chill of the November evening.

Alfonso's men were getting closer once more. Her body convulsed as she remembered the last time she huddled on this very spot, cocooned within her mother's warm embrace. As she stroked Clarice's hair, her mother said, "Do not be frightened, *ma chère*. God will protect us."

Well, she thought, as she repositioned herself on the cold dampness of the floor, God had not done a very good job at protecting either of them, had he? How much time had passed since the men had stormed the house where she and her mama had been hiding? Three days, she calculated. It seemed so long ago now.

Three days since she escaped to the alleyway a short distance away to see her mother dragged from the only home she had ever known. Three days since each soldier, in their turn, had straddled her mother, beating her face with their fists, while they rocked back and forth until they slumped with a yelp of victorious exhaustion.

She lost count of how many men there were. When the last one staggered away, Clarice crept to her mother's side. The ravaged woman was barely recognizable. Her bloodied and broken face stared with vacant eyes.

"Mama, mama, we must go!"

Nothing!

"Please, mama, please," Clarice said, attempting to shake her mother into wakefulness. Still no response. Shouts from the soldiers were not as distant. Were they returning?

Clarice did not care. She was not leaving without her mother. She could not. "Mama, please, we need to go."

Slender fingers encircled her small wrist. Clarice bent closer to pick up the words that her mother's cracked and battered lips attempted to form. "Mama, I cannot hear what you are saying."

Shouts of victorious, cruel pleasure echoed from somewhere just beyond the alleyway. Her mother gripped Clarice's hand. "Run, *ma petite ange*, run. It is too late for me. Run as fast as you can and hide."

"No, Mama, I will not leave you. Please, please, please get up. I will help you." A faint smile flashed up at Clarice. "No, *mon amour*, you cannot save me."

Stubborn resistance flooded Clarice's eyes. Her mother struggled to pull herself up on one elbow and raised her voice as much as she dared. "Do not disobey me an instant longer. Run, child. I command you. Go now!" She slumped to the ground. Clarice knew the warmth and safety of her mother were no more.

The dangerous thunder of boots grew closer. She touched the angelic face of her beloved mother, laying limp and lifeless on the cold, wet cobblestones and fled until the shrieks of the soldiers could no longer reach her.

To shake herself loose from this painful memory, Clarice inched her way to the window to peek out at the ravaged city. She realized that, at thirteen, she was completely alone. There was no one left to look after her. She must now fend for herself, and she was resolved, beyond any doubt, that if God did not have time to save her mother, then she would never have time for Him.

Under the weight of this new understanding, Clarice concluded that she must find a less conspicuous place to hide. She stared into the street below. Not a soul in sight, but she sensed they were near. Where would she be safe? Mama would have known, but she was no longer there.

Clarice stood, straightened her shoulders, and crept from her childhood home without taking one backward glance.

Chapter Fifteen

T HE PRIEST GLANCED down at his blood-encrusted hands as he walked the streets of Marseille in search of anyone who was still breathing.

The putrid reminder of death and human waste all around him produced a stomach-wrenching convulsion. He wiped his lips, but there was nothing left to wipe away. The entire contents of his gut had been projected onto an indiscriminate wall in one of the many alleyways filled with the mutilated remains of men, women, and children, their lifeless bodies left as fodder for voracious rats.

Faces frozen in permanent frenzy or disbelief had stared at him through the blur of carnage created over three short days. He closed his eyes to eradicate the memory of twisted bodies littering the blood-soaked ground.

The naked, mangled bodies of pre-pubescent girls lying spread-eagle, discarded along the side of streets, in houses, and alleyways, tortured his sensibility. The women he found in this condition were one thing…but the children…

He knew the answer, of course. Often, when spirits mixed with the lust of victory, men forgot the rules of decency. Reprisal against the defeated was the prize taken for granted by the victors. But who in God's name could—or would want to—claim victory for the senseless carnage, which was now imbued into the blackness of his cassock?

He slumped against the coolness of a nearby wall and took a drink from the flask concealed within the simplicity of his robes. His eyes caught the glint of the weak November sun reflected in the cross, which hung from his lean but substantial frame. It transported him back to the previous night as he cradled the dying form of a once beautiful woman. Her ebony eyes pleaded a request that her swollen lips could not utter.

He knelt beside her, trying to understand the appeal she wished to deliver, as her life- force seeped all around him. Before her battered body commended itself to God, he made out three words: Ma petite Clarice.

Raking a calloused hand across his eyes for the umpteenth time, he tried to wipe away the vagaries of this malicious attack by the Spaniard Alfonso V of Aragon. The slaughter and looting were nothing more than a peevish reprisal.

The weary priest straightened, resolved to offer aid and absolution to all that made the request. It was his duty and his penance for being a representative of a church that itself was in need of absolution.

—

Clarice stared into the night sky, blanketed by a million winking stars. How long had she lain there, surrounded by feces and debris? Her bruised and aching body hungered for food and the warmth of her mother's touch.

She wondered if she should get up and find a less conspicuous place to rest. To her fevered mind, there was warmth in the squalid sanctuary she had found. The crescendo of blood-curdling screams had died, replaced by an eerie, calm silence.

Why should she rise and try to find help? There was nothing left for her beyond the boundary of the alleyway she now found herself in. Her dear mama was no more. She had no family and no one willing to protect her.

Clarice sighed. She was alone in a hostile world. A world where men took what they wanted as they silenced any sound of joyous laughter with the repetitive slashing of their swords. It was a world in which God had forsaken her and everything she held sacred. A world where only the strong survived. There was no reason for her to stir from her present malaise. With that thought, she closed her world-weary eyes once more.

She jerked as a shadow fell over her, wrenching the momentary peace she had found.

She lay still, suspending her breath, hoping that whoever or whatever was looming over her would give her up for dead.

"*Ma petite*," she heard someone whisper. "*Ma petite*, wake up."

Even though the voice was soft with reassurance, there was no doubt it was male. She held on to the breath that only moments ago she had been willing to give up to the shadows of death.

"*Ma petite chou*, please, wake up."

The voice had a similar quality to that of her mother, but it belonged to a man. She did not dare peek at its owner.

When he rested a tentative hand on her shoulder, she could no longer ignore his gentle prompts. In cannonball fashion, she shot up. Slipping on feces, she closed her eyes and screamed repeatedly, "Please, Monsieur, I beg you, do not harm me."

"*Sois calme, ma petite. Je veux dire pas de mal.*"

He said he wished her no harm, but he was a man, and the past few days had taught her never again to trust them.

"Open your eyes, little one, and look at me. You need help, and I can give that to you."

What options did she have? She knew he could take whatever he wanted from her, and she would have no choice.

"*Ma petite*, come, open your eyes."

Despite her fear and reluctance, Clarice unlocked the hold on her eyelids and squinted at the large black figure squatting in front of her.

Neither one moved for what seemed an eternity.

Readjusted to the sunlight, she tried to take in the measure of the man. He was larger than any man she had ever known. Not fat like some fishermen on the wharves, but large all the same. His face held a sad weariness that made her feel both comfortable and comforted, but as he reached out to her with blood-encrusted hands, she jumped back, banging her head on the rough wall behind her.

He wiped his hand on his chest, then shrugged and offered a tentative smile. "I am sorry, *ma petite*. I have had little time to wash these past few days."

She reached toward his outstretched hand ever so slowly. Matching her cautious pace, he took her hand until he ensconced it within the warmth of his.

The glint of his cross caught her eye. A priest, she thought. Her rescuer was a priest. A fleeting smile crinkled her face at the thought that maybe God had not forsaken her after all. The vision of her mother fighting off her assailants erased the thought.

Clarice's knees buckled from under her. The priest swept her elfin frame into his arms.

Her body tensed, rigid with fear.

"*Ma petite*, I wish you no harm," he whispered. "My name is Father Philippe. Would you tell me yours?"

With her body still tense, Clarice opened her eyes for the briefest moment before whispering something he could not hear.

"I am sorry, *ma petite*, I cannot hear you," he said, bending closer to her face. "Would you tell me again what your name is?"

—

The faint croak that erupted from her lips was enough for him to understand. "Clarice."

The eyes he raised to heaven reflected both the pain and anguish he felt over the past days and the gratitude for the miraculous working of a God he still wholeheartedly believed in.

This trembling, filth-encrusted waif was the one he had been searching for. His only job from now on was to guide and protect her until she recognized and realized who she was!

—

Clarice peered over the priest's shoulder as he carried her from the gloomy solitude of the place where she believed she would die. She could have sworn that someone was there, observing what transpired between herself and the man who now carried her away to a new life. An odd feeling swept over her. She would never be alone again.

Chapter Sixteen

A convent north of Marseille, 1424

CLARICE'S KNEES WERE bloodied and swollen, but she would not repent. A year at the convent had provided her with ample opportunities to acknowledge the many purported sins she had committed.

"I give you one more chance, child. Confess your sins, and you may rise," Sister Bernadette said, not bothering to conceal her distaste for the young woman who knelt before her.

"But, Sister, surely it is not a sin to read," Clarice responded. She bent her head in part to hide the anger and disdain that burned in the depths of her eyes and to appear contrite to this mean-spirited hulk of a woman standing over her.

"How dare you talk back to me, you wicked, wretched child? Conceived in sin, you will die in its cesspool. You, who God has marked with a soul blacker than muck, your baseness evidenced by the events of your life!" Sister Bernadette's eyes bulged with puritanical indignation.

As she inhaled deeply, the nun appeared to choke back her anger before continuing in a more controlled tone. "Your reading offends God. When will you know your place?"

"But Sister, Papa gave the book to me on his last visit."

"Enough. Father Philippe does little to save your soul from the clutches of Satan. You will remain here praying for forgiveness until you see the error of your ways. You are a despicable, malignant sinner. If it is the last thing I do, I will save your soul despite your sin-filled life, no matter who or what your mother was. I believe the mother you revere was nothing more than a harlot who set herself up as a healer with healing powers greater than Christ's. A heretic who believed her prophecies foretold the future. Oh yes, believe me, I know all about your infamous mama."

As Clarice catapulted to her feet, the pain from genuflecting on the cold, wet, uneven stones of the chapel floor overnight shot through her like a bolt of lightning.

"How dare you speak of my mother that way! She was as kind and warm a Christian as you are a shriveled, old hag who pretends to love the Lord when, in reality, you despise everything."

As quickly as she had shot to her feet, a resounding slap sent her reeling to the floor once more.

"Sinful girl! You will obey me. You will learn to know your place. You will learn to do as I say, or you will perish. Trust me, if it weren't for your guardian, I would have seen you in Hell well before now."

Clarice waited until she could no longer hear the thumps of Sister Bernadette's receding footfalls before she permitted herself to grimace at the pain in her head, legs, and knees.

Her eyes welled with tears, contradicting the tenacity she had carefully constructed during her time at the convent. She would not live wallowing in any cesspool, whether it be full of sin or self-recrimination.

Breathing in the strength of that thought, she heard Papa's gentle voice in her head, reminding her that Sister Bernadette was also a child of God and should be treated with loving kindness. He always ruffled her hair as he told her that everyone had a cross to bear and maybe Sister Bernadette was hers.

Sensing a presence, she thought one of the other nuns had entered the chapel but saw no one.

CHAPTER SEVENTEEN

IT FELT LIKE someone had yanked her from a lucid dream and dumped her into a vat of acid. Dazed and more than a little confused, Tara realized she was again standing on the Hill of Tara.

What is happening to me? She glanced down at the hands of her watch. Shit! Only minutes had passed since the last time she'd looked at it!

With her heart thumping in a wild cadence, her breathing grew shallow, captured within the confines of her chest. A rhythmic trembling churned in her solar plexus, threatening to erupt and spew from her bowels.

Despite her attempts to make sense of what just happened, waves of imagination pounded the shores of all she knew to be true, filling her with an irrational and irrevocable sensation of being trapped.

Her body was wracked with convulsions and her mind alight with surging confusion. It took all the energy she could muster to redirect her present bewilderment to survey the hill and valley below. All appeared as it had been.

The electrifying intensity of the earth was receding whence it had sprung, like a snake that had delivered a lethal bite and recoiled to the darkness of its pit.

Shaking her head, she grabbed a bottle of water from her backpack and slowed her breathing to regain normalcy and calm.

She thought of the wretched way the old nun had treated the girl. "God, if only I had the strength of mind and the boldness of character of Clarice, my life might look and feel a lot different."

She wiped the back of her hand across her brow. Droplets of salty panic invaded her eyes as she attempted to shrug off the last vestige of emotion, which only seconds ago threatened to devour her. She forced herself to refocus her attention on the map in her hands to decide where to explore next.

Just to the north and outside the bounds of Ráith na Ríogh stood another ring fort hedged by three banks known as Ráith na Seanadh or Rath of the Synods, and to the north of that stood the rectangular Teach Miodhchuarta.

She turned the map over and read that the Teach Miodhchuarta, known as the Banqueting Hall, may not have been a hall at all. More likely it was a ceremonial avenue where the soon-to-be-crowned high kings would walk on the way to their inaugurations.

She turned back to the map and saw that south of Ráith na Ríogh was the hill fort named Laoghaire, with Ráith Maeve less than a mile south of it. Tara read that Ráith Maeve was linked to the mythological goddess figure of Medb Lethderg, who they believed married nine successive high kings of Ireland, including Fedlimid Rechtmar, Art mac Cuinn, and Cormac mac Airt. The idea of exploring where goddesses once walked intrigued her.

Unsettled and spent from her hilltop experience, she let her feet take her where they willed. Without hesitation, they headed toward the center of Ráith na Ríogh.

Before long, she was inches away from the infamous Lia Fáil, or the Stone of Destiny, as Dana described it.

Skepticism sprang up in her. There was no expert consensus that this hunk of stone was the real Stone of Destiny. There are experts who believe someone excavated it from the bottom of the trench surrounding the Forradh, where it lay flat on its face for centuries.

Thoughts of Clarice filled her mind. Feeling bold, she stretched her hand out and laid it against the side of the stone. She waited. Nothing. Not a flicker or spark of insight. Nada! Not ready to give up, she reminded herself of the legend of Cú Chulainn and how he'd split the stone in half with his sword when the stone had refused to cry out for his protégé, Lugaid Riab nDerg. Cú Chulainn believed this action would forever destroy the stone's power. Legend also had it that one hundred years later, Conn of the Hundred Battles tread upon the stone, either by intention or accident, and it roared once again, sealing the fate of his destiny as the reigning king of Ireland.

After a quick glance to make sure no one was watching, Tara put her foot against the enormous erection.

"Absolutely nothing," she whispered to the stone. What was she thinking? Overcome with a mixture of unrequited hope and anger, Tara spun around. "God, I'm stupid!"

Without looking back, she stomped down the hill, retracing her steps through the woodlands and meadow to the sanctuary of her little stone cottage. She trod along with a determination she was far from feeling, ignoring the quickening electrical pulse that vibrated in waves from her toes through her body and threatened to blow the top of her skull sky-high while her heart thundered against the walls of her chest.

At last, the safety of her temporary haven was in sight. Tara saw that the asylum she craved would have to wait. From a distance of about a hundred meters, she could make out a figure, Dana, waiting outside the cottage.

By the time she reached her unwelcome visitor, she had quelled the desire to tell Dana to bugger off. She even conjured up what she believed was a welcoming smile.

CHAPTER EIGHTEEN

DANA REALLY DIDN'T know why Mamó believed spending time here, at her ancestral home, would be good for either herself or Tara. And sensing the less-than-welcoming energy bouncing off her approaching host, she felt her suspicions were well-founded. But, determined to complete her mission, she straightened her shoulders and shrugged off any vestige of doubt. Her face radiated with childlike sweetness, like someone excited about the chance meeting of a long-lost friend.

"A fine good day to you," Dana said. "I wasn't expecting to see you today."

Taking in Tara's wild, disheveled hair and the thick brown paste of mud splatter that obliterated the pristine green of her Wellington boots, Dana said, "I was nearby and thought you might like some company. Been for a bit of a walkabout, have you?"

Her host raised a hand to smooth the havoc of her hair. "Finally made it up the hill."

"It's a fair old trek from here. Did you get what you wanted from your visit?" Dana asked as nonchalantly as she could, already knowing the answer.

Tara's hands trembled and the muscle in the corner of her left eye twitched as she sidestepped Dana's question. "I was hoping you'd drop by soon. I was wondering if you wouldn't mind filling me in on the journey of your Celtic ancestors."

Not waiting for a reply, Tara continued. "Shall we go sit under the hawthorn? I'll get some lemonade."

"Oh, that would be grand! I have all the time this world offers and more."

"So, where would you like me to start?" Dana asked a few minutes later as Tara handed her a glass chocked to the brim with pink lemonade.

"From the beginning would be great!"

"Well then, I will start with a question. Where do you think the Celts in Ireland came from?"

"Sure, no problem at all. From what I've gathered so far, some scholars believe Celtic origins emanate from the Late Bronze Age Urnfield culture, which was preeminent throughout Central Europe during the period between 1200 and 800 BC. Then, an offshoot of the Urnfield culture, which had all the evident characteristics of being Celtic, came into notoriety all over the same region. They dubbed this 'the Hallstatt period' because of the rich Celtic treasure troves found in grave sites south of the Alps, in and around Hallstatt, Austria. Archaeological finds have linked the Urnfield and Celtic cultures through a strong resemblance in metalwork, tools, and jewelry. These similarities suggest that the ancestors of the Hallstatt Celts were in that area by the late second millennia BC."

Tara's pulse quickened as she spoke. With the escape of a low, understated sigh, the last vestige of disquiet she suffered during her morning excursion released. It was replaced by a swell of excitement that coursed through her veins as she shared her discoveries about the Celts, further fueling her imagination and warming her heart.

"In the eighth century BC, the Greeks began a great age of

colonization across the Mediterranean and around the Black Sea. One area the Phocaea Greeks migrated to in 600 BC was the Celtic stronghold of Massalia, which is now, of course, modern-day Marseille."

Ever since she'd discovered this part of Celtic history, the mention of Marseille always incited a great pounding in her chest. She felt an unmitigated familiarity with that city, although she had only visited it briefly a few years earlier.

Without warning, Tara felt a tingle of energy vibrate in waves in the lower half of her body. Her feeble cry, "Oh, for the love of God, not again!" vanished, as did she, into the ether, leaving Dana alone under the hawthorn.

Chapter Nineteen

Convent, north of Marseille, 1431

Yet again, Sister Bernadette had ordered Clarice to retreat to the garden to contemplate her sinful life. Instead, Clarice sat, considering her future. For the past year or two, members of the order had made not-so-subtle attempts to force a decision. The abbess was pressuring her to choose a direction for her life.

One of the several challenges was the limited "directions" on offer. Tradition dictated most women became wives, mothers, artisans, or nuns. Few held influential roles, such as abbess or queen.

Becoming a wife and mother held no appeal to her at present. She allowed a momentary smile to play on her lips, amused by the thought of how vehemently Sister Bernadette would lobby against the choice of becoming a nun. She envisioned the aging nun as she scrambled to petition the wealthier patrons of the convent, as was sometimes the custom, to provide a substantial dowry to marry her off to some oaf twice her age.

The thought of a life shackled to a man she did not love disgusted her. How could she love someone she did not know? A man who would parade her innocence like a well-earned, paid-for trophy. That kind of life would leave her feeling like a skinned carcass of meat left hanging from a butcher's hook in the slaughterhouse.

Clarice had never experienced deep feelings of love for a man. Ugly, twisted memories of her mother being raped repeatedly in the dirty streets of blood-soaked Marseille had convinced her that the mere act of sexual intercourse was in no way the ultimate expression of love. The simple act of taking another person's body was a far cry from consummating deep and abiding heartfelt love.

She could not imagine giving her unbridled love and body to a man for worldly possessions and the outward trappings of security and success. She was sure that was no life at all, and that would, without doubt, lead to a deadening of her soul from spiritual hunger and thirst.

No, she would never sell herself to the highest bidder. Never! It would represent dishonesty and cowardice.

She returned the image of her loving mother to the recesses of her mind and reflected on her choices. Living a life of contemplation, cloistered behind these walls, praying for her own salvation and the salvation of others attracted her even less than marriage.

What she desired was a life of exploring, learning, and service, but how this might be achieved was far from clear. She was fascinated by the study of the medicinal properties of plants and herbs and the works of Hildegard von Bingen. What first drew her to this woman's work was Hildegard's assertion that every human being deserved the opportunity to develop his or her individual and unique set of talents and potential. Those words were music to her ears. Hildegard was a revolutionary visionary who spoke up against any and every injustice she witnessed. She even had the courageous audacity to demand change and reformation from the church authorities of her day.

More than once, Clarice had asked herself if she possessed such courage. The audacity to simply be herself. At the age of twenty, she still had no answer to that question.

She devoured the now-worn pages of Hildegard's two volumes on natural history. Some scholars believed these were not Hildegard's work because of their practical rather than visionary nature. But Clarice did not care how much of Hildegard lived within these volumes. The knowledge they contained opened a world of study for her and resonated with things she intuitively knew to be true.

Clarice believed Hildegard's assertion that all manifestations of nature, which, of course, included both humanity and plants, were closely related and interconnected. The nuns in the convent believed that prayer and penance led to healing and health, but Clarice had learned much about the healing properties of plants and herbs.

She now knew that yarrow and blackwort had unique and subtle powers in healing certain types of injuries. More than once, she had used the healing properties of lungwort to dispel the malaise brought on by severe chest infections. Parsley-honey wine had proven to help when a patient felt pain in their heart, spleen, or side. Those who suffered from severe heart pain benefited from taking two or three pinches of yellow gentian in spelt flour soup. This herb helped strengthen the heart and acted as a stimulant to the digestive system.

Through her study, Clarice came to realize that the path to health started first by eliminating or purging the cause of the disease with natural remedies and then administrating the right nutrients.

As the sun warmed her hands resting on her lap, her heart radiated with the memory of her dear mama. She remembered the days when she would accompany her mother on what she affectionately called "her rounds." Clarice would cling to the softness of her mother's hand as they visited the homes of the sick.

She relived how her mother would first consult the potions contained within the softness of her well-worn, oversized pouch and the gentle kindness with which she lifted the head of the one suffering to administer whatever was needed. Some said her mother had the healing sight. At the time, Clarice did not understand what they meant, but she was beginning to see.

A sound just behind Clarice made her turn around. There was no one to be found. Or no one she could see. She exhaled quietly and said, "I wish you would show yourself. I am not afraid."

CHAPTER TWENTY

TARA'S EYELIDS, LEADEN with strange, interrupted sleep, struggled to open. Frightened by the sensation of partial blindness, she employed her other senses to search her surroundings. The hardness of the hawthorn bit into her rigid spine. Its immense root system, which wove in and out of the muddied ground on her left, gripped the earth with tough, powerful limbs.

Replaying what just transpired, she was choked with remorse for Clarice, who was offered so few choices. Yet, the young woman's determination to carve out a meaningful and fulfilling life filled Tara with an inexplicable sense of pride and a touch of jealousy.

If only she had the same audacity. How different her life would be.

She considered the last words Clarice spoke. Even if she knew how to "show herself," did she have the ability or the courage? Her eyes regained their focus. She glanced over her shoulder to find Dana staring back. Her face wore an odd expression of both intrigued inquiry and something else Tara couldn't identify.

To quell the last trace of turbulent thumping in her chest and bring it to a calm, regular beat, her nostrils drew in a healthy serving of air, held it for a moment, and allowed it to escape from her mouth in a slow, controlled exhale. She could only speculate how strange her behavior appeared to her visitor. The vivid images still fresh in her mind's eye were not easy to erase.

Tara attempted a feeble laugh. "Sorry about that. I dozed off for a minute."

"Ah, do not concern yourself. You have had an eventful morning that appears to have crept into your afternoon as well."

"I'm not sure what you mean by that."

Dana's eyes twinkled with mischief, but the evenness of her voice gave nothing away. "Don't trouble your noodle! All I meant was that you've had a long trek today. No wonder you're feeling knackered!"

Straightening her spine and softening her tone, Tara conceded, "Yes, I guess I've had a bit of a journey. I'm happy to continue if you're up for it?"

"Definitely!"

"Okay. So, where was I? Ah, yes, I'd just finished talking about the Greeks' colonization of Massalia. Well, it's said that over the next decades, the Greeks spread trade routes out from Massalia because of its strategic positioning at the mouth of the Rhône River. This affected the Celts north of the Alps, bringing luxury goods to them for the first time."

Tara felt the buzz of her cell phone reverberate against her skin. Out of habit, she pulled it from her back pocket and read the text.

Where the fuck are you? Why haven't you returned any of my texts or calls? I am not amused. Call me…now!

She groaned and slumped against the hardness of the tree. Too drained to face the raging storm that was Guy, she turned off her phone.

"Everything okay?" Dana asked.

"Yes, no worries. Just something I'd rather not deal with right now." Tara shivered.

"Mamó always says 'there's no time like the present to deal with the vagaries of life.'"

"Well, answering that text is one vagary I choose to put off if it's all right with you and your grandmother. Sometimes, life gives us more than we can handle. I said I don't want to deal with it right now." Tara flung the words at her visitor without censoring herself.

After an awkward moment of silence, Tara said, "Crap, I'm sorry. I'm suffering from foot-in-mouth disease. I shouldn't take my frustration out on you. Can we just forget my outburst?"

Her words quieted the furor of emotion that threatened to consume Dana. "As you say, no worries. It's forgotten. Now, where were you?"

Tara fell back into stride. "For almost two centuries, the Celtic elite, living on the edge of the Alps, enjoyed exotic wares that the peoples of the Mediterranean brought in trade. Meanwhile, their more warlike cousins to the north were getting jealous. They grew tired of the superior attitude of their relatives to the south and resented paying them a premium for acquiring olives, wine, and other items. They decided it was time to raise their banners of war and overrun these Hallstatt Celts. So, by 450 BC, the Hallstatt way of life came crashing to an abrupt end and the La Tène period began and lasted until the Roman conquest."

Tara took a deep breath. Her eyes crinkled as she burst into laughter. "Christ, I sound like a bloody encyclopedia!"

Dana looked amused. "It seems you have done a lot of homework for your book already. But it still doesn't explain the presence of Celts in Ireland."

"I was just getting to that part!" Tara's face flushed as she realized her response was curt and childish. She continued in a softer tone. "According to historians, it was during the La Tène period that the Celtic culture, both by diffusion and migration, spread to most of Central Europe, the Iberian Peninsula of Spain, Northern Italy, France, and what we now know as the United Kingdom and Northern Ireland. By the third century BC, they even inhabited an area of modern-day Turkey."

"So, do you think the indigenous people of Brittany, Wales, England, Ireland, and Scotland have their ancestry rooted in Celtic Central Europe?" Dana asked.

Tara brushed dirt from the knee of her jeans. "Well, that's one theory a few experts maintain."

"Did you know that recent DNA tests performed on a class of students from Wales were compared to the results gathered from bones of the Central European Celts, and they were not similar? Genetic studies show that the Irish, who have inhabited this island for thousands of years, are closer to the people of the Iberian Peninsula in northern Spain."

It bothered Tara that months of research hadn't unearthed this tidbit of information. She repressed a yawn. Her muscles ached with fatigue.

"Well, since the Celts wrote nothing down, it's a wonder we know anything about them at all!" said Tara.

"Yes, that is true. Accounts of the Celts were written by their victorious enemies, like the Greeks and Romans. But factual histories have been passed down from mother to daughter and father to son for millennia, keeping our rich collective heritage alive in our hearts and minds through our oral tradition." Dana leaped to her feet with the elegance of a deer. "Would you see that? The sun is near to setting. I best be on my way and let you rest. We can continue this discussion another day. I'll tell you what I know about the lives of our ancestors. Would that be a good place to start next time?"

Before Tara could respond, Dana sprinted toward the labyrinth garden to the left of the cottage and disappeared.

Tara rose from her shady spot beneath the dense-leaved crown of the hawthorn. An involuntary shudder traveled through her, followed by a slight tremor of energy vibrating from the soles of her feet.

She retraced her steps toward the cottage, overcome with such exhaustion it would take more than one good night's sleep to cure.

Her fervent prayer was that its cool darkness would obliterate any further introspection.

Like most nights, she tossed and turned in a transitional state between wakefulness and sleep. Her mind wandered and wondered as she experienced the highs and lows of imaginings that dwelled in the shadowlands of consciousness. Here she was, neither awake nor asleep, a place of perpetual limbo. Sleep wasn't a place of rest but more like a torturous place that conjured a legion of unsightly phantoms.

She hadn't had a good night's sleep since early childhood when sleep had been a blissful adventure, a time when the familiar and not-so-familiar would glide through her existence, offering comfort, solace, and the wild abandon of freedom.

A familiar uprising of resentful anger flooded her consciousness. God, she wanted to be in control of her life, both awake and asleep!

On some sort of surreal cue, the tenacious tingling surged upward from the soles of her feet in waves. Without preamble, she found herself in unrecognizable terrain. As with most of her recent nocturnal escapades, she realized she was dreaming, with no control over what she was observing. She became the one who watched.

A girl and an old woman squatted beside an open-pit fire. Tara felt a swell of frustrated boredom rise from the girl's belly as she tried, with all her might, to focus on the old woman's instruction. It was clear she wanted to be anywhere but where she was.

"That makes two of —"

Tara's thought was unfinished as she became absorbed by the vision unfolding before her.

CHAPTER TWENTY-ONE

Numantia, Iberian Peninsula, 153 BC

THE WIND HOWLED and hissed, swooping up and through the large cache of tall mossy pines that flanked the east side of Upper Citadel's mud-caked boulder walls.

The woman-child attempted to conceal a yawn by running long, pale fingers across her upper lip. Impatient anger crept up from the pit of her stomach. If it reached her throat, she might lash out, say something she'd regret, which was often the case in her brief life. To release the tension, she expelled a breath. But her eyes could not hide the storm that raged just below the surface. With a face more wrinkled than the clothes she wore, the old woman challenged the girl's indignant glare in strong rebuke.

"I know that look, Ama. It will not release you from your oral instruction. You have worn that look since you slid from your mother's womb, screeching and howling in a fitful rage of temper. So, it has no effect on me."

As the old woman rose to tend to the pot above the flame, she raised her weathered, purple-veined hand, attempting to restrain the fading curls of her once flaming red hair, and whispered to the bubbling stew, "Sad is the memory that your wailing was the last thing your dear mother ever heard."

The heightened intensity of the wind echoed the ferocity of Ama's desire to rip the immediacy of her confines asunder. The only warmth she felt was a passionate desire to be free. In her mind's eye, she wielded the beautiful sword her father had given her as she and the other warriors ran their Roman enemies into the ground.

At seventeen, she knew she was ready, able, and willing to join the warrior elite. Her heart ached with the desire to defend their lands while pillaging neighboring domains to harvest vast wealth for her nation. In her mind, anyone not of their tribe was an enemy to be cut down.

Ama had no desire to become one of the many who would choose to journey forth from the walls and ditches of her hilltop home to spend monotonous hours herding and watching over cattle. That was no life!

The howls coming from Cado, the tufted-haired wolf the old woman rescued as a pup, reverberated through Ama, echoing her longing. She ached to join in fellowship with her own kind, the warriors of her tribe. She craved the savage ecstasy of both victory and downfall in battle. The horror of defeat and ultimate death were more favorable than living a passive existence as a shepherd or, even worse, being confined in a matrimonial home, awaiting the return of her lord and master from his latest fight, subjugated to attend to his every need.

"If you do not listen to what I am telling you, Ama, how will you share the ancient tales of our people with your daughters? You must pay heed, or I will not excuse you in time for your sword lesson. I mean it this time! You must be attentive." Her grandmother leaned forward, an air of menace dancing in her eyes, to impress the girl with the seriousness of her warning.

Ama feigned contriteness.

"Baba, I am sorry. I just cannot stop thinking about the Roman scoundrels invading our lands. I want to join the fight. We have the right—"

"To defend ourselves," Baba finished her sentence for her. "Child, I have heard that same speech spewing from your lips more times than I care to count on my tally stick! You not only descended from a noble line of warriors. You were birthed from a long line of healers and wise women. Why do you lust for conflict? Why do you embrace the agony of war, regarding it as a noble and just path?"

Unable to conceal her rage, Ama bolted to her feet and strode to the door. "My vow, Baba, is to slay anyone who threatens our way of life. You and your healers can follow behind and bring them back to life!" The girl's hasty footfalls drowned out the weary sigh of her grandmother as she stomped from the home they shared.

Beyond the confines of the circular, stone-walled hut, the frenzied wind whipped Ama's face. Aware of what would happen when her father learned of her insolence, she did not care.

She sensed her time there was limited.

Ama had long dreamed of leaving the ancient stand of holm oak, which grew amid the mountainous cliffs and crags that rimmed the plateau of her home. She wanted nothing more than to fight alongside the other warriors. She felt a keen anticipation. Her heart pounded, thumping like a celebratory drum. The hairs on her sun-soaked arms stood at attention. Warmth tingled and paraded up and down the curve of her spine. Freedom was at hand now that the Roman Consul Marcus Claudius Marcellus had declared war on the Belli. Conflict was inevitable.

At last, release from the monotony of her life was within reach. Freedom from the expectations of a father, who, at the sight of her, cursed his fate for never siring a son and who never missed an opportunity to remind Ama that she was not even a marginal consolation for his lot in life.

Below her, the waters of the Douro ebbed and flowed against

its banks. The rush of the water reminded her of the conversation she overheard among the tribal elders. A Roman dog by the name of Quintus Fabius Nobilitor had landed at the coastal settlement of Tarraco with an army of thirty thousand fighting men. Their intention was to march along the shores of the Ebro until they got to one of its main tributaries, the Jalón River, and head straight up the valley to Sekeida, a major stronghold for their kin—the Belli.

Ama knew that her own Arevaci tribe would join the fray to support the Belli because they were part of a confederation determined to eradicate the Roman swine from their lands. And she intended to be there, fighting with the best of them. A sense of pride and victory washed over her. She could almost taste the acrid smell of blood as she separated the head of her first Roman captive from the rest of his worthless…

Pain seared, burning hot, on the left side of her head. Crashing to the ground, she writhed in waves of agony. The skin on her knees was a shredded mass of blood and sinew. Her head lolled to one side as she fought to breathe, spitting blood that now gushed from the gash in her tongue inflicted by her own teeth. Ama's body shook with electrifying pain and the shock of the sudden attack.

Hugging the ground on all fours, she sought to slow her breathing and calm the immensity of the fear that gripped her. She would not give her attacker cause to celebrate. In the name of Neito, why had she dropped her guard and allowed him to creep up behind her?

"Get up, you sniveling piece of excrement. You think yourself a great warrior. You could not even hear your own father approach. In the name of Cernunnos, why was I not granted a son? Get up, you whimpering bitch! You will never be worthy of the sword I gave you."

Pain raced through her body mercilessly and without escape. She dragged herself to a sitting position and, with great effort, hobbled to a defiant and defensive stance. It had been a long time since she allowed a whimper to escape in response to her father's merciless attacks.

His breath reeked of wine. Even filled to the brim with the vile stuff, her father was a formidable enemy. Some claimed even more so.

Father moved closer. Ama smelled his nauseous spittle as it landed on her determined face.

"You think yourself a great warrior," he sneered. "It makes my sides split with laughter! You will never see the battlefield. I promise you that. I have, on this day, promised you to Carus of the Belli tribe at Sekeida. He will fight for you both. It will strengthen the bonds between our tribes. It is time you compensated me for your wretched existence by birthing me a male heir."

Her father spat at her feet and marched off.

In that moment, the face of her father replaced Ama's vision of the decapitated Roman. She imagined him lying in a pool of his own blood, his face contorted in disbelief as she butchered him like the animal he was. With that vivid image embedded in her mind, she limped back to Baba's hut, followed by a trail of blood.

Chapter Twenty-Two

TARA AWOKE TO a violent throbbing pain in her head. A refrain of voices rife with accusation and condemnation repeated: "When are you going to do as you are told?" "Who do you think you are?" "When will you know your place?" "It is time you paid me back for your wretched existence by birthing me a male heir."

"How dare others think they may control someone's life? To squash someone's dreams is barbaric!" She flung the words into the vacuous darkness of her bedroom.

Rage consumed her as she realized she knew how Ama and Clarice felt. "We should all have the right to choose how we spend our time on this bloody planet!" Tara screamed out loud, exacerbating the knifing pain that slashed through her cranium.

The words "for time is not of the essence, but your essence is" came floating back to her. They quelled the ferocity of her anger. Sliding her feet off the bed and onto the bedroom floor, she rose in search of her supply of painkillers.

As soon as her feet hit the cold stone floor, she winced. Sucking in her already labored breath, she looked down. Both knees were badly scraped and tinged brown with congealed blood.

Her eyes widened and her pulse quickened while her heart thudded frantically in her breast. She clenched her fists and shook her head. "What the fuck is happening to me?"

She hobbled to the kitchen, retrieved pills from the confines of her purse, and made her way to the counter to pour herself a glass of water.

As she popped the pills into her mouth, she glanced out at the world beyond. The iridescent glow of the full moon hung like a pearl and played peek-a-boo with meandering bullet-gray clouds. It was in that moment that she heard it. Tara shook her head in disbelief. The lilt of graceful, haunting lyrics tantalized her ears and consumed all other sounds. It ebbed and flowed like waves on the moonlit landscape.

"Are you going bonkers?" she asked herself, peering out into the shadowy night. But there it was again!

I am the wind on the sea;
I am the wave of the sea;
I am the bull of seven battles;
I am the eagle on the rock
I am a flash from the sun;
I am the most beautiful of plants;
I am a strong wild boar;
I am a salmon in the water;
I am a lake in the plain;
I am the word of knowledge;
I am the head of the spear in battle;
I am the god that puts fire in the head;
Who spreads light in the gathering on the hills?
Who can tell the ages of the moon?
Who can tell the place where the sun rests?

The sweet softness of the incantation overpowered Tara's senses. She leaned forward until her nose all but rested on the kitchen windowpane. The sound came from the weed-entangled garden. Her fingers still grasped the faucet as water cascaded into her glass. Her fear was subdued by the urgent need to investigate the source of melody wafting innocuously into the night. She padded to the front door, lifted its latch, and stepped outside.

Tara made her way to the side of the stone cottage set aflame by the orbed white radiance above. Peering around the corner, she surveyed the scene and couldn't believe her eyes. The garden had been transformed into an oasis of fragrant color. Long, slender boulders that had lain broken in the soil now stood in a circle as though they had risen to greet the night sky.

Her caution vanished in a haze of astonishment as she confronted the old woman, who sat cross-legged and naked in the middle of the circle. Before she could say anything, she was met by a jovial smile that radiated such liveliness that Tara didn't notice the telltale creases of age etched on the old woman's face.

Tara was mesmerized by the glow emanating from her unwanted guest. Not that she was lit up like one of those cheap, over-decorated Christmas trees that beckoned consumers to buy, buy, buy. The luminosity emanating from this woman was much more subtle. In fact, the writer in her was challenged to find adequate words to describe it. Tara flinched as a shadowy creature rose and stretched beside the woman. Stunned, she realized it was a wolf.

Before she could turn and run to safety, the intruder said, "Oh, do not mind Cado. He will not harm you. He's an excellent judge of character. Welcome, child. I have been waiting for you. At last, we meet again!"

A colossal wave of irritation overcame Tara. "Who do you think you are?"

"Ah, now that is a most interesting question to explore." The old woman shot her a quizzical look. "I suppose it would be a fair place to start if I asked you the same thing."

"Look, I don't know who you think I am, but we've never met

before. And I would appreciate knowing who you are and how this godforsaken garden looks the way it does. Just this afternoon, it was full of weeds and discarded debris! And why are you here in the middle of the night, naked, singing?"

"You can see the garden in all its splendor, then?"

"Of course I can. It's right here in front of my eyes. It would be hard to miss. What I can't believe is how you whipped it into shape so fast."

"I did not whip it into any kind of shape. You and I are seeing the essential manifestation of its eternal consciousness. And I am so glad that you can see it. It means you have not forgotten how to witness the world around you!"

As she rose from her lotus position, the woman stretched her lithe, sinuous frame. The swiftness of her movement defied the age etched into the pale softness of her face.

"Let me introduce myself. One name I go by is Mamó, and I am the grandmother of Dana. I believe you two have already met. This is the home of my most recent ancestors. I come here often on the days leading up to Lá Bealtaine, as it is known today, to celebrate the vitality and ever-existent nature of life in all its forms. That is why I was singing an ancient mystical poem uttered by the bard Amairgen Glanglun, who walked upon these lands so long ago. For me, it is a way to honor and respect the essence of life, which flows through all sentient and non-sentient beings."

Tara reacted with a petulance she hadn't felt since childhood. "Well, I know that Lá Bealtaine, as you call it, isn't a celebration of life. It marked the start of the pastoral summer season, not a celebration of life!"

"And are not cattle and crops an expression of life, just as much as you and me, my child?" Mamó asked with the lilting softness of a flowing stream. The old woman was beside her now, as was the panting wolf, baring the sharpness of his teeth. Tara sincerely hoped the beast had already eaten his supper. The old woman touched Tara's arm with long and surprisingly supple fingers, like the hands of a concert pianist.

The unexplained nature of Tara's experiences over the past few days shrieked into the forefront of her consciousness, imbuing her being with lethargy. As the woman's eyes, filled with concern, stared back at her, Tara conceded, "You'll have to excuse me. I need to go back to bed and rest. I don't have the time or energy for this right now."

"Now is the only moment of time any of us have, dear one," Mamó said, caressing the curve of Tara's cheek. "Rest, my child. But understand, you will realize who you are and why you are here."

"The only reason I'm here is to write a book, and that seems to be going nowhere fast." Tara turned, retracing her footsteps. Before skirting the corner of the cottage, she heard Mamó sigh. "You were also birthed from a long line of healers and wise women, my dear. Soon, you will realize the importance of your life!"

As she beat a path to the asylum of her bed, Tara heard the whir of her cell phone before seeing its iridescent glow on the wooden kitchen table. *Fuck, just what I need!* She glared down at the screen. It was a text from Guy. Instead of switching the phone off, she glanced down at the message.

Where in God's name are you? Who do you think you are? We need to talk. Call me when you get this.

"Great questions, dude." Limping back to the amniotic warmth of her comforter, she decided that calling was far south of any willingness she felt to deal with life's vagary called "Guy." Within minutes of falling into bed, Tara found herself, once again, far removed from the reality of her current life.

CHAPTER TWENTY-THREE

"LEAVE WHAT YOU are doing and come with me," Sister Bernadette commanded as she strode across the chapel's stone floor.

"But Sister, I have not yet finished my task here, and you instructed me not to rise from my knees until every inch of floor was without dirt."

"Do not vex me, you insolent mongrel. The abbess has charged you with a new task. Now hurry!"

Clarice rose from all fours and scurried as quickly as possible to lessen the distance between herself and the old nun.

"But what is my new task, Sister?"

"For the love of God, must you always ask so many questions? A woman found slumped against the convent's door is suffering from exhaustion and severe dehydration. While we do not minister to the weak and infirm, the abbess has decided that you must tend to this heathen until she is well."

The old woman stopped as if she had run into an invisible wall. With the swiftness of someone much younger, she whirled around and met Clarice's eyes as words spat from her lips. "A fitting task, would you not say, one heathen attending to another? Now hasten. We have set up a makeshift infirmary in the disused stable."

An hour later, Clarice glanced down at her new charge. The woman's exhaustion was the least of what ailed her. Great swelling nodes distorted the contour of her scalp, limbs, and chest. The ulcers in her mouth made swallowing even small spoons of water almost impossible. The frailty of her rotting shins refused to support her. As Clarice gently bathed the feverish woman's body, she discovered an array of foul-smelling abscesses.

Prior to leaving her to her ministrations, Sister Bernadette told Clarice that the abbess had summoned the local surgeon, Guillaume Accart. "It is my sincere hope he will dispatch this vile woman to where she belongs, which is definitely not within the sanctity of these walls." As the old nun shuffled from the stable, Clarice wondered where the vileness truly lay.

The sun was falling behind the horizon when the surgeon graced the stable with his presence. He lifted a lace handkerchief to his enormous nose and glared first at Clarice and then at the woman writhing on the swiftly constructed, straw-infused bed. Not bothering to come closer to perform even a cursory examination, he pronounced, "It is my considered opinion that this wretched woman suffers from the onset of leprosy."

"Marie," Clarice offered.

"Excuse me?" The surgeon countered, looking down his long nose at her. "Her name is Marie."

"It is of no consequence. We must send this woman as soon as possible to the leprosy hospital beyond the city walls. In the meantime, you are to administer the ointment of mercury. I will have my servant deliver it directly."

Clarice knew the malaise of leprosy and was quite confident that what afflicted her charge was something decidedly different. After a hesitant pause, she spoke. "Monsieur Accart, I am not convinced that Marie is suffering from the malady of leprosy."

"Oh, really? And what expert knowledge has led you to this conclusion?"

His reaction was no great surprise. Medicine was the precious territory of men. For centuries, women had practiced the healing arts through conventional and not-so-conventional means, but those days were over. In fact, in recent times, women who practiced the healing arts—whether in the religious or the secular world—were maliciously linked to witchcraft and black magic, although the general populace preferred their remedies over the cures of male surgeons.

"Monsieur Accart, please believe me. I mean no disrespect concerning your knowledge and opinion," she said, hoping to calm the mushrooming dilation of his pupils.

"Mademoiselle, I am not sure where you studied medicine? Those livid lumps that have attacked this woman's body, the bloodshot nature of her eyes, the hoarseness of her speech, and the drastic thinning of her hair are all indications of leprosy. Perhaps you should leave the diagnosis to the professionals and focus on a more suitable occupation? I might suggest weaving or milking cows." He turned his back on her with an attitude dripping with venomous disdain.

"But Monsieur—"

Incensed, the physician spun around. "I would not deign to waste my time on such a matter had it not been at the request of the abbess. Now do as I say!"

"But Monsieur—"

"I know all about you and your whore of a mother. Know your place. Do as I say. It will not bode well if you defy me. I promise you that!"

"Do not speak of my mother in such a manner, Monsieur," she said, unable to contain her rage any longer. "Mama was a kind and learned healer. She helped many of the 'wretched' people you are so quick to dismiss. You will never hold a candle to her!"

His gray eyes blazed with fury. "It would not be in your best interest to cross me. I can make life extremely difficult for you if I choose. You best do what I say in matters that do not concern you."

He stepped toward her, stopping mere inches from her face. "If you do not show the respect my station deserves, I promise you, I will crush you like an unwanted insect! Now, I assume you feel capable of administering the ointment of mercury when it arrives? If not, I will suggest the abbess find someone more suitable to attend to this wretched woman." His words stung.

Once he left the infirmary, Clarice allowed her pent-up, anger-fueled silence to erupt. "Of all the conceited malcontents! He is the epitome of the arrogant attitude of the medical profession. He would not know the nature of a disease if it bit him on the cheek." After taking a moment to catch her breath, she continued her rant. "Of course, that will never happen! He is too pompous to get close enough to see Marie's symptoms are not the same as those who suffer from leprosy."

With her anger sufficiently spent, she slumped onto a nearby wooden bench and focused on the differences between Marie's state and the condition of leprosy victims. Leprosy sufferers were insensitive to touch and related pain. However, her current ward cringed every time Clarice attempted to cleanse her body. Also, Marie seemed to have no trouble moving the parts of her body afflicted by her illness. Leprosy victims could not move parts of their bodies. This symptom began with the inability to close their eyes. In the cases of leprosy she had treated, the disease affected the victim's arms and hands, but this was not the primary area of affliction for her current patient.

Clarice had also noticed that the illness affected the bones in Marie's head and the shaft of her limbs rather than the bones of her extremities, as with leprosy sufferers. There were other symptoms that did not align with Accart's flippant diagnosis: Marie was feverish, had swollen lymph glands, a sore throat, and violent headaches. The sagging of her skin heralded the loss of a considerable amount of weight over a short period. Something else fueled Clarice's suspicions. She had found several faint grayish raised lesions inside the woman's mouth, under her armpits, and in her groin area. None of these matched the symptoms exhibited by leprosy. Her final thought, before rising to tend to Marie, was that leprosy victims experienced the constant expulsion of waste from their bowels. However, this symptom had not occurred in her current patient.

"No." Clarice fumed as she paced around the makeshift bed. "The only diarrhea witnessed today spouted forth from the mouth of one self-absorbed surgeon."

She set out to investigate Marie's ailment. Using the pretext that she needed supplies, she was granted permission to visit town. Clarice found that her patient was one of many with similar symptoms. She questioned as many of the afflicted as she could, attempting to identify common relationships, activities, or dwelling places. She determined that many of them frequented the docks; most of the men worked portside, and the women had dalliances with sailors on shore leave. She shifted her focus to the men, reviewing what she had learned. The major discovery that linked them to the woman in her care was that they had relations with prostitutes who worked the docks. Perplexed by this finding, Clarice wondered why this pox was rearing its ugly head now. She couldn't help but think that if this was the price these women must pay for plying their trade, then it was too high.

As she sat in the warmth of the afternoon sun, she recalled something her mother had told her. It was a declaration from the King's Council almost a hundred years earlier, "Les pêcheurs sont absolument nécessaires à la terre." Clarice mused that if fishermen really were a necessity, then someone must find a cure for this ailment, or they'd eat no more fish!

Raising her eyes to the heavens, she witnessed a single cloud, reminding her of white marble, as it moved across the blue satin of the sky in slow motion. Transfixed, she knew she must dig deeper into the original source of the disease. That would require gaining permission from the abbess, no mean feat! Abbess Héloïse was not easily swayed. Nor was she willing to deal in trivialities or unfounded truths put forth by anyone under her authority, especially a lowly postulant. Héloïse was an adept protector of both her community's interests and the authority of her office. Even amid the rage of the current political battle between competing royal family interests, the church, and the state, she had been unrelenting. From what Clarice gathered, royalty's desire to increase control and institute-sweeping monastic reform fueled this tension.

Since her altercation with Accart, she learned he was one of the most ardent local advocates for this institutional change. He believed women within monastic service did not need education, should know their place, and should serve as handmaidens for the priests.

"*Cochon!*" She listened at the closed door of her makeshift infirmary to hear if there were any pleas for help. Her anger deflated and her heart softened, but her conviction remained resolute. "I can beg an audience," she whispered. "Once I have collected substantial evidence, I can beg an audience with her. I must base my suspicions on more than intuition and current observations."

Motivated by the knowledge that she would have to visit the dock area to continue her investigation, she prayed for a way to be granted leave of the convent. Part of her role was to source and procure medicinal supplies. Clarice needed to get a fresh supply of bishopwort and wormwood to mix with equal parts of radish, garlic, helenium, cropleek, and hollow leek in order to refill the mixture she kept in a brass pot. Her supply was almost depleted, and filling it would serve as her escape route to further her investigation dockside. This excuse would work because, over the last few weeks, the concoction had proven to be a great relief for Sister Bernadette, as well as for others, when their heads and joints ached. She was certain the aging nun would grudgingly grant her permission to leave the confines of the convent walls to get what she needed to make a new batch.

As if on cue, Sister Bernadette appeared, robbing Clarice of any warmth she felt. "You insipid wretch, is this how you spend your time? Get up. I need some salve."

CHAPTER TWENTY-FOUR

CLARICE'S HEART RACED as she rose to attention. She could not falter in her mission. Not now, when so many depended on her.

"Sister Bernadette, I stand before you, contrite. My new charges have kept me so busy, I have not had time to replenish the potion. I am sorry to admit I do not even have all the ingredients needed for its preparation. It is my humble request to send Sister Adatte to the herbalist who lives near the docks to purchase bishopwort and wormwood. Although the last time, she did not remember what I required and came back with the wrong herbs."

Sister Bernadette lashed out. "You stupid, incompetent girl. I do not care about the condition of your 'new charges.' Their sickness is a divine reaction to their countless sins. There should be less ministering to them and more prayers asking the Lord, the Virgin Mary, and the saints for forgiveness."

Winching from pain, the elderly nun exploded. "You know full well I have directed you to keep a supply of this medication available at all times! Sister Adatte is busy with other duties and is not at your beck and call. You will stop what you are doing this instant and get what you need with haste." Sister Bernadette walked out of the infirmary with as much swagger as her bent, frail body and aching limbs would allow.

Victorious but also cautious not to waste a precious minute, Clarice called on Sister Simone, who was lovingly tending vegetable beds, to come and look after the needs of her patients while she visited the docks.

A postulant was not restricted to wear the habit of a novice or nun, and Clarice found herself humming with joy as she prepared to leave the choking confines of monastic life behind. Long ago, she realized she would never consider entering the novitiate and would never endure the years of intense study, contemplation, and prayer. Even further from her mind was taking vows to become a nun, despite Sister Bernadette's constant and brutal reminders of the abject need for her to find an acceptable way of "being" in the world.

As the massive front gate of the convent slammed shut behind her, Clarice's heart soared.

From the streets below, the savory smells of Guinea pepper, ginger, and beef greeted her. Inhaling deep into her belly, she caught a hint of saffron that perfumed the air, mixed with cooking cabbage, a staple of the less-affluent members of Marseille's society. The smell of fresh fish being unloaded from boats below assailed her senses and blended with an olfactory medley of olive oil, alkali, and sea salt that wafted from the city's latest enterprise, a soap factory.

The odors grew less aromatic as Clarice made her way into the bowels of the crowded city. Marseille's gutters overflowed with free-floating feces. The city was afflicted with contaminated water. Sanitation of any description was nonexistent. Diseases infested the docks, carried from far-away lands by the mercantile and trading ships which commandeered the inlet below. As she navigated streets and alleyways, she realized there should be a committee of local dignitaries and physicians who board and inspect all incoming ships before allowing them to dock in the harbor. If she had her way, this inspection would include cargo, passengers, and crew to make sure they disembarked disease-free. The pervasive male voice of authority would see this as a costly and frivolous waste of time. Especially if the idea came from a humble postulant.

Clarice set all notions of the unsavory, unsanitary nature of Marseille aside to concentrate on her descent to the lower part of the city, through the labyrinth of steep, narrow streets inhabited by the city's seafaring population. Laundry hanging overhead on lines strung from balcony to balcony competed for the warmth of the sun. She imagined the Marseille of old. The Marseille that had thrived since the Greeks founded it sometime around 600 BC. The Marseille before Alfonso and his thugs had sacked it.

She stopped to catch her breath beside an unimpressive doorway, weathered and crumbling, amid a row of similar entryways. Clarice understood that to find out what was going on, it was best to sit down where people gathered and listen, and she planned to do so today.

In the port, the seamless, uninterrupted blueness of sky stretched across the full extent of her field of vision. The peaceful view was a sharp contrast to the frenetic commercial hubbub that rose and fell from the harbor and lower town. She found an unobtrusive spot near the stalls at the entrance to the harbor, where young and old, male and female, Muslim, Jew, and Christian, came to buy, swap, and ply their trade in relative harmony.

The *Saint Marie*, heavily fortified with rams, catapults, and cannons, was making slow, arduous progress under oar to its anchorage in the harbor's southeast. The galley's owners had accumulated excessive wealth from yearly trading journeys to Alexandria in Egypt.

From her vantage point, she had a magnificent view of the comings and goings on the dock. And, if she turned ever-so-slightly, she looked out into the bay and saw two of the four islands that made up the limestone L'archipel du Frioul. The smallest of the four islands was Île d'If, and just behind it, was Île Ratonneau.

The vibrant expanse of turquoise water stretched out in every direction until it was contained by the arms of the horizon. Because of its accessible mooring, she believed Île Ratonneau would be the perfect spot for incoming ships to lay anchor while being inspected for contagious diseases. The easy access to its eastern shore would make it an excellent location to build an infirmary for the care of infected crew or passengers.

Turning her attention to her immediate surroundings, Clarice caught her first break. Amid the noise of men mending fishing nets and vendors selling grain, nuts, and olives, she heard a woman, a purveyor of every kind of spice, conversing with her neighbor.

"Did you hear about Marie? I told her not to go with any of those filthy heathens off that boat from Africa. Now she is up there at the convent wasting away, oozing pus, and who knows what else. I do not know why we let those godforsaken men come ashore." Gaining momentum, she added, "I do not know why we have to trade with the likes of them at all!"

"Well, *ma chère*, if we did not trade with them, where would you get those spices you sell for exorbitant prices?" the other woman asked. "Besides, the poor woman felt she had no other choice, living with that lazy, worthless husband of hers!"

The first woman straightened the grayness of the once-pristine white linen cap adorning her head, then tightened the belt on her high-waisted tunic that held her sagging breasts in place.

"And she is not the only one. Whatever malady is devouring her, she gave it to her husband, she did. Some of the other *putains* plying their trade hereabouts have found their way up the hill to the care of those pious nuns."

Crossing herself, the other woman sighed. "By the grace of God, we have been spared from a life of selling our bodies and souls to the highest, or should I say lowest, bidder."

The gossip monger clamped her calloused, saffron-stained hands on her ample hips. "Well, I do not care what you say! Whatever it is, this pox is divine retribution for a life of sin." She turned her attention to a young woman who approached her stall.

Clarice sat for a few minutes and observed the interaction between this woman and her customer. The girl's clothing revealed that she worked as a servant at one of the noble houses in the upper town. Although sumptuary laws enforced wearing clothing appropriate to one's station in life, the girl wore a newish gown made from more refined cloth than she looked like she could ever afford.

The dress was most likely part of her yearly upkeep, given by her employer. This was not charity given by the well-off families in town but a way of ensuring their servants were fit to be seen by household visitors.

"Pardonnez-moi madame, puis-je prendre un peu de votre temps?" Clarice asked.

The woman shot her a scathing look even Sister Bernadette would envy. *"Qu'est-ce que tu veux?"*

The aggressive retort made Clarice recoil, but she recovered and stood her ground. "Madame, a moment of your time, please. That is all I seek."

"Well, *ma petite*, if it is my time you want, it will cost you."

"But Madame, the only money I had, I spent to buy a piece of bread earlier. I have no money to give you."

"Well, be off with you, then. I have no time for idle gossip."

"Madame, I must insist on speaking with you further. It is not for myself I seek your audience, but for the benefit of the patients in my infirmary. I am in charge of the infirmary at the convent to the north of the city and have in my care Marie, of whom I heard you speak, as well as others who suffer from the same malaise."

"Well, if you were indeed listening, then you know I have no time to help such sinners."

A nearby hemp vendor, who had just dispatched a burly fisherman looking to broker a deal for material to mend his nets, with a perfunctory *"imbecile stupide,"* looked over and sighed. "Come, Agnesot, for once in your miserable life, do someone some kindness. She only wants to talk. It is not like she is looking for you to hand over that sizeable horde of money we all know you have."

"You leave my horde or lack thereof alone, Jehannette," the woman said. "I was just having some fun with little madame here."

Turning to Clarice, she said, "Ask what you will. But do it quick. I have no time to idle my day away with trivial rumor."

"Do you know which vessel the men came from who had…um… relations with Marie and the other women?"

"Relations," the woman scoffed. "Is that what you call it? Very well, it was the *Vertbois* out of Lo Vivièr. But that will do you no good. That bucket of sin upped anchor for Africa again."

"How long ago did the ship leave?"

"*Quoi?*"

"Madame, how long has it been since the *Vertbois* weighed anchor?"

"How would I know? I'm not their keeper! Got enough on my plate, just keeping hearth and home together and food on the table."

Jehannette scoffed, "Yes, *mon amie*, we can all see you are wasting away to nothing! For God's sake, just answer the girl."

"Gone about a month thereabouts, I would guess. Now bugger off! I have no more time for the likes of you."

With a smile of thanks to Jehannette, Clarice hurried away.

A month. She picked her way among the stalls, purveying wares meant to entice the citizenry of Marseille to part with their hard-earned francs. As her foot landed on the first of the many steps that led back to the convent, she had an idea. Administering healthy doses of sarsaparilla to her patients would be much more effective than the mercury ointment and vapor remedy the surgeon prescribed, which was not helping her patients' recovery. She smiled, acknowledging it would not be the first time she went against the advice of the medical profession.

Clarice halted, sensing a presence. "I know you. And I know you are there. Do not be afraid to show yourself to me."

CHAPTER TWENTY-FIVE

TARA'S EYELIDS SPRANG open. Had it all been a dream? It had seemed so vivid, so detailed! How the hell did Clarice know she was there? The vintage wrought-iron bed creaked in protest as she kicked off the luscious warmth of her comforter. She pulled back the ancient curtains as the vibrant lavender and amber of sunrise merged into a soft, pink-infused peach.

Stretching her arms, Tara acknowledged that Clarice's courage to place the needs of others above her own safety was inspiring, if not misplaced. It was challenging for a woman to stand her ground in the present world. If Accart discovered what Clarice was doing, the consequences could be lethal. After all, in the fifteenth century, women had to toe the line.

Her feet felt the floor with more caution than usual, remembering the searing pain of the night before.

"Oh, my frigging God!" Her cry shattered any hope of calm.

She scanned both knees, spreading her hands like starfish over them. The bruised, raw- redness of the prior night had vanished into a flawless sheen.

As the pale dawn transformed into full-blown daylight, her shaking hands kept pace with her racing mind as she attempted to understand what was happening to her. Was the isolation wreaking havoc on the stability of her mind and senses? That couldn't be it. She wasn't really alone. Not with Dana, Mamó, and Cado, her perpetual visitors who turned up whenever they bloody well liked.

Straining to remember how to breathe, she staggered to the kitchen like a condemned prisoner traveling to the guillotine.

An hour later, after a coffee and a bath in the old-fashioned copper tub, she dressed in faded blue jeans and a white T-shirt. She searched among the piles of clothing strewn across the two suitcases for the warm coziness of her favorite periwinkle jumper. She nuzzled into its familiar comfort and felt the tension unwind a bit.

As she carried the last sloshing bucket of bath water to the front of the cottage to dump it, she laughed at her daily activity. One of the "luxuries" of living in the middle of nowhere in a cottage last upgraded at the end of the nineteenth century.

Dana came around the corner. "Good morning. How goes your day?"

The innocence of Dana's question was the only catalyst Tara needed. Unable to maintain control over the vulnerability she was feeling, she spewed words with the red-hot velocity of an erupting volcano.

"To be honest, I've no bloody idea! Weird and not-so-wonderful things have been happening since I climbed that wretched hill. Oh, and your grandmother used some sort of magic to clear the land in the garden last night before I met her, sitting starkers in the middle of a stone labyrinth, chanting obscure poetry to the moon. How can someone so old have the physical strength to do that? And to top it all off, I'm having bloody visions now. So, run for the hills because I'm becoming a raving lunatic!"

As the molten energy receded, Tara realized Dana was attempting to stifle a fit of laughter.

"It's not funny!"

Like Tara's tirade, Dana's amusement was not slow to surface.

Her laughter exploded as if charged by dynamite, filling the immediate space between them and spilling out into the sunshine of the early morning.

Her hilarity subsided into the smiling creases of her upturned mouth. "I can see you are more than a bit upset, my friend. But I can assure you of four things. One—the garden has not risen from the dead. Two—Mamó can and will turn up at the oddest times. Three— you are not going mad! And four…" Dana dialed down her sarcastic tone for the final assurance. "You are blessed, Tara, more than you realize."

Not sure which of her companion's assertions fueled the fresh flush of anger that swept from her solar plexus, Tara clenched her fists. "Right. If you don't believe me, let me show you. The godforsaken garden is now a pristine refuge!"

Without waiting, Tara stomped to the garden at the side of the house.

By the time she caught up, Tara stood statue still, eyes glazed, mouth wide open.

"But I saw it…with my two eyes. What the fuck is going on? What is this place? I…" Tara's voice faded. Shoulders slumped, temper spent, she faced her visitor. Any remnants of tranquility disappeared. Her voice dropped to a hollow murmur. "I just don't understand any of this."

The whir of her cell phone, lodged in the confines of her jeans, made her jump. As if on autopilot, she wriggled her fingers into the recesses of her front pocket to extract it. Looking down at the caller ID, she choked as if starved of oxygen, gasping, each breath a short, shallow burst.

"Oh, for the sake of God! This is not what I need right now!" The call was from Guy. She looked for Dana and saw her walking toward the front of the cottage. Tara hit the green button.

"What?"

"Finally! Where the hell have you been? I've been calling for the last week. What, you don't answer my calls anymore?"

She bit her initial response of "What business is it of yours?" and composed herself enough to say, "Well, good morning to you too!"

"I know that tone. Don't patronize me. I'm in no mood."

"Well, what I can surmise from your tone is you're in one hell of a stinking mood!"

Clutching the phone tighter, she waited for Guy's blazing comeback. She didn't have to wait long.

"For God's sake, who the fuck do you think you are? You leave in the middle of the night for Christ knows where without even so much as a note. And now you're giving me attitude? I have a right to know where you are and when you'll be back!"

The skin on her knuckles grew white. Sucking in her labored breath, her words bounced off the phone with the ferocity of thunderous rain.

"You, of all people, have no right at all!" Bile rose in her throat. "How's your personal assistant doing? What's her name again? Oh yes, Charlotte, that's it, isn't it? Still looking after all your needs, is she?"

"Oh, for Christ's sake, I told you it didn't mean a thing. And we hadn't had sex for ages. A man has needs, Tara. Anyway, I thought you got over that incident. Can we move on from the tedium of this tired discussion?"

She should have expected that response. Guy wasn't someone to lament over past or present indiscretions. Weariness crept over her like a platoon of ants converging on oil-soaked concrete. With everything else, she didn't have the energy to deal with Guy's misogynistic self-obsession.

Sighing into the phone, all she could muster was a feeble, "Look, Guy, can we talk later? I have someone here right now."

"Who's there? You pick up a boy toy treat for your little rebellious time away?"

"Guy, please! I don't have energy for this or us right now." Her tone sounded as deflated as her spirit. "I need to—"

"Forget us for the moment. I'm your agent. I have a right to know how the book is coming along."

"It's not." Tara clicked the red button on her phone.

Unsure if disgust or pent-up longing fueled it, a craving overcame her, not based on sexual release, but one that surged from a deep sense of loss. She no longer knew what she hoped to find. Shivering despite the warmth of the morning sun, she was overwhelmed with desolate loneliness.

She looked toward the front of the cottage, wondering where her unwanted company had disappeared to and decided that Dana's intrusion was better than exploring the depths of her sadness. Her guest was lounging under the hawthorn. Tara resolved to banish all unpleasantness from her mind.

"Sorry about that!"

"No bother at all. I am the one interrupting your day!"

She noticed the ground was still dew-clad as she lowered herself to sit near Dana. "Can I get you a cup of tea or anything?"

Dana declined. "Thank you all the same. My eyes will float if I have another cuppa. But please, don't let that stop you."

"No, it's okay. I'm not bothered." Thorny leaves prickled her backside. Tara swept them away and resettled on the ground. To dispel any lingering discomfort from her recent phone call and divert the conversation away from her escalating nighttime wanderings, she asked, "Are you still willing to tell me a bit about your ancestors?"

"Of course, if you have the time?"

"Well, it's not like I'm writing up a storm at the moment," Tara said, surprised at the genuine heartiness of her laughter.

"Before I start, I must explain that some of what I will share predates history. They have handed these tales down from mother to daughter over generations, so you cannot verify the 'facts.'"

"No worries. It's possible my agent's insistence on producing 'historical facts' is causing my writer's block. Thinking about it now, I must admit it bores me rigid! Being privy to the everyday lives of women and men who can no longer speak for themselves would enliven both me and the storyline."

The thin lines of Dana's brows knit together in concentration, still and silent, as if contemplating where she might begin her tale. Within a matter of seconds, she smiled. "Best to begin as far back as the tales go. But let me warn you, our matriarchal line has not always been a picture of subservient meekness. It has more than its fair share of warrior women and healers condemned as witches. Both saints and sinners populate our long history." She chuckled.

Intrigued, Tara relaxed into the cool, damp earth beneath her.

"Well then, let me see. My foremothers came from the Iberian Peninsula, and I'll begin with one of the more colorful ancestors. No one remembers her name, but in her day, no one would ever forget it. Her story comes from a time some hundred-and-sixty-odd years before the birth of our Lord, Jesus Christ." Dana stopped long enough to cross herself before continuing.

"She was the only offspring of a fearsome Celtiberian warrior chief who lived in the mountainous region of what today is called northeastern Spain. Although day-to-day life revolved around raising and herding cattle, the warrior aristocracy, of which her father was one, claimed untold wealth as they raided the lands and herds of neighboring tribes and held vicious control over access to winter grazing pastures. She was born into a proud family who would rather die than surrender their swords. Being raised in that environment, it is no surprise she became fearsome, too."

"Humankind has not always been 'human-like' or 'kind' over the millennia, have they?"

Her eyes glazed over. For a moment, she appeared to be lost somewhere far beyond the present. When her eyes cleared, Dana's cheeks flushed with either excitement or embarrassment. Tara couldn't be sure.

"You will excuse me. Sometimes my thoughts distract me. Now, where was I? Ah, yes. I was talking about the fearsome and fearless woman-child. It is told that, at nine years of age, she challenged a boy almost twice her age and size to a duel. Dispatching him within moments, she raised her sword to take his right hand as a trophy. Had it not been for a group of tribal women, the lad would never have fought again." She took a quick breath and continued. "But the crux of her story does not start until the eve of her womanhood. For years, she ached for the victorious thrill of combat. It was a hundred-and-fifty-odd years before the birth of our Lord, Jesus Christ."

Dana shifted as if seeking a more comfortable position on the ground. "It was the time of great Roman expansion, and their lustful greed for power, wealth, and conquest had reached the borders of the girl's homeland. Now, she was a smart one, always eavesdropping on the conversations of the warriors. She knew there would soon be a call for every able-bodied person, including women, to defend their way of life. The story goes she found out a scoundrel named Marcellus had declared war on their neighbors, and she knew her tribe would rally to their aid. She was ready, able, and willing to die for the glory of her tribe and—"

Without preamble or apology, Tara jumped in. "Are you talking about the Roman Consul Marcus Claudius Marcellus and his declaration of war on the Belli tribe, which heralded the Second Celtiberian War?"

Dana responded, "Yes, but how do you know that?"

"I have no idea. I've never researched the Iberian Peninsula. Not for this book or any other I've written!"

Silence dangled between them, raw and out of control, like a wildfire threatening to consume them. The stillness spread to Tara's bloodstream and immobilized her brain. Her pupils dilated. Her hands trembled. A familiar tingle started at the tip of her toes and emanated in waves throughout her body. Before she disappeared, she felt her blood boil with anger at Guy, at her writer's block, and her entire life.

Chapter Twenty-Six

THE CELESTIAL ORB had waxed and waned six times since Ama's hilltop encounter with her father. To her, it was a lifetime ago. Since then, she had left Baba's hut and hidden in the thick underbrush of the nearby forest in fear of being handed off to Carus, the Sekeidian leader under whom she now served.

Her eyes narrowed. She tilted her head. Her lips tugged upward and to the left in a momentary smirk. She was sure neither her father, who fought at Carus's side, nor the exalted leader himself had any idea where she was.

Much had transpired since she escaped the drudgery of her existence. Quintus Fabius Nobilitor and his thirty thousand men had marched on Sekeida only to find it deserted. In retribution, the swine razed it to the ground and marched toward Ama's home of Numantia, where the people of Sekeida had fled and turned the earth black with soot as they scrambled to safety.

All those events had brought her to that moment. She stood and surveyed the blood-soaked earth of the forest near Ribarroya, a day's march from home. The enemy's mutilated and decapitated bodies were strewn like garbage. The defeat of the Roman troops was a massacre.

Serves the scum right, she thought, being defeated on the day they celebrated Vulcan, their God of fire!

Shaking off exhaustion and the ache in her bones, Ama removed her helmet with a blood-soaked hand. Long, beautiful tresses should have tumbled down her back. But all that was revealed was dagger-sheared hair, hacked off to conceal her identity before joining the twenty-thousand-strong infantry under Carus's command.

Her senses snapped to full alert. Adrenaline swam through her veins like fish through water. A pulse banged in her ears and sweat formed rivulets that cascaded down her spine. For several seconds, she dared not move a muscle.

There it was again. A distinct rustle from behind a cluster of nearby oaks, their branches dense with leaves. Feigning an air of cautious nonchalance, Ama scanned the surrounding area, realizing that all of her comrades were gone. She cursed herself for not noticing she was alone. The sound could be an approaching wolf pack. Ama scanned her surroundings again. A multitude of bloodied corpses were easy prey. The wolves would not delay such a sumptuous meal!

Her breath came in short, thin breaks. With as much bravado as she could muster, she exhaled and shouted, "Come out, you sniveling dog. I know you are there. Show yourself or I will cut you down like the vermin you are!"

She waited. The only response was the swish of long-dead underbrush tossed by sporadic gusts of wind as it wove through the trees. The soulless creak of her sword being drawn from its sheath answered back. And once again, whispered swirls of silence saturated the landscape.

Raising her sword above her head, she cried out in the frenzied, bloodthirsty howls that warriors of her tribe used to intimidate and paralyze their enemy. She clutched the hilt tighter. The moisture in her lungs evaporated as she ran toward the unseen threat. But her sprint stopped as suddenly as it began. A scene unfolded before her, inconceivable to fathom. In the shadows, a form appeared. Cowering with fright was a girl not much younger than herself, heavy with child. By the clothes she wore, Ama knew this girl was Roman or perhaps a captive slave forced to become a camp whore.

"In the name of Cosus, what are you doing here?"

The girl wailed as she fell to her knees, "In the name of Endovelicus, spare me and my unborn child!"

"Get up! I asked you what you are doing here. Where did you come from? Answer me now before I run you and your unborn child through!"

"I beg you, do not hurt us! The Romans captured me after an attack on my tribe." Tremors of fear erupted into convulsive sobs as she continued. "I…I…am…of the Paesuri tribe from the far west… near a…wide expanse…of water." The girl's breathing slowed. Her eyes glistened with tears of fear. She begged, "All I desire is to be returned to the arms of my people and to raise my babe in peace."

Ama stared with cold, rigid determination at the pleading eyes of this desperate mother-child. A bleeding heart would get her nowhere.

"Of what origin is the father of your child?"

"A Roman swine," the girl spat, but her malice transformed to unmitigated affection as she caressed her swollen belly and whispered in tender tones, "But I will love and cherish this little one forever!"

Upon hearing that the girl would spawn the offspring of her enemy, without hesitation or a flicker of doubt, Ama raised her sword once again. Her swift sword came crashing down to the red earth beneath her feet. A blinding flash of colored spots appeared without warning, as they had before.

"In the name of Trebopala, not now! I have no time for these intrusions!" The excruciating pain between her eyes intensified until Ama was no longer…

When she regained awareness, she was crouching, her limbs taut and ready for action. Eyes wide, alert, she surveyed her environs in search of any danger that lurked in the shadows. She found no immediate cause for alarm and allowed the air trapped in her lungs to escape in one slow exhale.

The harsh pounding of many feet had worn the small rocks that blanketed the main corridor smooth. She stomped over their cold unevenness, seeking a way back to the forest. But she knew her search was in vain. When these visions came, she was at their mercy. She despised not being in control. It was one of the fundamental reasons she shunned the path Baba so often declared she would tread.

A chorus of blood-curdling cries of victory drew Ama's lips upward in delightful recognition. *That is a glorious sound*, she thought with a smirk.

In an effortless, choreographed motion, similar to the wolves of her native land, she stalked another discernible noise. Unlike the victorious howl of the warriors, this grief-stricken sound was the wail of a child in distress. She had never heard such mournful longing. It wrenched at her gut. Still, she needed to be on guard. It might be a trap.

Ama crept forward to discover the source of the commotion. A small silhouette was crouched over a heap on the ground. Taking in the mud-caked hair, the filthy, tattered tunic, and the devastated silhouette, she realized the girl was only a few years younger than herself.

A distant haze of recognition arose, mingled with a sudden and scorching jolt so severe it threatened to split Ama's skull wide apart. She was not witnessing the scene; she had become part of it. No longer an observer, she had become one with the young girl. She saw what the girl saw and felt her intense emotions.

As one body, she and the young girl wept.

"Mama, Mama, wake up," they whispered in unison. Nothing.

Ama felt the clamminess of approaching death as they attempted to shake the woman back to wakefulness, sobbing, "Mama, please wake up."

Still, there was no response.

"Please, Mama, please wake up," they screamed, not knowing what else to do.

The shouts of marauding men grew closer. The young girl did not seem to care. She could not leave without her mother. She would not.

Frantic, they shrieked, "Mama, please wake up! We need to go."

Slender fingers encircled their hand. Bending close to hear the words the mother's lips were forming, they cried, "Mama, I cannot hear what you are saying."

Shouts of victorious, cruel pleasure echoed from the other side of the alleyway.

The woman clasped their hand more firmly. "Run, *ma petite ange*, run. It is too late for me. Run as fast as you can, and hide."

"No, Mama, I will not leave you. Please, please, please get up. I will help you," they begged.

Mama flashed a faint smile. "No, *mon amour*, you cannot save me."

In a flash of searing pain, Ama was once again standing, sword in hand, on the blood-splattered earth of the forest near Ribarroya, staring down at the lifeless body of the woman-child and her round belly.

Wiping the fresh blood from her sword onto her tunic, Ama knew no remorse. Nothing! All she felt was sheer and utter defiance. She could not, would not capitulate to the sobbing cries of anyone, however remote their association with the enemy was. It was her duty as a warrior to annihilate the Roman vermin, no matter what their age.

With quick, practiced efficiency, Ama yanked at the girl's hair and severed the head from the body with no notice of her latest victim's open eyes or the slackness of her mouth.

Her swift feet barely felt the ground as she marched away, knowing that her father would be proud of her warrior skills!

Chapter Twenty-Seven

TARA AWOKE. AIR rippled across the freckled bareness of her skin as the sun dropped behind the horizon, dyeing the sky a shade of pomegranate pink. She glanced at her hands, grateful not to find any remnants of blood splatter. Her icy fingers trembled, resisting any warmth that lingered in the air as she dragged her body to an upright position.

Her stomach heaved. Acting on instinct, she drew her knees toward her chest until they nestled under her chin and clasped her arms around them, desperate to attain calm. Her stomach spasmed again. It gripped her with more intensity this time as she relived the gruesome horror of Ama slashing through the fragile existence of mother and child, ending their life together with one hack of her blood-drenched sword.

Covering her aching eyes, still swollen with sleep, she realized she hadn't just been observing the scene from a distance, as in her other dreams. She had morphed into the angry, sword-wielding skin of this ferocious young woman, a female so fueled with unrepentant rage that she could take the lives of her enemy without an ounce of compunction.

Tara's stomach heaved again, but this time, she wasn't able to swallow its contents back down. A thick, fluid mass of partially digested food sprayed across the ground in front of her. Some chunks landed on her shoes. On all fours, she heaved again, her projectile vomit spraying even farther afield. Her body shook at the violent expulsion of the contents of her stomach, which continued until it produced harsh bile.

As she attempted to breathe, the vivid echo of what she'd just experienced reverberated in her head. Stunned beyond belief, she shrieked, "How the hell is any of this fucking possible? How can Ama, who lived long before Clarice, be privy to visions from Clarice's childhood?"

In marionette fashion, her hand jerked as she swiped at the sick at the corner of her mouth. Another thought struck her as she attempted to connect the dots that refused to form a unified pattern. How in God's name was she privy to both experiences? She wanted out of whatever was happening. And she wanted out now!

Exhaustion overwhelmed her as she flopped back onto the hard surface beneath her. Her throat was dry and sore from the stomach acid that laced it. All she could taste was acrid vomit. She rose to her feet and stumbled toward the cottage in need of water to wash away the stench from her mouth and to bathe, hoping to drown the vision that now haunted every step.

Before releasing the ancient door latch of the cottage, Tara turned to look at the hawthorn. Nothing had changed. "Well, only the decorated earth," she attempted a feeble quip. Something that had changed was the frequency of these dreams, visions, or hallucinations. They were escalating. She wasn't sure what to call them, these…episodes. Yes, they were definitely "episodes."

It was then that she realized Dana had vanished like Houdini. A vice-like grip of loneliness seized her heart and threatened to cut off its vitality. She needed to talk to someone about the source of the vibration that consumed her body, mind, and soul ever since her visit to the hill. But she was nowhere near ready or able to share with anyone, much less explore the origins of her episodes.

After a hot bath and sweet tea, Tara sat staring at the glare of her laptop. Her body ached for rest, but her mind demanded answers. Why was this vibrational hum becoming part of the normalcy of her life? And why did this powerful energy herald the onslaught of frequent episodic visions?

She rubbed the weariness from her eyes, not sure how long she had sat there. The watery white-silver glow of the waxing moon spilled through the panes of the kitchen window. Tara stretched to loosen the aching in her legs and sipped the dregs of her lukewarm tea. Despite the stiffness, she rose, gently shaking out the remaining kinks in her legs. With no express intent, she walked toward the front door. In one fluid motion, she opened it and herself up to the beauty and solitude of the cloudless night. An abundance of stars freckled the sky.

As she gazed upward, a soft, wistful voice whispered to her from somewhere just beyond the cottage. She craned her neck as if doing so would improve the clarity of the sound. The fear, which scant seconds earlier contorted her face into a pale mask, relaxed. She knew that sound and whence it came.

I am the sea blast
I am the tidal wave
I am the thunderous surf
I am the stag of the seven tines
I am the cliff hawk…

Tara tiptoed along the path. Each damp step reminded her she was shoeless. As she rounded the corner of the cottage, it was no surprise to find the derelict garden transformed once again into a breathtaking haven of beauty and calm. Caressed by rays of a slivered moon, Mamó rested against the charcoal-gray of one of the now-erect standing stones in the middle of the circle. As usual, her trusted Cado was not far away. She was not naked. A simple tunic sheathed her lithe frame, not unlike the one her granddaughter Dana wore.

Mamó's gentle greeting floated in the space between them. "Welcome, child. I have been waiting for you!"

"How did you know I was here? I'm barefooted. I didn't make a single sound!"

"Dear one, our eyes are not the only means of seeing, are they?"

Tara walked over and slid down beside the ancient woman. "Well, my eyes have always been the only way for me to see!"

Mamó's face grew animated with an impish grin. "Maybe that is something you might change sometime soon?"

"Don't hold your breath! I have a few more pressing issues right now."

Mamó took Tara's trembling hand in hers and stroked it with a rhythmic tenderness Tara had never experienced. The old woman's hazel eyes brimmed with warmth and concern.

"Tell me. What troubles you so, child?"

Without hesitation, Tara collapsed onto Mamó's shoulder and wept. Each sob swept away a lifetime of unacknowledged despair and superficial bravado.

And there they stayed, lost in time. The moon, their only witness, illuminated the serenity of the scene. Two women. One, older and tireless, embraced and soothed the shuddering heap of the other.

CHAPTER TWENTY-EIGHT

GUY FLICKED A manicured hand as he dismissed the server without even looking up. The anticipation of a double shot of twenty-five-year-old Glenmorangie made him salivate.

His initial concern about whether the platinum card would cover this extravagance was mollified by the ambience of Alain Ducasse's establishment and everything it represented to him. Its shimmering design and three Michelin stars offering exquisite gourmet master-pieces were just what Guy needed to signal his success. That he was someone worth being noticed.

Guy shifted his eyes aloft and smiled. Not only was he in one of the most famous restaurants in London, but he sat directly beneath the five-star opulent luxury of The Dorchester, where the likes of Cecil Day-Lewis, William Somerset Maugham, Elizabeth Taylor, Richard Burton, and Queen Elizabeth had graced the halls.

As the server delivered a crystal glass, Guy scoffed at the notion that cretins who lacked any nuance of sophistication or refined taste might call The Dorchester simply a "hotel."

Savoring the liquid velvet of the single malt on his tongue, he considered that any such observation was like saying champagne was a fizzy drink and caviar a sandwich spread.

He turned his head to admire his surroundings. Of course, he had reserved the Table Lumière, the centerpiece of the restaurant cocooned by a luminescent curtain of forty-five hundred shimmering fiber optics. From this extraordinary perch, he could enjoy the ambient buzz of the establishment screened from view. He adored this lifestyle.

Another mouthful of whisky reaffirmed his long-held belief that he deserved to live in this manner every moment of his life. On the heels of that affirmation, he made a solemn vow to make sure his most recent meal ticket did as she was told.

Just after ten o'clock, Guy struggled to keep his balance and decorum as he stumbled down the steps of The Dorchester, trading its cosseted intimacy for the noisy bustle of Park Lane. Bleary vision made him conclude he was much too inebriated to negotiate the ten-minute walk through the evening chaos of Curzon Street, a favorite thoroughfare, to Green Park tube station. He opted to turn southwest along Park Lane until he reached Louisa Duckworth Walk and entered Hyde Park.

The sharp shadows of the entryway lampposts faded into the darkness of the asphalt walkway. The damp night air, laced with a delicate hint of exhaust fumes, served as a cool salve for the grogginess of his mind as he staggered along the path. Its nocturnal solitude offered reassurance that he could shake off his drunken stupor unobserved.

When his legs refused to obey any further command to work, he slid onto the coldness of a black metallic bench in front of the park's famous bandstand. Swathed in an alcoholic haze, Guy concocted a grandiose fantasy of sharing the platform with the likes of Queen, Elton John, Eric Clapton, Madonna, Paul McCartney, and Coldplay as they graced its stage.

"These are the people I should live among," he announced to the empty park, slurring his words, "not the common riffraff I have to deal with daily."

This proclamation turned his thoughts to Tara. He began a tug of war with the front pocket of his perfectly creased pants to emancipate his phone. The numb fingers of his right hand brought an abrupt end to the struggle. Guy's skin was like ice. The temperature was dropping. He struggled to get up and, with some effort, found his feet. The quietude of the park, so welcoming only moments before, now felt threatening, isolated. He held his breath. His ears strained. He could have sworn he heard—

The suddenness of the attack paralyzed him. He fell faster than a cement-booted corpse being thrown overboard. A hairy fist lashed out, pulverizing his face. Down on all fours, Guy experienced a nausea that threatened to liberate his lavish meal and exquisite whisky.

He screamed at the gray outline of his attacker, "What the fuck?"

A hammering took up residence in his head. As he spat blood onto the cold asphalt, Guy attempted to rise and failed.

"Take what you want and leave me in peace," he slurred.

"I'd rather leave you in pieces. I don't want your fuckin' Rolex, and I'm sure, by now, your wallet is more than empty after your extravagant dinner. No, I want what I'm due, Guy. Did you really think you could get away with not returnin' my calls, you fuckin' wanker? I have eyes and ears everywhere, you bloody moron. How do you think I tracked you down tonight?"

Grabbing his nose to stem the blood, Guy attempted, once again, to lumber to his feet. "Just give me what's mine, and all this hurt will go away."

He collapsed onto the bench, reflecting that he had known this moment would come. "Look, Max," he pleaded, "I intend to pay you back, every penny. You have my word. I just need a bit more time. Once I get an advance from BBC for the miniseries, you'll be paid in spades."

"Funny you should use the word 'spades.' Because if you don't pay me back, that's what I'll use to bury your sorry ass."

Without warning, Max landed another heavy-fisted punch to his prey's gut. "You have a month. And don't even think about runnin'. I'll hunt you down like the weasel you are!" Like a ghost, Max vanished.

Sobered up by fear and adrenaline, not to mention excruciating pain, Guy retrieved his cell phone and texted:

Don't make me hunt you down

CHAPTER TWENTY-NINE

THE DAMP MORNING dew seeped into the flimsy fabric of her night dress, drenching it.

Tara shot up and away from the warmth of Mamó's arms, disturbing Cado, who nestled across her feet. The weak softness of the sun's orange-hued rays painted the horizon. Tribes of birds had begun their morning ritual of heralding in the day's newness. But none of this brought clarity to the haze of her confusion. Then she remembered. Embarrassment inflamed the pallor of her cheeks. Distancing herself even farther from the woman beside her, all she could muster was a feeble "Sorry."

"Dear one, there is no reason for you to be sorry! It was a privilege to be the one to hold you as you expelled a lifetime of suppressed grief."

"No! It wasn't like that." Tara's voice rose. "It was stupid of me to break down like that. I have no idea what came over me. Tears are a senseless waste of time! I assure you it won't happen again!"

Mamó whispered, "Pity! But we shall see!"

Shifting gears, the old woman then asked, "So what brought you outside so late last evening?"

Glad for this new direction, Tara offered, "Oh, I'd been researching any strange energetic anomalies experienced by people on or near the Hill of Tara, and I just needed to stretch my legs."

"And did you find anything?"

"No, not really. Just some rubbish about ley lines and their magical powers. There's not one iota of scientific proof of their existence. I think anyone who believes in such nonsense should get a life!"

"And what type of life would that be, Tara?"

"A real one!"

"And what, I wonder, is your concept of reality?"

"Don't tell me you believe in all this hocus pocus?"

As she watched her companion cross her arms in defiance, the old woman's voice took on a lilting huskiness, a strength that belied the ancient fragility of her frame. Her eyes glazed over as if she saw something the naked eye could not.

"Not only do I not consider it hocus pocus, but I know the wonder of the vibrational force. Believe me when I say, my dear, that it is quite true, and its power is extreme!"

"What? You believe in ley lines?"

"Well, I'm not sure about the expression 'ley lines,' but I know there are energetic patterns that run above and beneath this wonderful, mysterious world of ours. For as long as the Earth has existed, they have served as conduits of energy transfer and communication. They are the nervous system of this living planet. But it has been eons since most people have understood how to tap into the power of this network. And, over time, it is no longer intact, but shorn into many threads or tendrils, so much so, it no longer makes 'sense' or is easy to 'prove' to exist."

"Oh, my god!" Tara stared in disbelief. "You actually believe this rubbish!"

Exhaling, the old woman continued, ignoring the comment.

"These ley lines, as you call them, are not constant. They are forever shifting because of the structure of the Earth's crust, the energy of the sun, and the natural occurrence of energetic fields created from minerals and the decomposition of organic matter. These energies flow along the meridians within the sacred body of the Earth."

Inhaling, Mamó fell into a contemplative silence after saying, "Structures built on them, designed by sacred geometry, attract the energetic power that runs just above or beneath the crust of the Earth."

Stunned by disbelief, Tara remained silent. What was this crazy old woman saying? There was no empirical proof that these veins of energetic power existed. Still, it vexed her because, somewhere deep within her being, she knew Mamó had spoken the truth. And this line of thinking was intolerable to her no-nonsense approach to life. If you couldn't see it, then it didn't exist. It was as simple as that!

Tara needed to distance herself from her confusion and the old woman who contributed to it. She stumbled, with the coordination of a drunkard, back toward the cottage.

The old woman's voice followed her. "I am sure you have felt its power by now. In fact, dear one, I know you have. When you are ready to talk, you know where I will be."

Inside the cottage, Tara struggled to relate her own concept of reality with what Mamó had said, but an incoming phone message interrupted her thoughts. The ten words that glared at her from its screen put everything into perspective.

Don't make me hunt you down. It won't be pretty!!!

Tara hurried toward the quiet solitude of her bed, desperate to smother her confused thoughts under the blanket of sleep. But her dreams refused to bring solace to the ache in her body and mind.

"For the love of God, n–"

Sucked into a vibrational conduit, Tara traveled once more to a reality far from her own.

She felt a chill on her skin…but she knew it wasn't her skin. It was Clarice's, wasn't it? All rational thought melted as she found herself in the grayness of impending dusk.

CHAPTER THIRTY

Convent, north of Marseille

THE SUN WAS waning. The cool nip of evening had begun. Clarice knew the bells would soon call her to Vespers. Her heart stirred at the thought of the wondrous sound of chanting, the part of this nightly ritual that never failed to lift her spirits heavenward. At first, she balked at having to attend, but Papa reminded her it was a sacred time to gather and give thanks for the day just passing.

No matter how fond she was of Vespers, today she wanted a few more minutes of silent contemplation before the heavy footedness of Sister Bernadette shattered her peace. With that resolve, she let her mind wander. She reflected on the meaning and purpose of her visions: why she knew something would happen before it did. Risking another wrathful outburst from Sister Bernadette, she sat even longer, pondering why she had inherited this dubious gift of "sight" and what useful purpose it might serve her and the rest of humanity.

Clarice thought of the young woman she had heard so much about, Jehanne d'Arc. Over the last few years, Jehanne had not only announced her verbal and visual communications from saints and angels to the world, but she had also acted on them.

Clarice recalled standing in silence, absently rubbing the area just above and between her ring and baby finger, while Sister Bernadette maligned this peasant's daughter, who they quoted as saying, "I heard the voice on my right, in the direction of the church, and rarely do I hear it without a light. This light comes from the same side as the voice. It seemed to me a worthy voice, and I believed it was sent to me by God. After I heard this voice the third time, I knew it was the voice of an angel."

The aging nun's scathing condemnation of d'Arc had permeated Clarice's world, heralding the things she had known would come to pass. She knew, beyond a shadow of a doubt, that d'Arc would burn at the stake as a relapsed heretic. Her visions had shown that many people would fall in the struggle over the sovereignty of France. Gazing into the fading light, she knew that no angel, let alone God, could save Jehanne from her ultimate fate.

Clarice thought of her own life and knew that Papa would be the only one she trusted to act as confidante about the growing intensity of her dreams and visions.

As if her thoughts summoned him, the priest appeared. His lion-like movements were sleek and smooth, and his thick black mane shimmered in the pre-dusk sun. He appeared not a day older than when she first encountered him. His frame was neither tall nor short but forever reassuring, with a face faintly pocked by childhood illness. His large, calloused hands were always tender to the touch. Still, it was his eyes that took her breath away. They were brown pools of quietude, emitting a depth of kindness and wisdom. She believed those eyes had existed since time began.

"You look so tired, *ma petite ange*," her mentor said, touching her lightly on the hand.

She hesitated for the briefest of moments before saying, "I am so exhausted, Papa. I do not sleep so well sometimes."

He reached out and collected her into a fatherly embrace, "But why is this, *ma chère*? Does Sister Bernadette not permit you a decent night's sleep?"

"No, Papa. Well, often Sister tasks me with scrubbing the chapel floor after evening prayers, but that is not the reason for my tiredness."

"Then what is it, my child?"

A voice inside Clarice's head warned her not to divulge her secret, but the loving concern in Papa's countenance reassured her. His familiar scent, the perfumery collaboration of pine shrubs, spicy herbs, and sweet flowers, which grew in abundance from Carcassonne to Marseille, bolstered her decision.

"Papa, I have something to tell you. But I am afraid you will not like me afterward."

"*Mon trésor*, do not concern yourself on that account. Nothing, and I mean nothing that you feel compelled to share with me could or would ever stop my love from flowing in your direction."

That was all it took. The floodgates, fueled by the terror of her dream visions, burst open. Clarice's words poured out like the ferocious pounding of a springtime waterfall that consumed everything in its wake.

"Oh, Papa, I have dreams and visions so real they scare me… and sometimes I dream of things to come…and they do, they do come to pass. More and more, I am afraid to fall asleep…Often, I wake up thrashing and screaming at the things I have seen with my eyes shut…"

Out of breath, she inhaled, pulling air deep into her belly as her diminutive frame attempted to shrug off the heavy weight of concern.

"And, Papa, sometimes I see things, not just when I sleep, but when I am awake. Sometimes I know something is ailing a person before they show any symptoms, and I know precisely what they need to recover. Mama had what she called a 'gift' of sight…but Papa, for me, this is not anything like a gift."

Clarice slumped against the cold stone bench where they now sat and held her breath. She glanced at her companion to gauge his reaction to what she had just shared. To her surprise, his face showed only that he loved her without condition, without censure or condemnation.

He took her hand in his. "Such a burden for one so young to keep shut up inside, *ma petite*. It is no wonder you feel exhausted."

At his pronouncement, some of the tension she had carried for such a long time was released. "But Papa, if anyone knew of my gift, I am certain it would not end well for me. I can imagine how someone like Sister Bernadette would use this knowledge against me." At this assertion, the corners of her protector's mouth curved slightly upward.

"Of course, you are quite right, *ma chérie*. Some would not understand the nature of this gift. They would use it against you to make you conform to what they see as the correct way of being in this world of ours."

Her heart sank. He had confirmed her worst fears. "Papa, what should I do with these visions…this curse?"

Papa ruffled Clarice's hair and smiled. "What do you think God is calling you to do? You can either continue to see this as a curse or you can focus on why you have been given this gift. I know you have studied the works of our most venerated Hildegard von Bingen. She, too, struggled to comprehend why God had given her special sight. Do you remember the passage in her work that addressed her doubts?"

Clarice nodded. She had read and reread it, hoping to find some answers for herself. "Yes, Papa, I am very familiar with the passage. I know it off by heart."

Taking a deep breath, she recited the passage. "O mortal—speak the things you see and hear; and write them not according to yourself or any other person, but according to the will of the One who knows, sees, and disposes all things in the hidden places of his mysteries. And again, I heard a voice from heaven saying to me, *'Therefore speak these wonderful things and write and say them in the manner they were taught.'"*

When she finished her recitation, Clarice gathered her thoughts. "Papa, I am just a lowly servant. What contributions to humankind can my visions make? I am not as strong, not as resilient as our blessed Hildegard. I do not have the courage to speak, let alone write, about what I see in my sleeping and waking states."

The priest patted her hand. "There are many ways to share what we have with the world, my child. We can announce them through our words or our deeds. No one can choose for you. It is up to you how you express your gift. The choice is, and must always be, yours."

They rose in unison and strolled through the fragranced, cloistered confines of the monastic grounds. The hair on the back of Clarice's hand bristled as she remembered the brutal audacity of the male victors who had taken her mother's life. A fleeting image crossed the canvas of her mind. It was a pack of male wolves. They lifted their legs to mark out what they believed was their rightful territory. Such a sad but fitting image, she mused as she walked along the path to the chapel.

Before entering, Clarice looked up to the heavens to offer her fervent prayer that Papa would be part of her life for an extremely long time!

CHAPTER THIRTY-ONE

TARA STRETCHED FULL length under the cozy warmth of her olive-green eiderdown. Checking the antiquated clock on the bedside table, she calculated that she'd been out for almost twenty-four hours.

The pungent musk scent from the dense blackthorn hedgerow that lived in amicable bliss next to her favorite hawthorn permeated the air.

"Today," she declared, "is a day to get some rational answers to what is going on! God, gifts, and destinies have nothing to do with it."

Sliding her legs over the side of the bed, she rubbed any remnants of sleep from her eyes as she planned a strategy for the day. She decided she would indulge in a leisurely breakfast before traveling to Dublin to keep the appointment she'd arranged in haste the evening before with one Professor Aine Ruaidhrí. The woman was an expert on the effects of the Earth's magnetic field on humans. The recent data she presented proved a definitive correlation.

Perhaps some sort of electromagnetic current caused the tingling and visions Tara experienced since visiting the hill.

Tara walked into the kitchen and spied the last of the croissants she'd brought with her. She prodded two of them with her index finger. Yup! Just as she'd guessed, they were turning to stone. Never mind, she thought. Nothing a few minutes in the oven wouldn't cure.

Ten minutes later, she sat hugging a cup of coffee and munched on the now-edible croissants slathered with raspberry jam. Licking the corner of her mouth to recover a renegade dollop of pitted red-ness, she studied a crinkled expanse of a map. The only question on her mind at present was which route she'd choose to journey into Dublin.

If she followed the ruts of the old road a kilometer or two from the cottage until she picked up the R154, she could explore the medieval town of Trim. Afterward, she'd turn left onto the R158, passing Summerhill and Kilcock. From there, she would turn right onto the M4, passing villages and towns with names such as Maynooth, Leixlip, Lucan, and Palmerstown, after which she'd join the R148 and travel past Ballyfermot and onto the Guinness Storehouse in Dublin to keep her rendezvous with Professor Ruaidhrí. With the route sorted, she made no plans to stop anywhere other than Trim, deciding to play it by ear.

An hour later, as Tara drew closer to Trim, she decided her first stop would be its castle and the medieval centerpiece of the town. She'd read that not only was it the earliest stone castle to be built in Ireland, but it was also one of the largest Norman castles in Europe. It was the dream child of Hugh de Lacy; he began construction in 1176, four years after King Henry II granted him "the liberty of Meath." This gift was not borne from generosity but from the king's fear that the powerful de Lacy would deny his allegiance and declare himself the king of Ireland. The project took thirty years from de Lacy's start until his son, Walter, finished the job.

After touring for forty-five minutes, Tara decided her last stop in the keep would be the rooms farthest from the main door, those set aside for the lord of the castle and his family. Oh honey, she thought, what's the point? If your enemy was clever enough to get inside, would you feel safe in any room?

Referring to the informational pamphlet, she realized the stairwells in the keep had a clockwise rotation, which meant the defenders who came down the stairs could use swords gripped in their right hand. This meant that any attacker coming up the stairs would have their sword hand against the inner wall, making it next to impossible to wield it. As added protection, the height and depth of the steps varied, with some steps a different size to trip up anyone unfamiliar with the building.

"No slouch, that Hugh de Lacy!" Tara stepped from the stairs into a room with walls the thickness of two people lying feet-to-feet.

Drawn to an alcove on the left of a deep, recessed window, she stood and peered into the darkness of the hole at its bottom, wondering what purpose it served.

As if on cue, a larger-than-life, middle-aged woman, bearing all the telltale signs of an enthusiast, came bounding in. The creased folds of a well-used guidebook were glued by sweat to fingers that could never be described as bony. The flush-faced interloper burst out in raucous laughter, which sounded like a TNT explosion.

"I wouldn't touch that if I were you," she warned.

Tara's hackles shot up. Pulling herself into a full, upright, and rigid Sergeant Major stance, she looked disinterested and asked, "And why might that be?"

"That's the toilet chute! It goes down to a room at the bottom of the keep."

"Is that right?"

"Yes. And, at the bottom, there would have been a man whose sole purpose in life was to dig out and remove all human excrement from the privies and cesspits of the castle. Yuck! What a way to make a living! They called him the 'Gong Farmer.'"

Tara relaxed her stance and became engaged in the conversation. "Why the term 'gong'?"

"I don't know. I just know that 'gong' was used to describe both a privy and its contents. Wait, maybe my book will tell…"

Tara heard the unmistakable footfalls of several others ascending the stairwell. Not wanting to get caught in their wake, she smiled at the woman. "Thanks, but you needn't bother. I'll look it up later."

Without waiting for the woman to respond, she beat a hasty retreat away from the confines of the keep. She could either spend another hour or two investigating the castle, or she could explore Saint Patrick's Anglican Cathedral across the river. Her feet decided for her. Soon, she was crossing over the River Boyne via the pedestrian-only Millennium Footbridge. Turning onto Leman Street, she arrived at the nineteenth-century cathedral a few minutes later and wandered around its grounds before exploring its interior.

To the southeast were ruinous walls that embraced the remains of the medieval portion of the church. Her feet crunched the hard blackness of crushed stone. As she entered the ruins, the all-too-familiar waves of vibration convulsed through her body.

"Oh, for Christ's sake, not now!" She reached for the steadiness of the moss-covered wall just behind her.

Chapter Thirty-Two

CLARICE REFLECTED ON how long she had been the focus of Sister Bernadette's particular brand of attention, as she shifted her weight on the jagged stones of the chapel floor. Oh goodness, had it been six years since Papa had brought her almost-lifeless body to the convent that housed the Poor Clares?

Shortly after her arrival at the convent, Clarice met a pious and stern woman, Sister Colette, who was in charge of all the Poor Clare convents. By her behavior, it grew clear Sister Colette had little time for young girls of questionable faith and pedigree.

Much later, Papa shared this woman's story with Clarice as they sat in the cloisters on a warm spring day, just after one of the Sister's visits.

"Did you see Sister Colette on her last visit?"

"No, Papa, I hid. I am not that brave. She frightens me."

"Ah, *ma petite*, but you both have something in common. You are brave and so is she. Do you know how she came to be in charge?"

"No."

"By the time she was seventeen, she had lost both her parents. Left in the care of a Benedictine abbot, her guardian desired her to marry, as was the custom, but Colette gravitated to a life of contemplation, penance, and prayer. After failing several times in her spiritual vocation, she renounced the world and became an anchoress."

"What is an anchoress?"

"Ah, *ma petite*, always one with the questions," he replied, ruffling her hair. "An anchoress is a woman who barricades herself within a church cell with only a small window opening. There, she focuses on penance and prayer."

"But they would have no books to read. How would they ever learn about the world?"

"Some people are not as curious as you," he said. "And this is not the end of the story of how Sister Colette came to be in charge. In contemplative silence, she had visions. Saint Francis of Assisi appeared to her. He ordered her to restore the original Rule of Saint Clare, which proclaimed the need for a life filled with penance and prayer. When she did not heed him, she became blind and mute."

"Oh, my!"

"Ah, do not worry. She saw this as a sign to take action. And that was when her genuine challenge began. At first, her attempts were in vain. Still, she did not give up. After a time, she walked from Corbie to Nice barefoot, clothed in a ragged habit, to ask for the aid of Pope Innocent III. He was so impressed by her he declared her a 'Poor' Clare and made her superioress over all convents."

"*Mon Dieu*," Tara gasped.

"But that is not all. Even with the Pope's blessing, it was difficult for her. The Sister braved much abuse, slander, and accusations of sorcery until she gained support for her reforms. Change of any kind is never easy. Do not confuse her dedication with severity. Going against the norm is a challenge. There is always a price to be paid."

As Clarice shifted her weight to ease the pain, she acknowledged that, once again, she was paying the price for "going against the norms" of Sister Bernadette. Forever defiant, she refused to give up reading the works of the women she admired. Women like Sister

Colette had struggled to stay faithful to their vision, while those like Hildegard von Bingen had visions that would have a positive impact on the world. Clarice vowed she would continue to learn and grow no matter how often she suffered raw rubbed knees or weariness from deprived sleep.

Thank God Papa believed education was an essential part of the spiritual path. He brought her copies of sacred texts to read and reflect on. The latest was a translated copy of Hildegard's *Scivias*, describing the twenty-six religious visions she experienced.

Clarice wondered, not for the first time, how Sister Bernadette would react if she knew her sinful young nemesis had her own gift of healing and vision. Of one thing, she was sure. If the Sister ever became aware, Clarice would meet with even more brutality to save her from herself.

Although skeptical about her commitment to God, Clarice admired the tenacity of faith and courage of women like Hildegard and Sister Colette.

"Oh, come now, Clarice. You should at least be honest with yourself," she chided.

Skepticism was such a mild term to describe what Clarice felt in her heart of hearts. She was still furious with a God who had allowed her sweet mother to die in such a violent way while giving the likes of Sister Bernadette free rein to terrorize her and others.

Kneeling in the coldness of pre-dawn, she went over the text she had memorized from Hildegard's musings about her reluctance to pay attention to or do anything about her visions. Clarice reminded herself that she had no desire to sense or hear the voice of God. She had witnessed the lives destroyed in the glory of his name. And yet there was joy, too. She reflected on the women who had stood up for what they believed.

With that thought embedded in her mind, she once again redistributed her weight, squared her shoulders, and awaited the dawn of a new day. As she marveled at the fading carpet of stars, she fantasized about the world beyond the convent's cloistered walls. She under-stood it was less than perfect, scarred by war and crowded with men who took what they wanted, considered it their due. Lurking some-where deep within, she sensed there was more. An abundant world filled with wonder, awe, and adventure. She had no intention of staying with the likes of Sister Bernadette and focusing on penance and prayer. Each night, she prayed for the freedom to explore and dedicate herself to learning and knowledge.

Chilled and exhausted, Clarice mouthed the words that perplexed her since the cracked and bloodied lips of her dying mother uttered them. "Remember who you are and all that I have taught you, *ma chérie*. You are part of a great and noble lineage. Always allow your thoughts and actions to be directed by the source of all things. Let the strength of who you are guide you to all that you will become." Although she did not understand how her mother's words applied to her current situation, they made her feel special, proud, and loved.

Before she let her head drop against her chest in fitful repose, one thing was unmistakable. No matter how great and noble her lineage and gifts were, she was not ready to expose her daily visions. Clarice believed they were something to contain, to stifle, to keep within her inner life. A life far more colorfully expansive than her current reality.

CHAPTER THIRTY-THREE

SOMEONE, PROBABLY THAT horrid Sister Bernadette, was attempting to shake her from sleep.

"*Ma chérie*, are you well? What is your name? Do you have the strength to stand on your own?"

Certainly not Sister Bernadette's voice!

"Should I send my husband into the town to bring a *médecin*?"

In the background, Tara heard the voice of a man. "Marie, *mon amour*, shall I go for the doctor?"

Struggling to open her eyes, she blinked into the warmth of the sunlight, whose source, at present, was obscured by a kind and worried face. These people were not violating her personal space; they were offering help. Tara looked around to get her bearings. She was ensconced within the walls of the fourteenth-century chancel, a mere stone's throw from the cathedral. Exactly where she'd been before the blackness. Embarrassment replaced bewilderment.

Tara was polite in her refusal of help. The middle-aged woman who had crouched in front of her, face creased with concern, rose to her feet. "Are you sure?"

"Yes, really, I'm fine. Too much sun and too little water," she laughed, trying to quell the panic in her solar plexus. "Thank you for stopping, for making sure I was all right. I'm very grateful. But I'll be fine. Nothing that a good cup of tea won't cure, I'm sure."

With a look that shouted she wasn't the least bit convinced, the woman offered, "Well then, *mon mari* and I will leave you in peace. We only have a short time left to explore this *région magnifique* before flying home to Marseille."

She watched the couple retreat. After a few steps, the woman turned back to Tara and said, "*Soyez gentille avec vous-même lorsque vous revenez d'où vous êtes venue.*"

Stunned, Tara stood beside a window with carved heads on both sides and stared as her would-be saviors vanished from view. It was a bloody odd way to wish her well on the journey back to her car. Whatever did the woman mean? If her French served, it roughly translated to "be kind to yourself when you come back from where you came." What did they think she was going to do to herself on the way back to the parking lot?

Weirder and weirder was all she could think as she glanced at her watch. Shit! How had almost two hours passed since she'd last checked her watch? There was no time for idle dalliance. If luck was on her side, she might be on time for her appointment with Professor Ruaidhrí.

Gathering her bag, water bottle, and any wits she had left, she fled the chancel and all that had happened there.

"What happens at Trim stays in Trim," she quipped under her breath with more bluster than she felt. She strode away with purpose, determined to leave everything behind her.

An hour later, she was thumping the steering wheel in utter frustration. Her frivolous excess of time at Trim made her late, and she hated being late. Although it was only three kilometers to Saint James Avenue, the GPS announced it would take twenty-five minutes to get from where she was to her destination.

With one hand guiding the wheel, she rummaged in her bag for the slip of paper with Professor Ruaidhrí's cell phone number on it. Her frantic search produced no results. She slammed the side of her fist against the black leather of the steering wheel cover. It did little to dispel her frustration, which bubbled up and threatened to explode into her throat and out of her mouth. She slowed her breath to quell the frantic uprising within. Her breath stuttered in her lungs until she let it go and some of the tension drained away. Expelling the last trace of stale air, she hoped the professor was a patient woman.

Tara parked in an area offered to Guinness Storehouse customers and clambered out of her car. She dashed across the smoothness of a cobblestone alleyway, crisscrossed by veins of long-disused train tracks that ran between the grayish-brown bricks of two brewery buildings. A sign, flanked by nineteenth-century gas lamps, informed her, with the international standardized symbol of a person walking and a huge arrow, that she was headed in the right direction.

Inside the Storehouse, she was enveloped by a gaggle of avid enthusiasts as they listened to what their guide was saying. Even though she was not taking the tour, Tara paid the twenty-euro entry fee and made her way to the Gravity Bar on the seventh floor.

Her eyes widened as she took in the massive maze of blue-green steel riveted beams that consumed the interior. They branched off from a central smudge-free glazed atrium designed in the shape of a pint of Guinness. Like gleaming polished tentacles, a series of escalators swept visitors along each corridor of this Disney-like wonder.

Like a sailor who'd just come ashore after an extensive ocean journey, she felt as if she were wobbling at the incongruity between where she stood now and her travels through the ancient world of Trim.

As she rode a series of escalators to the top, her lips curled into a blend of sneer and smile at the sight of a mural wall to her left. It was a black and white seascape with a dramatic sky full of clouds, from wispy white to menacing dark. Streaked across it in enormous, bold, black letters: "Not Everything in Black and White Makes Sense."

"Well, they got it partially right," she whispered as she passed.

"Nothing, whether black, white, or any other hue in between, makes sense. At least, that's how it looks and feels in my life right now!"

The seventh floor greeted her with the glare of white paint spread atop the imperfections of a brownstone wall. The sign proclaimed that at the St. James's Gate Brewery, Guinness used one hundred thousand tons of Irish-grown barley each year.

With that factoid squirreled away in her memory bank, Tara stepped forward to search for Professor Ruaidhrí in the throng of tourists enjoying their "free" beer, included in the price of admission. Thank God she had the foresight to download a picture from the university website. She spotted the professor on a bench, with her back to the panoramic view of Dublin. Her long auburn hair cascaded around her slender shoulders and framed her freckled face.

With confidence she wasn't even close to feeling, Tara extended a hand and blurted out, "Professor Ruaidhrí, I'm so sorry for my lateness...I know how busy you must be...Thank you so much for seeing me at such short notice..."

"Aine, please," the woman responded, as she extended her own hand in warm welcome. The woman's slender hands were fragile in appearance only. She had one hell of a strong grip. "How exciting! Writing a book on the migration patterns of the Celts is no small feat. Just a friendly word of advice, if you don't mind. Be careful about interchanging the words 'Celt' and 'Irish' when talking to folks hereabouts. Many are sensitive about their heritage."

"Thanks for the heads-up."

A group of twenty-something tourists ordering another round of Guinness drowned out any means of communication other than screaming at the top of their lungs. Aine pointed at the escalator and Tara understood what she was proposing. They tunneled their way through the merriment that accompanied the boisterous mixture of youth and alcohol and arrived at the escalators, where the din was somewhat diminished.

"Might I suggest we go to the Brewers' Dining Hall on the fifth floor? It's much quieter, and the food is quite good."

"Great plan! But this one's on me." Noticing Aine's hesitation, Tara added, "Please, it's the least I can do to thank you for your time and knowledge, not to mention patience! I won't take no for an answer."

Laughter exploded from the pale pink softness of the professor's mouth. The gold-tinged green of her eyes, shielded by long, unaffected lashes, sparkled with amusement. "Well, if you put it like that! I just wish I'd starved myself over the last couple of days to build up more of an appetite."

When they arrived on the fifth floor, the hostess seated them at a snug table away from the entrance beside an original stone wall. As they settled, Aine asked, "So, what can I do to help with your research?"

"Well, that's the million-dollar, or should I say million-euro question!"

"Yes, sometimes we start out researching one thing and our exploration takes us in quite different directions."

The anxiety that had risen during her trip from Trim to Dublin, bolstered by the idea of meeting with a well-respected expert like Aine, began to melt away. Tara let go of her breath in a slow and purposeful way and returned the woman's smile.

"I'm so glad you said that. I was afraid you'd think me an absolute flake and weirdo!"

"Well, if it makes you feel any better, in certain areas of science, I'm considered the ultimate in 'flakedom.' But my thoughts are that today, weird is the new normal!"

Tara began to giggle, which raised eyebrows from fellow diners at the next table. Sobering slightly, she admitted, "God, I haven't laughed in a long time."

"Glad to oblige!"

As a waiter sauntered toward them, Aine suggested, "Shall we order first? I must admit to being quite famished. Being an oddball takes a lot of energetic fuel."

After they'd heard the young man rhyme off the specials of the day in a less-than-interested monotone, they both ordered a hamburger marinated in Guinness with a side Caesar salad and a glass of tap water.

Tara decided to bite the bullet and dive straight in. "Speaking of energetic fuel, I've been staying at a cottage a short distance from the Hill of Tara and getting some really weird vibes from the place. A woman I've met there thinks it's all about ley lines. I, for one, am far from convinced! I'd love to hear your views on the matter."

Tara was pleased to see that Aine wasn't discretely picking up her bag in preparation for flight.

As Aine's long auburn hair cascaded around slender shoulders, her eyes narrowed slightly and danced with the intensity of someone fully engaged.

So, not doing a runner then, Tara silently mused and sighed in relief.

Aine sat silent for only a moment before saying, "I know the notion of ley lines is, in some realms, hotly contested. Some say that the concept is complete bunkum with no scientific evidence to back it up. I—"

Tara interjected, feeling a sudden pang of unexpected disappointment. "I knew it was a pile of sheep's dung. But I'm not sure how to explain the weirdness that's been happening ever since I went to the hill. Maybe just—"

Reaching over and softly touching Tara's hand, Aine continued. "I was about to say that whatever anyone wishes to call them, there are electromagnetic pulses, both natural and artificial, emanating in, through, and around this wondrous planet of ours! And just to put your mind at rest, no, I don't think you're crazy."

Going even further out on the sanity limb, Tara decided to ask, "And do you think these electromagnetic pulses can affect humans? I read that you recently presented a paper on the effects of the Earth's magnetic field on our lives."

"Hah, now that *is* a million-euro question! However, my research has convinced me that certain frequencies of electromagnetic waves, or radiation, can interfere with the way our brain functions, for good as well as ill."

"But how could that be?"

"Well, think about it for a moment. We're all electromagnetic beings, vibrating at different levels of frequency. So, it might stand to reason that if the frequency of the electromagnetic impulses around us aren't pulsing at the same rate as we are, then they will affect our own pattern of vibration, including our biological tissue, which means our brains."

Tara decided to disclose what had happened to her on the verge of the hill. "As I got closer to the hill, I began to feel some kind of electric charge emanating from the ground beneath my feet. It was so strong I had to sit down until my head stopped spinning."

"Hmm…interesting!"

"Interesting in a weird way?"

"No, in a fascinating kind of way!"

"Is there a cure, doctor?" Tara offered up, half-mocking with a side dish of serious.

She wasn't sure Aine heard the comment, as she continued, hardly skipping a beat, "Have you read the research that suggests the low-intensity electromagnetic disturbances in the Earth's magnetic field caused by gusts of solar wind may have a subtle but measurable influence on the rate of suicide incidence in women?"

Tara shook her head.

"If you like, I can send you a copy."

"That would be great! I'll give you my email address after lunch."

As if on cue, the waiter appeared with two heaping plates.

"Oh my god, I'll never be able to eat all this," Tara gasped.

"Well, I, for one, am going to give it my best shot!" Aine

responded, just before sinking her teeth into the juiciness of her hamburger.

Thirty minutes later, the staff had efficiently swept away the juice-stained plates, and Aine and Tara sat with cups of expertly brewed coffee.

"So, where were we?" Aine asked of no one in particular. "Ah yes, that's right. I was telling you about how disturbances in the Earth's magnetic field have an effect on some women."

"Do you really think, from your scientific perspective, that we can be affected by the intensity of these electromagnetic pulsed frequencies? And that they can also affect the level at which our own frequency vibrates?"

"Just between you and me, my answer would be a resounding yes!"

Stunned into silence, Tara began to process the information. On some level, she was beginning to believe that the energetic frequency at the hill was so strong it had somehow affected her own level of vibration. But why was she feeling these surges even when she wasn't near the hill? And what about all the bloody visions, or dreams, or hallucinations she'd been experiencing?

Tara decided that talking about her visions might be a step too far, even for the broad-minded professor, so instead, she opted to ask, "Aine, do you think that once our electromagnetic frequency is somehow tuned to a higher level, it stays there?"

"Yes, I absolutely believe that to be a possibility."

CHAPTER THIRTY-FOUR

O
N THE DRIVE back to the cottage, any previous tension Tara had felt left her body. She couldn't put words to her sense of relief. But somehow, it was possible that the surge of power she first experienced on the hill had made a permanent, irrevocable change to the way she viewed life and her relationship with it.

The muscles in her throat constricted as she realized she was no closer to solving the riddle of the increasing sporadic frequency of her visions. Still, it was a shock when she realized she wasn't so fearful of them.

An unfamiliar car was parked in a small indentation off the road amid the line of pine trees near the cottage. Mental and physical exhaustion from her day had put her in no mood for company. She considered reversing down the track to wait for the interloper to leave. But the need for a warm soak and the comfort of her pajamas outweighed the childish impulse. She backed into the space reserved for parking, turned off the ignition, opened the door, and squared her shoulders, determined to dispatch whoever it was in haste.

As Tara rounded the corner of the cottage, the force of a heavy mass hit her square on and slammed her to the ground, knocking the wind out of her. On all fours, like a panting dog, she gasped for air. The skin of her knees bled, the contents of her bag were scattered on the ground, and research papers floated like a burst feather pillow.

"What the fuck, Tara! Can't you watch where you're going? You made me drop my bloody phone," Guy exploded.

Clambering to stand while picking shards of earth from her bloody, grazed knees, she almost achieved a modicum of civility. "Hello to you, too. How nice of you to drop by. Not! As usual, you were on your bloody phone and didn't bother to look where you were going. Now do us both a favor and get back in your car and go back to London! I'm more than sure Charlotte is waiting and wondering where you are."

Guy wiped dirt from his phone with a starched white handkerchief he pulled from the pocket of his crisp, ironed jeans. His sigh emphasized his exasperation.

As Tara retrieved the contents of her bag, she took in the full measure of this man. She couldn't believe that not so long ago, he had been her sun and moon! All she saw now was an indolent, self-absorbed child with an old-fashioned steam kettle temper, which now looked ready to blow. The ebony curls of his hair, tinged gray at the temples, ruffled in the breeze as she picked up the last of her papers. He prattled on.

"Oh, come on. Don't be such a bitch. Just admit it; it was your fault. No point in getting your knickers in such a twist. As your boyfriend, I have an absolute right to visit you whenever I like. Besides, I warned you not to make me hunt you down. My being here can be no surprise. You know I always get my way."

"The last time I checked, we were no longer an item! So, describing yourself as 'boyfriend' is inaccurate. I mean it, Guy. Get back in your car and leave me alone!"

The blood that trickled across her lip and into her mouth was a too-late reminder that she should have known the reaction her tirade would bring. But she was too tired to be cautious or to choose her words with care.

"Now look what you've made me do!" His tone softened as he came so close that the heat of his breath cooled the sweat on her face. Moving backward, she cringed as he caught both her wrists in a vice-grip hold, forcing her body hard against his.

"You never minded it a little rough before, Tara. Why don't you show me just how glad you are that I've come all this way to see you?"

Forcing the slightest of gaps between them, she heaved her chest.

"Guy, as I told you before I left, I need some time alone to think and to get a handle on this bloody book you want me to write. What I don't need are unnecessary distractions."

Guy released her, propelling her backward with such force that she once again found herself on the ground, but this time bottom first.

"You, my dear girl, are lucky to have such a fine distraction like me in your life. Do I need to remind you how many women are waiting to get a taste of what I offer?"

"No, Guy, you don't. I confronted that reality when we were together. And if I missed one of your potential conquests, you were always quick to point her out. Look, I'm asking you nicely. Leave. Life has become plenty peculiar since I've been here, and I need time to regroup and refocus." Her plea hadn't hit the right octave, so she added, "Guy, please!"

Cold, emotionless eyes below ample knitted brows examined her with an air of abject boredom and obvious disdain.

"Ah, you know I can't resist a desperate woman. Besides, I knew you'd be a total prig, so I've booked into a cozy B&B in Powderlough. You know, the girl on the reception desk there assured me my stay would be most pleasurable. I don't doubt it!" The depths of his eyes grew darker, more distant. He took a step back and wiped a spot of Tara's blood from one of his immaculate, manicured fingernails. "What I demand to know is how the book's coming along."

Tara's body sagged as the sheer futility of her existence flashed through her mind. "Guy, I told you, it has gone nowhere. I want to take it in a different direction. Bring in the human aspects of the Celtic migration. To transfuse the facts with the blood, sinew, sweat, tears, and fears of the people who made monumental journeys and sacrifices. I don't want to make this another academic exercise. I want to inject some soul!"

Once again, they were almost nose to nose as Guy said, "And I don't give a flying fuck what you want! May I remind you of the rather healthy advance I've extended? So, you'll write what I tell you to. And if you deviate from my express wishes, asking for you to return the advance won't be the only reprisal. Do I make myself clear?"

More than anything, she wanted the dark malignance of this egocentric narcissist to leave. Instead of telling him to fuck off, which was what she wanted to do, she mustered all her strength and said, "Yes, Guy, I understand. You will get the manuscript you want. I promise."

Placated by her contrite expression, he backed away and walked toward the sleek lines of the black Porsche he'd rented at Dublin Airport.

Before sinking into its plush comfort, he half stood, his hands caressing the top of the car door, and shouted, "My dear girl, I'm giving you two weeks to get it together, or believe me, there will be hell to pay!" He lowered his lithe frame into the car, slammed the door, and sped off.

Tara forced one foot in front of the other in the cottage's direction, certain that Guy had the wherewithal to carry out his threat. She believed even the police couldn't stop him once he had his mind set. People had commanded no less than absolute surrender from her during her lifetime and she was too bloody tired to revolt against the most recent demand.

CHAPTER THIRTY-FIVE

GUY HEARD THE loose stones and dirt ricochet against the underbelly, grill, and sides of the car he'd rented. However, the car was the least of his worries. Gnawing on the inside of his cheek, he remembered the credit was obliterated on his platinum card. For the past week, the only thought that consumed every waking moment was his dire need to access funds, and fast.

Since Tara stumbled across his path two years ago, he'd been living the life he believed he deserved. And why not? From the age of eight, like his distant ancestor Vercingetorix, the Gaulish Celtic king slaughtered by Julius Caesar for his part in the revolt against the Roman occupation, Guy had paid dearly to establish his rightful place in society.

The car jerked as he sped over another large hole in the dirt track. Tugging aggressively on the wheel to keep control, he acknowledged that his life was far less favorable now than it had been six months earlier. Not only was Tara not kowtowing to his every whim anymore, but Max promised to make an example of him if he didn't pay what he owed. Life was not good. He remembered how the young woman behind the reception desk at Powderlough had, with an air of superiority, declined his sexual advances. "Ew, I don't think so. You're old enough to be my father."

Her father, for Christ's sakes! He dragged his mind from the unfatherly images of what he'd like to do to her back to the issue at hand. He needed the book finished, and he needed it finished yesterday. The deal with BBC4 to turn it into a miniseries was already cut, based on the sole success of Tara's other penned efforts. If she didn't deliver, his life would be over.

Hitting yet another car-shattering crevice in the road, he snapped. The destructive power of his rage spewed faster than a volcanic emission. He swore to himself that she would pay for her petulant antics. He would do whatever it took to make her conform, to do what he needed her to do. Whatever it took!

Out of nowhere, a snarling gray mass leaped into the middle of the road, a few feet from the car. Guy's body jerked with adrenaline as he yanked the wheel to the right to avoid colliding with what looked like a wolf, baring its razor-sharp canines and thirsting for blood. In slow motion, he felt himself lose control as the tires hit an embankment and sent the car over its brink and into the stone wall that separated the dirt track from the green field just beyond.

"Fuck!" His body lunged forward. His face hit the airbag, and his nose shattered into a bloodied mess. Gasping for air, heart hammering in his head, dazed and bleeding, he peered to the left and up the track to see where the beast was. The shock of the accident sent tremors through his body as he scanned the road and terrain. The wolf's piercing hazel eyes, which only seconds earlier had heralded his imminent demise, were nowhere to be seen. Shuddering in disbelief, his shaking hand grabbed his wallet, wedged into the cup receptacle beside him, to extract his Roadside Rescue card. Although close to her cottage, there was no way he would ask Tara for help. That would expose a weakness and vulnerability he was unwilling to share.

CHAPTER THIRTY-SIX

HIDDEN AND PROTECTED by an ancient grove of oaks, Dana, Mamó, and Cado looked on. Mamó's smile illuminated her ancient face, but a deep-set scowl raged across Dana's. Turning, Dana saw her mentor's face awash with delight, which reminded her of the sun as it danced atop the gentle ripples of a stream in summer.

"Mamó, I see nothing to smile about. That man is a filthy muck. We must do something now before the swine hurts Tara. Our intervention must be stronger than just sending Cado to scare the bejesus out of him."

"May I remind you, child, our job is to guide someone to change their life. Taking matters into our own hands is only a last resort. We must give Tara the courtesy of time so that she can make whatever changes she deems appropriate for her. This is how it has been since time began."

"But—"

"There are no buts, dear one! We are guides, not changers of destiny. Our friend must realize that no one will ever come to make her life right and whole. She has to conclude that she is the 'one' she has been waiting for."

"But grandmother, we both know what it is like to suffer at the hands of those who do not understand what lies beyond their senses."

"Do you think these individuals do not suffer in their own lives because of this lack of understanding? They are as much victims of their ignorance as the ones on whom they attempt to inflict their will or their perception of what is right and proper."

"But —"

The old woman embraced her granddaughter. "Patience, my child. Our friend will come to appreciate the true nature of who she is. Now come, we must leave her in peace to figure out her next steps."

As the pair turned in unison, the sacred copse of oak trees enveloped them.

Chapter Thirty-Seven

TARA TURNED AWAY as Guy's car screeched along the track, like a great angry snake, tires spewing errant pieces of dirt caught in its wake. She heard Mamó's soft, melodic chant coming from the garden and clasped a hand over her mouth, attempting to subdue a frustrated yelp.

"In the name of all that's holy, this is all I need right now!" She could swear the old woman had been nowhere nearby just moments ago. *Where did she come from?*

Tara stomped to confront her unwelcome guest, but Mamó's quiet offer stopped her in her tracks. "Come sit with me, dear one. There is nothing more soothing than to abide with the mother of all that is natural and listen to the wisdom of her silence."

Phlegm filled Tara's mouth as she blurted out, "I have had enough of unannounced visitors for one day. I just want to be alone."

As if she hadn't heard, Mamó patted the ground on her left in invitation as Cado sauntered to her side, wagging his tail. Tara knew the woman wasn't going anywhere fast. She realized, for the second time in as many minutes, that resistance was futile. As if on auto pilot, she made her way to the unevenness of the spiked and pebbled earth just ahead.

Without turning to look at her companion, Mamó swept her hand across the immediate horizon. "It is sad, is it not, that most people have turned their awareness away from the rich bounty of the natural world and focused instead on the superficial, illusionary world they have created, both alone and together?"

Tara's voice cracked with anger and a side-serving of hopelessness. "Well, some of us spend all the time we have making our way and surviving. There just isn't any time for anything else! I learned long ago that the best way to carry on, in what you term the illusionary world, is to suck up the brutality of life and just get on with it the best you can. There's no time for navel gazing. There are no saviors, no one who will make it all better. Since childhood, I realized and accepted that there is no other way to exist."

"But dear one, why is it you stay with a man who demeans you in every way?"

"Were you spying on me? You have no right!"

The old woman did not respond. Tara's fury subsided. "He wasn't always like that, okay? At the start, he was incredible…romantic… charming…attentive to my every need. For the first time in my life, I felt special and loved."

"Well, he is not like that now. It is time for you to know your worth, your value. And that knowing, my child, will never come from anyone else but you."

"I owe him. I wouldn't be where I am today without his connections."

"And where exactly are you? In a relationship with someone who does not respect your talent or the natural beauty of who you are."

It was Tara's turn to resist responding. She knew the old woman was right. God, she must seem like a sniffling coward, but she had learned from an early age that men needed to feel superior at all times or there was hell to pay. And, right now, she just didn't have the strength to deal with the backlash that would come from severing yet another controlling relationship. Truth be told, she had no idea what it meant to be loved.

The old woman turned to face her and said, "Two tablespoons."

"Pardon me?"

"Did you know your modern science has proven that today people are only awake using a scant two percent, or two tablespoons, of their brain matter?"

Tara glanced sideways at Mamó. "I'm not following you."

"My child, do you not wonder what life would be like if humanity discovered ways to recapture some of the unused ninety-eight percent? I, for one, have found that to sit in silence in nature and listen to what it has to say has added much to my life. Often it has given me answers to questions I had not realized I sought."

"Does nature speak? I thought it was just out there, that's all!"

"Nature speaks to those who have the patience to listen. It speaks in all kinds of languages. However, it vibrates and communicates not with the two tablespoons of our external consciousness but with our inner eyes, ears, and innate, internal capacity to make sense of all life. And if we sit long enough, it reawakens the vitality of our intuition. Without abiding in nature, I do not see how people today will revive their intuitive knowing."

The defiance in Tara's voice was unmistakable. "I don't believe that I'd restore any kind of 'knowing' by communing with nature."

"You have not yet come to realize that Mother, the womb from which all earthly abundance flows, is the silent witness of our intuitive, deep sense of knowing, which lives at the core of our being. When we understand the value of who we truly are, taking time to 'navel gaze' becomes essential not only to our well-being but the well-being of others and the Earth."

A grudging acceptance of the wisdom of the woman's words flickered inside her, but Tara couldn't bring herself to agree, even slightly.

"Even if I began to navel gaze, it wouldn't change the attitude of people around me now, would it? What's the point of using more than these supposed two tablespoons when everyone else is still attached to that measurement?"

Without warning, Tara began convulsing from an unmitigated eruption of tears. "It bloody wouldn't stop…people treating me like shit…now…would…it?"

"Ah, you are talking of your man!"

Wiping the tears from her bloodshot eyes and the snot from her nose on her sleeve, Tara retorted, "Among others."

"All I can say is this. In a world fashioned by the speed of technological connectivity and shrinking geography, there seems to be a swell of intimate disconnection. Not only with others but with ourselves and especially with the Mother of all things natural."

"I don't get the connection between what you've just said and the way Guy thinks he can treat me."

"Dear one, do you not see that disconnection from the Earth and the natural world has translated into disrespect for and a diminishing of all things feminine? I am not talking here about gender, although that, of course, is important. I speak of violence or the love of it, in all its guises, perpetrated by a misdirected and unchecked masculine energy, which is taken as the normal mode of operating in modern society."

After taking a breath, she continued, "Again, this rampant masculine energy is not gender bound. I am sure you have encountered many females who wallow in its cesspool of coercive and corrosive authority."

"Great! So there's no way to reverse the trend then. People like Guy will continue to get away with abusing people like me because it's just the bloody way it is!"

"I do not know if Guy will change. But what I understand is this. It is when we use the receptivity of our feminine energy to listen to what Mother and our intuition have to tell us that we become aware and connected to the essence of who we are and the essence of all that is. And through this connection, we can become mindful of the choices we make in life."

"What about the wretchedness of others? Do I always have to subjugate myself at the altar of everyone else's needs? Are you saying it's all down to me? Great, just great!"

Leaning slightly, Mamó caressed the coldness of Tara's hand with the warmth of her own. "No, Tara, I am not saying that. What I mean is this. When we become still and silent, whether in nature or elsewhere, we access the receptive femininity of our intuition. From that place, we see and relate to ourselves, others, and the world from the inside out. Not the other way around. That is when we can live our lives with intention and purpose."

The old woman closed her eyes then and became silent. Tara pondered what had just passed between them. Her head exploded with a kaleidoscope of conflicting thoughts. Why should she pay any attention to this deranged woman, who believed that one could change the reality of his or her life by going inside oneself and listening? Hadn't she honed the skill of surviving in a world bent on suppression and control, thank you very much? And there was no way she could afford to change her ways now!

However appealing Mamó's ideas might be, she couldn't envision a way to live from a place of deeper meaning. Not in a world that didn't give a damn. No, it was only a fanciful notion, relegated to the world of dreamers. Straightening her spine, Tara reminded herself that above all, she wasn't a dreamer but a realist. The world dictated her role in it, and that was that. End of story!

On the heels of that conviction, niggling questions chipped away at its bravado. What if she were to move away from the distractions of the world and all its rigid, immutable truths?

Would she, in fact, hear answers to the longing she'd denied? Would this intuition that Mamó so ardently believed in softly whisper why she was here—not just in Ireland but on Earth? Would it give her the strength of an inner compass to traverse the ever-changing nuances of the world around her? Would it allow her to experience the deep unknown of her soul, whatever that was? A soul that encouraged and enabled her true nature to not only survive but thrive?

She surfaced from her reverie and shook her head. What utter nonsense! She'd learned the ways of the world the hard way, and she wasn't about to risk her survival on an unrealistic notion that there was something greater that waited for her somewhere within.

No! She couldn't risk the thin protective veneer she'd glazed over her existence. Any imagined idea of a world not bounded by a cavalcade of expectations and populated by either winners or losers would have to stop right here, right now!

Without hesitation or goodbye to the woman who sat next to her, eyes closed with serenity streaming across her face, Tara sprang to her feet and walked away.

As she stormed off, she heard Mamó say, "It would be nice if you would lend even a little credence to the power of your intuition. It might just prove to be a jumping-off spot for you to connect with your past, present, and future! But of course, the choice has always been and will continue to be yours!"

Tara fell into bed that night with her head and heart reeling from Guy's threats and Mamó's encouragement to create a different life. Her last thought, before she fell asleep, was how empty she felt. She must have missed dinner.

CHAPTER THIRTY-EIGHT

SUN-KISSED MORNING AIR wafted through the window above her head. It briefly lulled Tara into a sense of well-being that, to her surprise, seemed just shy of joy. But the moment was all too fleeting.

Jolting upright, she felt her face grow warm as memories of Guy's threats and what she now considered a shameful display of vulnerability in front of the old woman played across her mind. As she swung her legs over the bedside, she felt as if she'd been stabbed in the carotid artery with an adrenaline-filled needle.

Her heart pounded as incessant questions compounded the chaotic concoction of thoughts that crowded her mind. How could she free herself from Guy? Why was Mamó so adamant that she alone held the key to a different life? Who were Clarice and Ama, and why the hell were they haunting her day and night?

She wiped a residue of encrusted saliva from the corner of her mouth, frantic to know who these stalkers were and why they'd chosen to invade her life! Tara catapulted into a standing position, attempting to slam the door shut on this line of inquiry.

On her way to the kitchen, she obsessed over the interaction with Guy the day before. As her feet embraced the cold, stone-clad floor, she squared her shoulders. "Listen up, my girl. There's no use fixating or crying over the litany of disappointments that continue to sweep through the pages of your life. Just suck it up and move on!"

She knew she must come to accept that any childhood desire to create magic, awe, and wonder for the world through her writing had been drowned in the tedious banality of her life.

"So," her cry ricocheted off the stone walls, "just keep your head down and do what others want. That's the bloody ticket to a tranquil life!"

An hour had passed since Tara had made her declaration of obedience. Her neck ached from staring into the informational abyss of Google. She'd been searching for links between the indigenous people currently populating Ireland and the Celts of the Iberian Peninsula.

Aggravation threatened to flare into a full-blown tantrum. She hadn't found one iota of empirical evidence to tie the two cultures together. Frustrated, she took a break and walked to the stove and ignited the transitory promise of relief the kettle offered.

Waiting for the familiar whistle to erupt, she stared out the dirt-smeared window. Her line of vision darted over the panorama beyond.

"Where's Dana when I actually want her company?" she said.

As soon as she uttered the words, something caught the corner of her eye. "Oh, my...I don't believe it!"

As if on some surreal cue, Dana had materialized from around the corner and walked without hurry, until she stood in front of the kitchen window. The depth of her eyes radiated childlike, innocent mischief as she raised her slender hand to shield her sight from the sun's reflection. Her eyes sparkled with mirthful surprise and recognition as she spotted Tara with her mouth frozen open.

Her visitor breached the void of silence that hung between them. "It has been a while. I thought you might want to find out a wee bit more about our ancestry. Would you have the time today?"

The high, keening impatience of the kettle was enough to make

Tara jump into action. As she reached the source of the noise, she lifted the kettle into the air and placed it on the gray stone of the counter. She turned her head until it brushed against the softness of her hair and said, "Yes, I have the time. Would you like to come in and have some tea?"

"Ah, thanks. But I would rather watch the rays of the sun kiss the earth while it ushers in this new and glorious day. Would you mind having breakfast outside? The midges will not get you, I promise! I will be under the hawthorn tree."

And without waiting for any response, Dana turned her lithe frame and meandered over to her chosen destination.

Tara turned and dunked a Chai tea bag into the warmth of her cup as she thought, weirder and weirder!

A faint voice echoed from somewhere deep within, "There's nothing weird about the blooming of your innate knowing and the awareness of your connection to all that is!"

Flinging the defunct tea bag into the sink, the only response she could muster was, "Shut up! I've got enough in my life to deal with right now. I don't have time for philosophical claptrap."

With the cup clasped in her hand, Tara glanced at her bed and the faint promise of a cozy blanket of oblivion. Blowing to cool the steam rising in ringlets from her cup, she would have to forego that pleasure for now. Instead, she headed for the door. Duty called! She needed to get the facts about the Celtic experience of the Second Celtiberian War.

Tara twiddled her pendant, which hadn't left her neck for as long as she could remember. She did not know why that specific war had become essential to her research, but it had. Maybe, just maybe, it would hot wire her desire to write.

The sweet softness of Dana's singing halted her progress. She stood transfixed, enchanted by the melody.

O woman, washing beside the river,
Hush-a-by baby, babe not mine,

My woeful wail, do you pity never?
Hush-a-by baby, babe not mine,
A year ago I was snatched forever,
Hush-a-by baby, babe not mine,
From my home to the hill where hawthorns quiver,
Hush-a-by baby, babe not mine,
Shoheen sho, ulolo,
Shoheen sho, strange baby O!
Shoheen sho, ulolo,
You are not my own sweet baby O!

Tara's hand drifted upward to cover the overzealous thump of her heart.

'Tis there the fairy-court is holden,
Hush-a-by baby, babe not mine,
And there flow beor and ale so olden,
Hush-a-by baby, babe not mine,
And there are combs of honey golden,
Hush-a-by baby, babe not mine,
And there lie men in bonds enfolden,
Hush-a-by baby, babe not mine.
Shoheen sho, ulolo,
Shoheen sho, strange baby O!
Shoheen sho, ulolo,
You are not my own sweet baby O!
How many are there of fairest faces,
Hush-a-by baby, babe not mine…

Dana stopped. With no hint of embarrassment, the softness of her lips extended upward into a full-blown smile.

"Ah, I was just communing with the faeries. It's always a wise thing to acknowledge and respect things we know are there but cannot see with our eyes!"

"It's so beautiful. Don't stop on my account. Where do the lyrics come from? I think I've heard them somewhere before, but can't, for the life of me, remember where."

"It is ancient. But of course, any sense of age is relative, is it not?" Dana chuckled before going on. "It is an old Irish fairy lullaby."

As celestially painted oranges and reds faded into full-blown sunshine, Dana patted the earth beside her.

With this obvious invitation, Tara sauntered over, intent on extracting the information she needed for the book Guy demanded. She put all thoughts of faeries and the unforeseen out of her mind.

A voice, not unlike Mamó's, whispered, sending a reverberating shiver from her feet to the top of her head and back down to her core, "My child, when did you learn to run from what your soul craves?"

"I told you to shut up!"

"Beg your pardon," Dana said.

Plopping herself to the ground, Tara replied, "Sorry. Never mind. It's of no importance! Now, if you wouldn't mind, please tell me some more about your ancestors and the Second Celtiberian War."

"I would be more than happy to accommodate. Now, where were we?"

"You'd just told me the Roman Consul Marcus Claudius Marcellus had declared war on the Celtic tribe of the Belli for building fortified walls around their stronghold at Sekeida. You also said your ancestor saw this as her chance to break away from the expected role of women within her tribe."

"Ah, that is precisely where we were! Well, Marcellus dispatched Quintus Fabius Nobilitor and an army of thirty-thousand men to defeat the Belli."

There was a slight pause before she continued. "Of course, this army was not exclusively Roman. Almost two-thirds of them were auxiliary from Hispania or Roman allies."

"Crap, I can't imagine the Celtic forces being anywhere near that number. Seems to me like overkill!"

"True, but Rome wanted to wipe out Caros and his allied army before more tribes joined them in the fight against Roman occupation. Nobilitor marched on Sekeida only to find the defensive wall unfinished and the inhabitants gone. Angered by the loss of a good fight, he razed the town to the ground."

"Empty victory." Tara yawned as the brilliance of the sun seeped through her scalp, soothing her entire body.

"No doubt! Nobilitor was so intent on killing all the Celtiberian rebels he marched, with blind haste, to the Arevaci stronghold at Numantia, where the Belli men, women, and children from Sekeida had fled."

As Tara lay back onto the sweet fragrance of the earth beneath her, she thought of laundry left free to dry outside. With that picture of white linen sheets swaying in the breeze, the last thing Tara heard was Dana explaining how Caros and his army had ambushed the Roman legion twenty kilometers from Numantia. The Celtiberian forces slaughtered one in three of their number.

CHAPTER THIRTY-NINE

Numantia, 153 BC

AMA WATCHED AS women, children, and the elderly came out the next day to greet each wave of returning warriors, who carried effigies of Neito, their God of war. As she walked along Numantia's principal thoroughfare, the shortness of her hair and battle attire concealed her true identity. Her impassioned desire to show Baba that she had achieved her goal to be initiated into the art of war far outweighed the risk of being recognized. She found the old woman, as she squatted on her haunches, to the right of the entrance to the hut Ama had once called home. Her father, she knew, was cleaning up the fleeing Roman army alongside Caros.

Baba greeted her. "I have missed you, child. I suspect you are hungry. Come and sit by the fire while I prepare some food for you." With an agility that belied her age, the old woman sprang to her feet and entered the hut. In a resolute voice, she commanded, "But you can leave those outside. I will not permit the savagery of war to enter my home. Do you hear me?"

Ama balked at the idea of leaving her trophies to be pecked to the bone by circling airborne scavengers. However, she decided she was too tired to get into a battle of wills with her grandmother. And locking horns with the old woman would be one battle she had no hope of winning.

Leaving her victory tokens outside, she marched into the hut. A snarling blaze that leaped from the central fire pit welcomed her with its warmth. Fat from the wild boar roasting on the spit sent showers of fiery sparks into the air. Her belly grumbled in anticipation. She wondered how long it had been since she last filled it so full it ached. She stood just to the left of Baba, who was busy slicing off a piece of their feast to see how close it was to being done.

And there they stood, in silence. One shook, frustrated with life. Shrouded eyes, fueled by nervous restlessness, darted about, trying to foretell what was coming, desperate to be prepared. Her hand caressed the hilt of a blood-soaked sword she believed was her only line of defense and survival.

The other slouched. Deep, sagging lines on her face belied a sharpness of mind and ease of motion. Her cracked and weathered hands turned the spit with practiced agility. Her eyes gleamed with contented knowing and reflected the reassuring warmth of the fire.

The old woman turned, placing the warmth of her hand on her granddaughter's cheek. "Come, child, our feast is not ready. Let me tend to your injuries."

"Baba, I am fine! My wounds of battle will heal by themselves. And I will wear the scars with pride and honor. It is the way of the warrior, after all. I have no need for your magic!"

"Oh, my dear, sweet child!"

"I am not a child. Nor am I yours!"

Heaving a deep sigh, Baba continued. "I prayed that the reality of war would help you see its futility. I had hoped you would learn that there are ways to live in harmony with all that is around us. But I can see war has only kindled a bloodlust within you, and for that, my heart bleeds."

"Oh, for the love of Neito! You talk such nonsense. The power of the sword is mightier than all else! It is an honorable way to live and die. Like our ancestors, it is all we need to keep the precious peace you always talk about!"

Baba's eyes froze, like the iced surface of a winter puddle, and then shifted, with great speed, into pools of fire fueled by indignant anger that surged from her pupils and flashed at her granddaughter.

"And why, pray tell, did you find it necessary to sever the head of a girl not much younger than yourself!"

Baba's question was unexpected. Ama could feel her face turn crimson. Before she could regain her wits, her grandmother continued. "How is an action like that in any way honorable or peaceful?"

"She was the enemy," Ama screamed, "and a threat to our tribe and the other tribes of the confederation!"

"How, pray tell, was this child a risk to any tribe, whether ours or another?"

"For the love of all that is holy, you ignorant old woman, she was carrying the bastard child of a Roman dog."

Mouth agape, Baba stood while tears streamed into the ashen crevices of her dumbstruck face.

"Have you no heart? You ended the life of a girl heavy with child. A babe conceived in violence…in rape! The girl was a mere child herself, far from the protection of family. How could the child of my child do such a thing? Killing on the battlefield is one thing, but to slaughter a woman-child is the act of a coward! And in that, there can be no honor!"

"You old fool! I would strike down anyone who addressed me in such a manner. I am the warrior daughter of a warrior chief. It is my right and duty to kill anyone related to our enemy. And that includes a 'child' carrying the offspring of a sworn enemy."

"But you are not!"

"I am not what?"

Baba hung her head as if someone had just placed a heavy object across her neck. A deflated sigh lingered on her cracked lips. "You are not who you think you are. You are not the daughter of a warrior chief."

Stunned, Ama stared at the old woman. "For the sake of the gods, have you gone mad?"

"No, my child. I have not."

Shaking her weary head, Baba continued, "Have you never wondered why your 'father' treats you with so much disdain? Why he beats you at every opportunity?"

"He is just trying to make me a fierce warrior. One who has no time for sentiment or idle and futile ways of thinking, like you! That is all."

"No, child. That is not the reason. Your mother was just wed to your father when the Romans captured her as they marched across our lands. They ransomed her back into the folds of our tribe, but not before a group of legionnaires raped her. The true identity of the man who sired you is unknown. The man who conceived you was one of those legionnaires. Your mother and the man she had married could not rekindle the love they once had. But one thing this crazy old woman knows is that your mother loved you very much and would have marched into hell to save your life!" Baba slumped to the stone seat next to the fire pit.

Ama stood motionless. Flames of anger ripped through her, extinguishing any sense of wrongdoing. Without saying a word, she turned and marched out of the hut, her heart frozen by the realization that she was half-Roman.

The self-hatred that lurked in the shadows for most of her life consumed her. One thing she knew for sure was she would not rest until she killed every Roman swine or she herself lay in a pool of her own blood.

CHAPTER FORTY

"WELCOME BACK, TARA." Dana's voice was close yet distant. "If you keep this up, I am going to think I bore you into sleep!" Without taking a break, she continued as if she had not noticed the confusion on her companion's face. "So, are you going to weave the stories of our ancestors into your tale of Celtic migration? It would add some color to the story."

Bewildered, Tara scanned her surroundings. Where was Baba? Where was her home? Where, in the name of Neito, were her comrades-in-arms? Her right hand shot down to clasp her fingers around the hilt of her trusted sword, ready to kill all interlopers.

"I said welcome back."

The hackles on the back of Tara's neck bristled as she tried to fathom who in the name of the gods had just spoken.

"Are you all right?" a very female voice asked her.

As far as she knew, there were no other female warriors in the ranks.

"Tara, I just asked you if you are all right?" The voice grew more desperate.

Who was this "Tara," and what madness had beset her? She bolted upright and whirled around in the voice's direction. As she attempted to shake the heavy drowsiness from her limbs, she shot to her feet and lunged for her sword. It was not there. Squinting into the sun, Tara saw the figure of a woman dressed in a tunic and barefoot. As she spun around, everything in sight was foreign, save the warm rays of the sun on her skin.

"Tara, are you well?"

"For the love of all that is holy." She leaped forward to silence the intruder. The sudden action threw her off-kilter with such a force that she crashed to the ground, and the world went black.

When Tara came to, Dana was applying a cold compress to her aching head. As she opened her eyes, she saw relief flooding her companion's face.

"You had me worried. In a trance, so you were. Quite beside yourself, if you catch my meaning. Do you remember anything of what happened?"

Tara tore the cloth from her head. "No, I don't! Absolutely nothing! Not a jot!" she said, with childlike petulance.

An incredulous look spread across Dana's unblemished face. It was obvious she didn't believe one word she had just heard. Tara felt her face grow warm. She'd been caught in a lie. She whispered, "Sorry. I think I just need to go lie down for a while. Will you excuse me, please?" She turned, determined to reclaim the solitude of the cottage.

Before closing the wooden door on the world, both outside and in, Dana called to her. "Sometimes our greatest fears are our greatest allies. Do not be afraid of what lies deep within, my sister. You have so many just waiting for you to open your eyes and realize who you truly are!"

Once inside, the iridescence of her phone caught Tara's attention. It was a message from Guy.

Tick tock, tick tock. I hope for your sake you're not wasting the precious time you have left to give me what I want! Don't even think of not delivering!

Her bones and emotions ached with an exhaustion that sleep would never, ever quench.

She muttered, "No matter what Professor Ruaidhrí says, I must be stark raving mad. This madness must stop! All I want to do is to close my eyes forever."

As she flopped into the comfort of wrinkled sheets, she heard a soft voice whispering, "Ah, my child, when will you realize you are here for a specific purpose? It is not your time to go anywhere but into the wondrous depths of who you truly are!"

And with that came darkness.

CHAPTER FORTY-ONE

Convent, north of Marseille, Spring, 1435

CLARICE STOOD IN the infirmary as she sorted out her potions, making sure she had enough supplies to treat the constant flow of patients who now came and went from her care. Bending over the wooden bench where she stored most of her herbs and other ingredients, she smiled. Hope springs eternal, she thought, and today she felt hopeful.

The English had just dropped out of negotiations with representatives from France and the Burgundian Kingdom to end the bloody war, which had raged between them for almost a hundred years. But to her, the end was in sight. The reason for the abrupt departure of the English from Arras was to engage in combat with the forces of Étienne de Vignolles and Jean Poton de Xaintrailles at Gerberoy in the north of France. These two had long been ardent supporters of Charles VII and had served alongside Jehanne d'Arc before her execution. There was news that they had delivered a scathing defeat to the English.

Another significant piece of information that permeated the thick stone walls of the convent made her smile even more. The French delegation and leading clergy were urging Philip the Good of Burgundy to reconcile with Charles. Reaching across the well-scrubbed, pock-marked surface of her workbench for the remains of her Erica multiflora, Clarice experienced a surge of joyous anticipation. Despite Charles's treachery, it now looked favorable for Philip to swing his allegiance back to the royal court of France.

Absently picking up a jar of crushed sarsaparilla root, she kept in mind that outcomes, which at first might look promising, often became the fodder for disappointment. Just for the moment, she would not allow those thoughts to dampen her current mood.

Her focus shifted. She reflected on the past couple of years and how her life had settled into a comfortable rhythm of prayer, contemplation, and, best of all, healing the needy who came to the convent's wooden door. Even Sister Bernadette seemed to have accepted the usefulness of her role. Clarice often caught the old woman, now stooped, riddled with swollen joints and poor eyesight, looking in her direction wearing a secret smile.

Basking in the belief that conciliation with the elderly nun was imminent and reveling in the wonder of her life, she fiddled with the single strand of the gold necklace her mama had given her when she was eight years old. At its center hung a pendant made from an ivory-colored material she had never been able to identify.

According to Mama, the pendant had been handed down from mother to daughter in her family for as far back as anyone could recall. She also said that it held immense power for those who understood its true meaning. When she begged her mother to tell her what she meant, Mama ruffled her hair, kissed her forehead, and said, "All in good time, *ma petite*. All in good time."

This heirloom was the only object of material and emotional value she owned, a reminder of halcyon days, which now lay concealed under the dust of yesterday.

Clarice studied the pendant. Burned into the unknown material was a picture of a naked woman sitting cross-legged, leaning against the bark of an ancient tree. The tree appeared to be upside down, stuffed unceremoniously into the earth. She smiled. It always reminded her of a carrot. Its trunk was bald, but it sprouted branch-like vegetation at its apex. The woman in the image was holding an infant girl-child between her thighs. A boy-child stood off to the left, caressing the woman's ebony perfusion of spring-like hair.

She recalled something else her mother had told her about the pendant. She said it was her own personal talisman that kept her out of harm's way. Clarice did not want to tarnish the memory of her dear mama, but over the years, she accepted that this "talisman" had not done its job particularly well. For her mother or for her.

Squaring her shoulders, she sat up straighter on her stool. In gentle admonishment to herself, she whispered that there was no use in crying over the past. It could not be changed. She tucked the pendant under her blouse and returned to the duties at hand.

So engrossed in taking inventory, Clarice paid little attention to the ruckus outside until the door behind her came crashing inward. Alarmed, she turned to see Accart explode into the confines of the room, followed by three unkempt, burly guards from the jail. Two of the foul-smelling oafs dragged the battered bodies of Marie and her husband.

Sister Bernadette followed behind the entourage of brutes as swift as her old limbs would allow.

"Seize her!" The surgeon pointed in Clarice's direction.

The two loutish guards dumped Marie and her husband to the earthen floor. Smelling of a nauseous concoction of sweat, damp wool, cabbage, and garlic, they lunged at her. Charged with fear, Clarice moved in haste and evaded their filthy grasp. She stood in the furthest corner of the infirmary, every limb of her body shaking with surprise, terror, and contempt.

Feeling far from brave, Clarice steeled her voice. "How dare you force your oafish presence on me? I have work to do here and you are interfering with my duties. And what, pray tell, have you done to Marie and her husband, you poor excuse for a man?"

Accart raised his hand, signaling the guards to halt. His eyes raked over her body with icy contempt. The vengeful wrath in his eyes, the tightness in his jaw, and the involuntary twitching on the left side of his face belied his controlled demeanor.

"*Ma chère*," he said, bowing in mock civility. "Let me explain. It has come to the attention of the abbot of Saint Victor and me that several individuals have accused you of heresy and witchcraft."

She could not believe what she was hearing. It was all too absurd.

"And who, pray tell, is accusing me of such terrible things?" Despite her fear, her tone matched his, even and crisp.

The guards returned to the slumped bodies of their two charges and raised them into a limp standing position as the surgeon flicked his hand in a dismissive gesture in their direction.

"Allow me to edify you. Among other charges, these two have come forward to inform us you cured their pox with mystical potions and incantations. The woman, of her own volition, informed us that on many occasions while under your care, you sat with her, stroked her head, and whispered lyrical spells."

Clarice could not believe it. "By all things holy, you cannot equate lulling Marie into a blissful state of sleep by singing a song my mama sang to me as a child, as a spell. Of all the ridiculous things I have ever heard, this one reeks of fantastical untruth."

As the speed at which the angry veins in his face twitched increased, Accart took a step forward but then halted. As if he had taken too large a bite, he swallowed hard and continued. "Can you refute the accusation that you refused to follow the instruction given to you regarding administering mercury ointment and instead mixed your own concoction to remedy what ailed them?"

Shaken to the core by the level of vengefulness this pompous man had reached, Clarice could not control the venom in her voice. "No, I cannot. And if I had followed your instructions, Monsieur, these two and many others would be wasting away in the leper colony. It was intuition that guided me to make the tea from sarsaparilla root. Somehow, I knew it would be more effective. There is nothing magical or sinister about it. It has been around as a medicinal plant for a very long time. And may I point out, it worked!" The volume of her voice had risen to match that of his. "If your mind was open to different ideas, you might appreciate how effective the treatment was."

"Ah," he whispered as a churlish but immense expression of pleasure crossed his face. "So, you do not deny that you went against instruction and mixed your own potion to heal these wretched people?"

"No, I do not!"

"And do you admit to, as you say, singing to this pitiful woman while in your care?"

"Oh, for the sake of our dear Lord, I have already said as much!"

"Do not blaspheme, you insolent and vile little cockroach of a human being!" Accart appeared ready to explode.

Something made Clarice cease her assault. She attempted to moderate her tone to one conveying a modicum of civility. With feigned contrition, she said, "Monsieur, I meant no disrespect. It is the inaccuracy of these accusations that astounds me!"

"That will be up to the secular courts to decide. But there are other charges being leveled about your heretical actions."

Staring at the man as if he had grown another head, she could not believe her ears. Heresy? What on Earth had she done to have such charges laid at her feet?

"Who, on this God-given Earth, would accuse me of such a thing?" The moment the question was asked, she knew the answer. It was clear why Sister Bernadette had worn an uncustomary grin across her pinched face whenever she was in Clarice's presence.

"It has also come to the attention of the abbot and the secular authorities that, more than once, you have refused to supplicate yourself through prayer with the nuns in the chapel. We have witnesses who will swear that you have frequently desecrated the sacred chalice by mixing your ungodly potions in it. Also, we have an eyewitness who informed us you used the blessed host during a Black Mass celebrating the Witches' Sabbath."

Stunned into silence, she licked her lips and rubbed the sweat from her palms against her dress. Rivulets of perspiration cascaded down her hunched back. The impact of these fraudulent accusations knocked every wisp of air from her lungs. She struggled to control her uneven breaths. It was as if her body had forgotten how to inhale and exhale.

Quieting herself as best she could, she spoke, her voice rasped with fear and indignation. "Monsieur, sometimes I did not attend Vespers as I was tending to the ill."

"So, it is true. You put the need of mere mortals ahead of your dedication to God our Father. You make me want to vomit!"

Before she could conjure up further defense, he cut her off. "Enough! I am tired of your petulant antics. I will not waste any more time listening to your idiotic excuses. Guards, take this filthy ingrate from this sacred space to the jail. Throw her into a cell. I will join you anon."

He marched past the ailing Marie, landing a parting kick to her ribs. Clarice sprang to her patient's aid, but she was yanked by the arms and dragged from the sanctuary of her infirmary.

Sister Bernadette watched, her wrinkled face squeezed into a smirk, a mixture of distaste, hatred, and victory.

Chapter Forty-Two

Abbey of Saint Victor, south of Marseille

PAPA CONTINUED TO rehearse the conversation he was about to have while he trod up and down the length of the abbot's private chambers. The austere nature of his surroundings, dotted with a sparse collection of crude oak benches, mirrored the current abbot's commitment to the vows of simplicity, poverty, contemplation, and prayer.

The only piece of ornate furniture in the entire room was a carved oak chest, a present from the bishop. Papa knew the only reason the gift was tolerated was that its flat surface served multiple purposes as a seat, table, or desk. Its hollowness served as a trunk in which the abbot stored both personal and monastic documents.

To divert his attention from the current dilemma facing his cherished ward, the priest studied the carving on the front of the chest more intently than necessary. The image depicted a battle between two knights seated on coursers. Their drawn lances were aimed with no intention other than killing each other. Necks bent, nostrils flared, their stallions were pitched in a head-to-head battle for supremacy. The only relief to the scene's violence was carvings of indiscriminate trees on either side of the knights.

He hoped and prayed that his interaction with the abbot would end in a more conciliatory fashion. No matter what, he would do whatever it took to free his precious Clarice from the circumstances she now found herself in.

For four days, he had tried, without success, to visit her in prison. The jailers, drunk on self-importance and spirits, had denied him access. He did not know what state she was in or how she was being treated.

Diverting his attention from such unpleasant thoughts, he went over what he knew of the abbot. Pierre de Bourbon had been in situ at Saint Victor's for the past five years. His family origins were unclear. Some said his was a humble background, the son of a miller. It was general knowledge that, at ten years of age, de Bourbon was offered as an oblate to the Notre-Dame de Sénanque abbey, located one hundred kilometers to the northwest. Most abbots were elected by general consent of their monastic community, but de Bourbon was appointed on the grounds of his reputation of piety by the Bishop of Marseille himself. The bishop appreciated the abbot's zeal for enforcing strict regulations as he attempted to restore the primitive spirit of the order.

The abbot's pious nature was not the only reason the bishop gave him the position. His Excellency was far more self-serving than that. The underlying reason for the appointment was that, unlike some of his contemporaries, the abbot was a stranger to nepotism and scrupulous about any decisions made concerning the abbey. Possessed with neither piety nor scruples, the bishop appreciated being able to manipulate those who did. De Bourbon's appointment meant his Excellency would never have to worry about surreptitious politicking by the abbot in order to feather his own nest. And de Bourbon was more than satisfied to keep a narrow focus, which included following the instructions of the Holy See and the bishop, in that order, to the letter. This he did with great gusto and ensured others within the abbey followed suit.

Returning to the situation at hand, Papa believed the only reason the abbot agreed to see him was at the behest of the abbess, although he was uncertain what she said to get de Bourbon to agree. To quell the rising anxiety that threatened to crush his façade of outward composure, he lowered his weary frame onto a crude bench.

Anger and tension gripped his chest as he reflected on the events of the past few days. When he heard what Accart had done, he went to confront the weasel. To label a person in such a way was against the tenets of Christianity. But he also knew that Accart's wish to annihilate anyone he considered "different" was not part of the legacy of Jesus.

Straightening the hunch of his shoulders, he reminded himself that the basic tenet of all the holy books he had studied invited adherents to practice love in all matters. Calling Accart a "weasel" was not loving, but he allowed himself that little misdemeanor, for it was not God who was judgmental but humankind. Papa decided self-forgiveness was more than adequate in this situation.

The surgeon was another matter. When Papa entered Accart's rooms, the surgeon's face betrayed his anger: mottled crimson cheeks, eyes narrowed, nostrils flaring. The man spewed his furious venom before Papa could offer a single word of conciliation.

"There is no point in your visit. That *chienne* is going to pay for her insolence at last. How dare that spawn of a whore assume she knows better than the likes of me?"

Accart turned his back on his visitor and said, "And if you think you can take this matter to a higher authority, like the abbess or the abbot, you have overestimated your importance and that of your sniveling little ward."

Attempting to dampen the simmering anger that threatened to ignite into full-fledged rage, the priest approached the surgeon's retreating frame with slow, deliberate steps. Accart turned to confront Papa, but it did not deter him. He leaned in close, their facial hair almost touching, and with fierce composure, uttered, "May God forgive you. You think yourself all-powerful, Monsieur, and it is true you have many allies. But from what I know, I guarantee you not a soul in Marseille who will weep at your demise!" He departed without waiting for Accart's response.

Papa stared at the inlaid scene on the chest to his right as he shifted from this memory to relive his conversation with the abbess. It had not gone the way he wanted.

"Abbess Héloïse," he opened his plea, bowing in deference to her station, "thank you so much for taking the time to speak with me."

The abbess gestured a slight bow and spoke before the priest continued. "I appreciate your depth of compassion and love for your ward, Father, and that it is she who brings you here today." She half-smiled. "But you must appreciate that they accuse her of the most heinous crimes against the Church and all that is holy."

Unperturbed by the directness of her opening remarks, the priest took in the full measure of the tall and extremely thin figure before him. High jutting cheekbones that stood like sentinels over her gaunt, drawn mouth framed her hawklike nose.

Despite her fragile appearance and the caring nuance of her opening remark, he was aware of what lay just beneath the surface. Reputed to be rigid and headstrong, she had an ironclad will and a penchant for putting her accumulated political clout and power above all else.

"But, Abbess, I am sure you are aware of the splendid work Clarice has accomplished at the convent?" A sudden chill swept the room. He knew his rhetorical question had not moved the woman, and he continued before she could stop him. "She is a pure soul, Mother, destined to do important work with her healing. Her patients adore her. She takes nothing for herself and gives her all."

The abbess's pencil-thin lips contorted with the awkwardness of an unaccustomed smile, spotlighting the blackness of the sizable gap between her upper front teeth. Without blinking, she replied, "Let me be clear with you, Father, for I do not wish to waste your time or mine. Although Marseille has enjoyed great wealth and freedom to do as it pleases, unencumbered by the demands of the royal court of France, I and others can see what the future will bring."

He knew what she meant, but he persisted. "I am not sure I understand what that has to do with your intercession on Clarice's behalf, Mother."

The abbess straightened her frame, achieving an unimaginable stiffness, and rested her arms across her concave chest. Ill-concealed disdain replaced any sham of pleasantry. "Then let me put it in terms that you will understand. We are embroiled in a power struggle between France and Provence. A mêlée that has brewed for some time. The royal court of France means to have sovereignty over the Church. When Provence becomes just one more French province, which I guarantee you it will, Marseille will lose the independence it so covets." She looked away and, in that moment, her shoulders drooped, weighed down by this vision of the future.

Regaining her steely composure, she continued. "Even if Marseille refuses to join with the rest of Provence in swearing allegiance to the French monarchy, we fear we will lose the right to administer our own affairs. So, you see, our collective focus must be on using any means possible to repel anyone who threatens our current liberties. Therefore, I cannot and will not waste my time and political clout on rescuing one insignificant postulant, no matter how 'valuable' you think she is!"

The bitterness of rage rose in his throat, and his fingers gouged the skin of his palms. What on Earth had brought him to this moment? Why this place and why now?

He struggled to gain composure as he attempted to eradicate the vileness of his thoughts. He knew he needed to stay calm as he fought the urge to grab this woman, who was oblivious to the suffering of others, and shake her sanctimonious piety loose. But that would serve no useful purpose, so he changed direction.

"Abbess, I now understand you cannot divert attention from your current focus. It grieves me to think I have taken time from your dedication to the future of Marseille and its inhabitants."

At this point, he thought about adding a self-depreciating bow but knew the shrewd abbess would see the impudence of such a gesture. Instead, he continued. "One last indulgence, if you would be so kind. I beseech you to see your way clear to arrange an interview with the abbot for me. For this, I would be forever grateful."

She flicked her fingers toward the door behind her, dismissing him. "Very well. I will see what I can do. Now, I must bid you adieu. I have much more pressing matters to address." She turned her back and, with swift, regal grace, strode to the door.

Shaking off the memory and returning to the present, Papa looked up as one of the abbot's underlings strode toward him.

"The abbot has been detained after Mass longer than originally thought. Important church business," the pock-faced monk candidate stated. His tone was condescending, even derisive, conveying his belief that a lowly priest did not deserve to be granted an audience.

"Father has asked if you would wait for him in the central courtyard."

With a look of disdain, the emissary concluded, "I am sure he will hurry as quickly as possible to deal with the urgency of your needs!"

And with that, the pompous oaf departed.

As Papa sat in the placid, calm environs of the courtyard, he could find no respite from the rekindled anger-fueled tension he felt. He seethed with renewed vigor at both the ego-fueled vendetta Accart had mounted and at how the abbess deemed Clarice not worthy of her intervention. To her, Clarice's life was inconsequential when pitted against her zest for power and status.

With head bent and cradled in his upturned hands, he recognized what sparked the ferocity of this renewed anger. His misdirected rage, the fiery fury that burned within, was fueled by his belief that he had failed in his duty to Clarice. All those years ago, he had looked long and hard for her. And once he found her, among the refuse in that alleyway, he realized his sole purpose in this lifetime would be to protect and guide her until she recognized who she was. This task had proven to be his greatest challenge.

For the sake of all that is holy, he thought as he cast a despairing glance skyward, *I am not new to the role of shepherding souls, helping them to find a genuine sense of themselves and their role in life. It should get easier, should it not?*

He knew the answer, but sometimes he just did not like it. When he accepted this role so long ago, he understood that the learning was not strictly for the souls he nurtured through life; it was for himself as well. In this moment, however, he doubted his ability to be anyone's guide.

And as he again glanced aloft, he had no idea what his learning was or how it might benefit the current situation.

He exhaled, his breath shallow and jagged, and rose to shrug off his despair. The abbot was approaching, with his lackey lapping at his feet. Papa filled his lungs once again with fresh air. He could not allow his present negative mood to color the outcome of this meeting. Too much rode on its success.

Caterpillar eyebrows dwarfed the abbot's eyes. His sullen pallor and lean body made Papa think of the feral cats that prowled the passageways of Marseille in search of meager scraps.

The abbot had not bothered to remove the worn purple, sleeveless chasuble, a vestment he always wore over his alb during Mass. Both garments threatened to swallow the wiriness of his slight frame. Instead of white, the usual choice of priests for their alb, this austere man had opted for brown for his tunic, which encompassed his ankles and feet.

The only decorative pieces de Bourbon added to his otherwise dreary ensemble came from the pristine whiteness of a silk stole, which hung like a mantle around his neck. Its narrow width trickled over and down the front of his chasuble, its center dotted with four ornate embroidered crosses. The other spark of vibrant color came from the stiffness of his horned miter, bordered by a golden ornamental strip of silk, patterned with the elaborately embroidered faces of early saints. The beauty of this band, which fit snugly against his forehead, did little to relieve the crevices long since etched into an unrelenting face.

Papa guessed that the man was well into his fifth decade, and therefore, whatever his beliefs, they were entrenched and would be hard to affect.

The abbot left sufficient room for his visitor to bow before him. Even before Papa had straightened up, the abbot, his voice clipped and determined, began speaking. "Father Philippe, what brings you here today, my son?"

Papa reigned in his annoyance, for he was more than sure the man was apprised of the reason for his visit. He felt like a Christian being led into the arena for slaughter. His head pounded and his stomach ached with the need to have this go well for Clarice's sake. No time for shrinking into a sense of doomed inevitability. He needed to seize and hold on to the belief that something good would come from this encounter.

After leaving the abbey thirty minutes later, Papa felt neither joy nor abject disappointment. In the end, all it had taken for the abbot to become receptive to his request was the revelation that Accart had implicated him in his plans, saying the abbot had given full permission to have Clarice jailed.

As he walked to the center of town where the dank, dark judicial jail stood defiant of the sunlight overhead, he wondered why men like the surgeon spewed bilious venom toward such pure souls as Clarice, even to the point of risking their own safety.

Accart was exposed, and the abbot was far from pleased. The future did not bode well for the surgeon. No matter how extensive he believed his family connections to be, the wrathful clout of the abbot extended far beyond Marseille.

CHAPTER FORTY-THREE

DARKNESS HAD DESCENDED by the time Tara woke up. She rubbed her eyes, trying to make sense of recent events. Waking up had once been a lethargic pleasure. Now, any sense of peace seemed to evaporate quicker than summer rain bouncing off scorched earth. She ached with a desperate desire to be rid of the images that consumed her. Flopping back against the softness of her pillow offered no respite from the thoughts pounding in her brain.

What the flying fuck was going on with her?

She was tired. Not the kind of tired that needs a good night's sleep, but the kind that makes one ache for so much more. Hers was a fatigue that chipped away at body and soul until it became ingrained.

The passionate intensity of both Clarice's and Ama's desire to lead lives that differed from what others expected shone a spotlight on the dreariness of Tara's existence.

Oh my God. I've never really lived at all. I've just endured and survived!

This fledgling awareness took hold. Maybe, just maybe, life wasn't meant to be just "endured." From that thought sprung a desperate desire to leave her tiresome and stressed life behind. She wanted to experience how it felt to be truly alive. These ruminations were swiftly overpowered with a desire to understand how she could live in two, correction three, places at once.

Six hours later, Tara slumped over her laptop, overcome with physical and mental exhaustion, as she grasped for any sane explanation for what was happening to her. She rose to stretch the weariness from her limbs. Most of what she'd found was, in her opinion, a load of crap.

Like an aging pensioner, Tara shuffled across the room and lifted the kettle onto the stove. Igniting the stove's flame, she decided that what she'd uncovered ranged from the sublime to the ridiculous.

On the more plausible and rational end of what might cause her visions were things like emotional and physical distress, trauma, anxiety, and the level of dopamine in her body. The more surreal, out-of-this-world reasons were spiritual or paranormal experiences or having the special gift of sensitivity.

She'd even answered a forty-question quiz, which had taken over twenty minutes to complete, to see if she might have anxiety. The message, provided by an electronic, upbeat, empathic female voice, was that she managed stress well and in a positive way most of the time, didn't use alcohol or medication to excess, managed conflict well, and was an assertive communicator.

Tara extended her arms over her head and locked her cramped fingers together to crack away their fatigue. The same convivial voice had also informed her that although her anxiety level was within the realm of normal, she had things to work on. The voice further promised that once she registered her contact information, she'd receive the opportunity to learn additional life- management skills.

Her smile evaporated, like the steam from the kettle now in her left hand, as she reached up to the shelf above the stove for a sachet of tea. Her mind drifted to one of the thirty million results she'd dug up by tapping in the words "reasons for seeing visions" into Google.

Although past life regression, or PLR for short, was within the realm of the surreal, something had compelled her to spend considerable time and effort exploring the concept.

Lifting the warm tea to her lips, she reviewed what one website had suggested. You could use PLR as a vehicle to find the historical source of any current blocks you might be experiencing.

Tara meandered back to the chair and patted the faded, torn cushion that sat askew on the arm. Placing the chipped teacup on the edge of the table, she sat fixated, recalling what the website offered. It promised that PLR would provide the vehicle and the freedom to experience who they were on a much deeper level. She wasn't at all sure she wanted to become acquainted with her "deeper" self.

The section, which garnered some interest, stated, "Through PLR, you have a way to understand the root cause of any fears, impairments, and symptoms that are inhibiting you from living life to its fullest. When you experience, understand, and deal with the core reasons for an unfulfilled life, all symptoms disappear." For Tara, that was a promise worthy of exploration.

Flicking the laptop off, she thought that if, as the website suggested, the challenges of today had their roots in yesterday and that a journey down the PLR rabbit hole could also treat chronic musculoskeletal pain, headaches, asthma, and conditions related to one's immune system, then it might just be worth a shot.

The line that sealed the deal and the one she was still trying to ignore was "the challenges we humans experience in this lifetime are due to the fact that we have lost connection with our soul." Tara slammed the cover of the laptop shut with more force than she'd intended, rose, and walked to the bedroom.

The next morning, she phoned a PLR expert in Dublin to schedule an appointment.

Nothing ventured, nothing gained, she thought, as the person who answered the phone told her she was in luck. For 120 euros, there was a spot with her name on it at two o'clock that very afternoon. She glanced at the bedside clock and realized there was plenty of time to travel to Dublin, and she jotted down the directions to their offices.

Half an hour later, as Tara lay under the hawthorn with two hours to kill before setting off on her journey, her mouth became dry, her stomach began performing ungainly somersaults, and her mind ricocheted between firing off a barrage of self-deflating thoughts and complete blankness. Why had she picked up the phone that morning to make such a ludicrous appointment? What if she walked out of the PLR office no more enlightened than she'd been before? Well, all except for her wallet being lightened to the tune of 120 euros?

CHAPTER FORTY-FOUR

TARA APPROACHED THE offices of Bree Ó Ceallaigh GQHP, GHR, PLTA, IARRT. Seeing the letters behind the woman's name, she laughed at the thought that her own letters would read DHBCWIDH, which stood for "Don't Have a Bloody Clue What I'm Doing Here." She turned the doorknob with the firm belief that, for the next one-and-a-half to two hours, a Harry Potter world would envelop her.

The space on the other side of the portal didn't, by any stretch of the imagination, look or feel like Hogwarts. The dusky purple of the reception walls quelled any hesitation she'd felt before entering. A bookcase stood to the right of the low-slung reception area straight ahead.

Crafted from roughly hewn wood, its edges still kept their original bark. Half a dozen engraved birds flew across the smoothness of its sides, making it look and feel as if nature had been invited to roam freely through the three shelves of books with labels such as *The Power Within*, *Inner Child*, *Inner Peace*, *Meditation*, and *You Are More Than Enough*.

Farther to the right were several certificates

illustrating Ó Ceallaigh's expertise. There was a General Qualification in Hypnotherapy Practice and certificates denoting her up-to-date memberships in the General Hypnotherapy Standards Council and General Hypnotherapy Register and the International Association for Regression Research and Therapies.

Tara allowed her breath to flow more easily as she focused on the warm smile of a woman seated behind an antique mahogany desk.

"Good afternoon, Tara. My name is Colleen, and I'm so glad you found your way to us all right! Bree will be with you in a moment. She's just finishing up with another client. In the meantime, it would be great if you would fill out this form. I promise you it's not too invasive or tedious, but the law requires all new clients to give us some pertinent information. Here's a pen. There are plenty of chairs. Please make yourself comfortable while you complete it. Can I get you something to drink? Tea, coffee, water?"

Tara shook her head at the offer of a drink as she took the purple clipboard, the one-page questionnaire clipped to it, and headed toward the overstuffed comfort of the chair behind her.

A sweet-smelling bouquet of lavender on the table next to her lulled Tara into a sense of safety and comfort. And it was in that state that she focused on filling out the requisite form.

A few seconds later, two women emerged from an oatmeal-colored door behind the reception area. The only way she could tell the difference between the regressionist and the client was that one had telltale signs of emotions still trickling down the rose of her cheeks.

Tara took a moment to assess the woman she would spend the next couple of hours with. She wasn't sure what she'd expected, but the woman who was hugging her client was more than a pleasant surprise.

An inch or two taller and about ten years younger than her, the woman was a picture of calm composure. Her pocked face was free of makeup and her chestnut hair swung in the simplicity of a ponytail. Her willowy figure was draped in a loose white silk blouse tucked into a pair of matchstick jeans and, on her feet, a pair of classic black ballet flats. She wasn't beautiful in the luminous curls, ivory skin, or piercing green eyes kind of way. Still, something grounded and genuine radiated from within, which made her irresistible to anyone she met.

Bree walked over and extended her hand in greeting.

"Good afternoon, Tara. It's so nice to meet you. Why don't you come with me, and I'll show you into my inner sanctum."

Bree picked up the form placed at the corner of Colleen's desk and stepped aside to allow Tara to go in before her.

Crossing its threshold, Tara wasn't sure what she'd been expecting, but whatever it was, the reality of the interior of Bree's office didn't match. Its walls were the same soft oatmeal color as the door they'd just walked through. Brilliant pre-summer sunlight streamed through the multiple white panes in the two floor-to-ceiling arched windows. The sun's rays warmed the light-blue and smoke-white striped fabric of a couch, off-center and to the left of the windows, accessorized by a couple of deep sea-blue cushions.

Like a weary traveler coming home to rest, a rectangular, scuffed oak steamer trunk sat in front of the couch, linking it with two over-stuffed chairs reclining opposite. One matched the color of the walls, while the other carried large swirls of dark-blue paisley.

Tara felt her tense, tight neck muscles unraveling like a spool of wool taunted by a playful kitten. This place exuded warmth, safety, and caring.

"Beautiful. What a lovely room!"

"I'm so glad you like it. I know how important it is for my clients to feel safe and relaxed, especially if it's their first time. Please take a seat wherever you feel most comfortable."

"You mean you don't expect me to lie down on the couch?"

"Only if you think you must," Bree replied.

"No, it's all right. I think the chair over there will do just fine!"

"Okay, then. I'll be the one taking the couch. Can I get you a glass of water before we begin?"

"That would be kind. Thank you."

Bree poured two glasses and brought them back, placing them on the steamer trunk.

As Tara watched the woman relax into the couch, she became more open to thinking there just might be something in this past life regression stuff. But the pessimistic skeptic in her head clung to the notion that all of this was nothing more than a well-orchestrated scam.

"Would you like me to give you an overview of what you might experience during our time together?"

"Yes, please. That would be helpful. I've already researched online, but I'd like your slant on it."

"Well, we believe that if we explore our past, it may assist us to understand what is going on in our lives in the present and sometimes in the future. PLR can help us uncover the root cause of current challenges or symptoms, and while not eradicating those issues, just seeing them at a broader, deeper level can strengthen our strategies to cope. PLR and other regression therapies have even weeded out the root cause so that it dies." She leaned over to take a sip of water. "Is there anything else you need to know?"

Not yet trusting the woman enough to confide in her about the visions and dreams she'd been having, Tara opted for safety and said, "Would you tell me a bit about the process?"

"Of course! The session will take about ninety minutes. First, we'll focus on relaxing your body and mind. In this state, images from past lives will come more easily into your conscious awareness. The next step is to use hypnosis to assist you with recall."

"Hypnosis?"

"Yes. Hypnosis is just a form of focused awareness. It's an effective vehicle that enables us to access past life memories. Don't worry, Tara. It's a light trance. You'll be aware that you're reclining in that chair, hearing the birds and the sound of car horns outside, but your mind will be engrossed in past life memories. You can stop at any time. All you do is raise your index finger— not the middle one, mind you— on your right hand, and I'll bring you back."

"I'll try not to raise the wrong finger!" They both laughed.

"Much appreciated! Now, where was I? A lot of skeptics say that most of the PLR process is about the therapist planting suggestions in a person's mind. However, my approach is to ask you to describe everything you see, feel, smell, and think during the time you are here. I take you along the timeline of the experience so you can get a past, present, and future perspective. In the sessions I conduct, there's little or no asking of questions that could be deemed suggestive. Is there anything else you need to know before we begin?"

Tara realized she could ask questions until the cows came home, but that wouldn't get her the answers she was hoping for. So, she reclined even farther into the softness of the cushion behind her and said, "Let's go for it!"

Two-and-a-half hours after walking into Bree's office, Tara found herself in Dublin's afternoon rush-hour traffic. She'd forgotten what it was like to join a steady stream of motorists in varying states of hurried frustration as they made their way to the rest of their lives. The roadway was a noisy blur of honking horns, shouted expletives, and angry fingers shooting up into the space between the steering wheel and roof as she made her way back to Dunsany and her quiet sanctuary.

She shifted in her seat at yet another red light and attempted to expel the exhaustion that infiltrated her entire being. Although her body was weary, her mind wrestled with conflicting thoughts, ablaze with the images from her session. Instead of validating the notion that her visions and dreams were rooted in some distant past, the session brought up another potential life.

Stuck in a backlog of traffic that did not offer hope it would move soon, she reviewed the session. One hundred and twenty euros had bought more questions than answers, and it frustrated the hell out of her. A horn shrieked, jolting her back to the present. The light was green. Wiping her tears, she plunged the car into drive and inched through the intersection.

Half an hour later, she emerged from the drudgery of Dublin's traffic and ate up the distance between where she'd been and where she was going. Her mind raced as she wondered why she'd regressed to a place other than the ones she wished to explore. When asked, Bree was candid. She admitted she couldn't answer that question but suggested a good question to ponder instead: How can the vision from the regression shed rays of light and learnings about what was occurring in her life at present?

Not mentioning her daytime visions, Tara had said, "But that doesn't help me understand the dreams I've been experiencing ever since I got to Ireland."

"No, I suppose it doesn't. However, many have found it helpful to sit with both the details of a regression and their dreams. Often, insight and knowing come from being patient enough to let the answers float to the top of our awareness. I appreciate this is hard to swallow in a society that demands speed-of-light answers, like the fast execution of one's order at a McDonald's drive-through."

It was the rickety creak of a farm wagon stacked with fresh-brewed manure trying to overtake her that brought Tara back to the present. A few minutes later, she emerged from the stagnant atmosphere of the car and stretched into the fresh air of early evening. As she picked up her black leather bag from the passenger seat, she concluded that despite the wonderful Bree, her journey to Dublin had been one colossal waste of time!

Both surprised and annoyed at the tremor in her fingers as she pressed the fob to lock the car, she bit down on her lip to crush the avalanche of tears that threatened to erupt. Her heart raced. She straightened her shoulders and marched with determination away from both the vehicle and the unanswered questions.

"Maybe you should not focus on getting answers but hone the eloquence of your questions," a soft voice whispered.

"Not now. I have to find out what the hell is going on."

Realizing she was talking to herself, the tenacity of her resolve slipped as a dark thought crept through her mind. "Maybe I am going quite mad!"

Chapter Forty-Five

BEFORE EVEN LOOKING at the caller ID, she knew who it was. Tara glanced at the time on the fluorescent screen of her bedside clock. It was four in the morning. Dealing with a nocturnal rant via phone was less harrowing than face-to-face. She reached over, pushed the accept button, and raised the phone to her ear.

"Guy, do you know what time it is?"

"Of course I know. I'm the one making the effing call!"

Tara snapped her mouth shut to choke back a venomous retort, determined to make the call quick and painless.

"Stupid question, I guess. Guy, what can be so important that you're calling me at this ungodly hour?"

"How many pages have you got for me? At least tell me you have a detailed synopsis to present to the BBC producers!"

She could just imagine the scene at the other end. Smoke forming into artistic curls from a Hoyo de Monterrey Epicure No. 2 cigar would languish in a nearby ashtray. Beside it, a near-drained bottle of Glenfiddich. Guy, in some state of undress, slumped in a chair, his facial features collapsed into a drunken sulk.

The days of attempting to cajole him into lessening his

consumption of alcohol were long gone. She knew all too well what it was like to be around him at these times. Over the past months, she'd been privy to countless moments of waiting for the bomb of his temper to detonate while under the influence.

"Guy, I told you the other day the manuscript hasn't come to life yet. At least, not substantially. I just can't seem to—"

"Listen, here! You'd better get your finger out! You have just over a week to produce something of substance, as you put it, or I won't be responsible for the consequences. Do you follow my drift?"

At that moment, what Mamó had said came to her like a gentle whisper. "It is time for you to know your worth, your value. And that knowing will never come from anyone else but you."

Tara took a deep breath before saying, "I can't. No…I mean, I won't! What you want just isn't working for me anymore. Your idea is stale and without heart. It doesn't conjure—"

"Listen, if you don't give me what I want, you won't enjoy what I plan to conjure!"

And with that, the line went dead. Tara made two attempts before she hit the red disengage button. Although fearful about the fall-out from her declaration, she was exhilarated. She had, for the first time in her life, spoken her truth, and that felt pretty damn good! Climbing back into bed, she turned onto her left side and punched a determined hole in the pillow.

The last thing she remembered was that two hours had passed since Guy cut off any hope of an amicable resolution.

Chapter Forty-Six

CLARICE STRAINED AS she attempted to steal warmth from the tepid, golden rays of the spring sun that illuminated the grimy, barred window high above her.

She was wondering how many days she had spent in the tiny, rat-infested cell, surrounded by thick gray stone walls. The freshness of the breeze filtering down into her confined space did little to dispel the stench of human waste. Age-old straw, her makeshift bed, littered the cold, dank floor to the left of where she stood. Her only comfort was the thinness of a well-worn woolen blanket, alive with lice and nits.

Clarice convulsed, and her pulse quickened as screams from tortured inmates pierced the putrid air. Their cries layered on top of each other in a frenzied choir of pain.

Clarice did not know what was going on or what was to become of her. Her only visitor was one of the contemptible jailers who had dumped her against the clammy wall of this place. Their only interaction was his lecherous lip-licking as he threw a tin plate, garnished with rancid slop and moldy bread, in front of her twice a day.

A tremor of revulsion rose from the pit of her stomach as she relived the vile experience when she'd dared complain about the swill on offer. Clarice's hand caressed the swollen, reddish-purple bruise on her arm, willing the vileness of the experience away.

As she straightened her frame to full stature, she focused on counting herself as fortunate. After all, they could have thrown her into one of the many oubliettes that punctured the walls of Abbey Saint Victor. She had never seen them but knew they were in the basement of the abbey's towers. They were accessed through a low-hanging door, which led to a room with a sidewalk one meter wide, off a spiral staircase in each of the towers. In the center of this room was an inverted cone-shaped funnel, giving the captive within only enough girth to stand.

There were many stories of prisoners being stuffed into this orifice without food or water to contemplate the consequences of their alleged crimes. Many were never seen again.

A shiver convulsed her frame as she looked around her confinement and tried to convince herself that she, indeed, was one of the lucky ones.

CHAPTER FORTY-SEVEN

AMA'S EYES WERE emotionless pools of intent as she slithered down the embankment to hide behind the cover of brush. With wolflike dexterity, she crouched and waited for the first sign of her prey. Patience rewarded her. She spied the arrogant, beleaguered, and bloodied man as he sat astride his mount. Soon, he would be fodder for the wild dogs running feral in the neighboring woods.

Lying flat against the evenness of the windswept earth to avoid detection, Ama waited until after dark. By then, the lout would be clumsy with drink and much easier to butcher.

Feeling a peace she had never known, her body sank farther into the bowels of the earth as she gave way to exhaustion.

Ama felt a tremor of wakefulness erupt throughout her body as she bolted upright and attempted to get her bearings, peering into the darkness of the night sky.

Scrambling to her knees, she kept low and looked up and to the right to survey the top of the hill. Fires cast lazy, ever-smaller shadows over the land. The fervor of boisterous bragging from the returning warriors had died to a whimper.

It was time for action!

Ama knew the terrain like the back of her hand. She lessened the distance between herself and her prey with ease. No doubt he would be slumped either inside or near the house of his latest whore. Ama would spare her because they were once playmates.

She circumvented the town via one of the two thoroughfares ringing its boulder-clad protective walls, thicker than two men standing on one another's shoulders and higher than the tallest warrior. She had always felt safe behind the time-washed fortification.

But not tonight!

She squatted just to the rear and side of a house, which backed onto the exterior wall of the town. From her current viewpoint, she was at a definite disadvantage. She could see nothing. At the risk of being discovered, she took a measured breath and dislodged her sword from its sheath. If she left it at her side, it would scrape along the dirt and alert someone to her presence. Raising it with purpose above and to the right of her head, she crept along the side of the pebble- stone house in order to get a better look at any activity on its front face.

Ama felt the sting of the coarse, sharp earth piercing her hands as she stole forward, stopping just shy of the corner of the house.

As she glanced to the left, she faced a hairy, muscled leg. Looking up, she saw the sneering derision of the man she once called father.

"I was wondering when you would show your worthless backside around here. Not that I care, but your useless hag of a grandmother has been scouring the hills in search of you."

The muscles of her jaw flinched with suppressed rage as he continued.

"She has told me you now know who your bastard of a father was." His eyes glared with a look that froze her where she knelt.

Repressed anger and fear flowed upward, flooding her body and sweeping away the brief rush of vulnerability she had felt. Her current situation was tantamount to being forced to kneel in the middle of a winter storm, where every chunk of falling ice was a dagger piercing her skin.

Now on her feet, she looked at the hateful man slurring his words, unaware of or unconcerned about her discomfort.

"How relieved I am not to have to keep up the pretense any longer, you daughter of a whore," he said.

"You poor excuse for a man! My mother was not a whore. She was taken, another spoil of war, by who knows how many Roman dogs. Do not talk about my mother and the wife you once loved in that way, or I will cut you down where you stand."

"Loved! There was no love, you stupid girl. They gave your mother to me to cease years of bloodshed over a long-standing land dispute." His foot came crushing down onto the earth as he laughed. "She meant only that to me and even less when she became impregnated by Roman swine."

"But you must have loved her! You let her live even though the child she carried was not yours," she shrieked, eyes dark with disbelief and hatred.

His face clouded in a mist of bored disgust. "There are only two reasons you live today. The first is that I waited to see if your mother birthed a boy. At least that would have been some repayment for the damage done to my property." His laughter became shrill. "You would have followed her into the afterworld had it not been for your grandmother threatening to curse the rest of my existence."

Ama forgot all about her well-thought-out strategy. She thrust her sword into the night sky and flew at the beast. A crowd had gathered to witness what disturbed their sleep.

Although full of cheap wine, the ease with which he sidestepped and backed away from the viciousness of her attack surprised her. The momentum of her advance delivered her face-down in the dirt, her sword now five or six hands away. As she attempted to rise, the animal stomped down on the small of her back and kicked the sword farther away.

With his heavy foot on her, her face inches from the dirt, he yelled with lustful delight, "Well, my friends, now that the truth is out, looking down on the vixen, maybe I can find another, more pleasurable excuse to keep her alive for a short while."

Snickers erupted from the men, men she had fought beside who had witnessed her valor and should have known her worth. The swine released Ama from underfoot and allowed her to stand, cut and bruised, encircled by the jeers of men she once called comrades. She swallowed, unable to digest the humiliation of defeat. Several hands moved in quick and effortless unison to unsheathe their swords as she made a lunge for her own.

Death was preferable to whatever this cretin had in store for her, so she took her sword and, with all her might, plunged it against a nearby boulder, rendering it useless. She then turned and walked over to the man, who was still laughing. Lowering herself to the ground, she raised her head to the sky and offered her throat to him.

Taken by surprise, he looked down at the upturned face of the young woman who had passed as his daughter. For the briefest of moments, Ama believed she saw a flicker of admiration in his bloodshot eyes. But as quickly as it came, it went, replaced by the benevolent disgust of a victor who did not believe his opponent worthy of an honorable death.

"Do you think I would honor you with a warrior's death? You, my little whore-child, are not worthy of such an accolade. Go before I have you stripped and flogged for your feeble attempt to end my life."

Ama's heart hardened with embittered rage. With as much dignity as she could muster, she said, "I promise you one thing, Father, I will destroy you. It does not matter how, but I will live long enough to see your cold black eyes close for the last time."

She turned, picked up the bent sword and walked, body shaking, back the way she had come. Before she disappeared under the camouflage of night, she turned, looked the man straight in the eyes, and vowed, "Next time, do not think for one moment that I will play by the warrior's code. My sole intention is to see the vermin you are extinguished in any way possible. And I will do this in the name of my mother."

CHAPTER FORTY-EIGHT

"MAMÓ, WHY CAN we not instruct Tara on who she really is and why she came to this place? It is obvious she is waking up to the fact she has lived everyone else's dream of what her life should be and that it angers her."

"Dearest, our job is not one of instruction but of gentle guidance. You, of all people, should remember that one cannot be directed to change one's perception of oneself and one's relationship with the world. They must be moved to action by loving, self-knowing, and self-compassion. If not, the enhancement and enchantment of life will never happen."

"But—"

"There are no buts, my child. To create a life based on awareness and faith in one's authenticity, it will take as long as it takes. We are not here to tell anyone what her soulful potential might be. We are here to cradle her in love and patience."

CHAPTER FORTY-NINE

GUY WISHED TO hell he hadn't hit accept when his cell phone trilled *Dream Life, Life* by Colbie Caillat.

What the fuck had he been thinking?

"Did you think you could hide away in Ireland, you piece of shit? I know where you are. You have just one week to come up with my money or the Blarney Stone will be the last thing you kiss, except for the fucking earth I am going to bury you in. Tick tock, tick tock."

The man hadn't waited for a response.

The frenzy of the wind outside echoed the tumultuous despair and hatred eating at his stomach. This was all that bloody bitch's doing. She would not win. She could not! He grabbed his phone.

Chapter Fifty

I T HAD BEEN eighteen hours since Tara's defiant declaration and Guy's most recent threat.

She had risen this morning with the full intention of writing what she wanted. Yet here she was, six hours later, with nothing to show for her time except a blank page. The only signs of life on the screen were tiny deposits of croissant, which spewed from her lips earlier when she'd choked on tea.

The events of her waking and sleeping hours consumed her. Why the hell was her life reeling so chaotically out of control? Well, more chaotically than normal.

Feeling like a trapped bird with clipped wings, she slammed the laptop shut. A stint of relaxation under the branches of the hawthorn might help refocus her attention on the task at hand and stir her creativity.

It wasn't long before the rhythmic percussion of nature swept Tara away. The last thing she felt was the familiar tremor of energy rising from the soles of her feet. Before the waves of the unknown carried her away, she realized it was getting somewhat easier to let go. What choice did she have, anyway?

CHAPTER FIFTY-ONE

ACCART LICKED HIS lips to quell the nervous tension shooting through his entire body like sparks from a full-blown blaze. Sweat trickled down his forehead, although he stood in a cold cell.

Sunday. He knew the tiresome priest was, at this very moment, with the abbot. He also realized that no matter what the result was, it would not bode well for him. Still, this did not dissuade him from his current mission. In fact, it expedited it.

He was intent on inflicting as much pain on that little witch as he could. She must suffer and she must suffer now! It had cost him a small fortune, but he did not care. She would pay for her insolence, and it was that intent that led him to be standing in the putrid air of this hellhole.

But her misery was not his only aim today. He needed the vixen to confess to sins of witchcraft and heresy. Without that admission, his life would be far less favorable than it had been a week earlier. He could not afford to be consumed by the web of lies he had woven. Just that morning, he had learned that Marie, her husband, and their entire family had gone into hiding. That information did not bother him. He had the resources to brutalize false statements from others.

What troubled him most was what would happen if Sister Bernadette and the abbess found out he did not have the ear of the abbot. In fact, he had never been in his company. The reaction of the abbess would pale into insignificance when compared with the wrath of the abbot concerning his subterfuge.

Of course, his wealthy and influential family connections would grant him some clemency. But not enough to go unpunished for his outright fabrication of the truth. Holding a lace cloth over his nose and mouth to dispel the unsavory mixture of urine, feces, blood, and stale air, he was more than aware that his lies might demolish the life he had created. But for now, he needed to focus on the job at hand!

He shuddered amid the chill of the stoned walls, hewn with the express purpose of muffling the screams of the tortured. This avenue of thought only made his rage and intent inflate so much it threatened to engulf him. He could have no other ultimate end in mind but to extract a confession. If the wretched woman perished as a result, that would be a bonus.

Failure was not an option. That was why he was there. To make sure a confession happened.

As if on cue, he heard the distinctive sounds of someone being dragged over the cold stone slabs along the rat-infested tunnels.

The tightness, which had threatened to render him immobile, loosened. A faint smile elevated both the corners of his mouth and his mood. For the briefest moment, he allowed himself to believe victory would soon be his.

The two guards to whom he had paid a hefty sum came in, yanking Clarice's bruised and battered body between them. On seeing her clothing stripped from her body, he fumed.

"You idiots! I told you not to defile this bitch's body. I want no accusations coming back to haunt me. What you do with her after her confession is not my business or concern. But you had better not have deflowered her before we gained a witnessed declaration of guilt. I need the Sister to confirm that the wretch offered her admission being of sound mind and body!"

Sister Bernadette shuffled in. "Do not trouble yourself, Monsieur Accart. Believe me, her virtue is still intact."

Appeased, Accart ordered, "Get her on her feet. I want her to see what is in store if she refuses to confess her sins."

The guards did as commanded. Clarice's body hung limp, like damp laundry in the stillness of a windless day.

Accart walked to the bucket of fetid water just inside the cell and wrapped a fine embroidered silk handkerchief around his right hand. He leaned down and scooped a ladleful of the rancid water, strode over to the postulant, and flung the ladle's contents in her face.

As she spluttered into consciousness, Clarice flailed from side to side, trying to extricate herself from the iron-fisted confines of the guards. Through bloodshot eyes that sunk into the pasty hollowness of her face, she took stock of her surroundings. Her eyes darted back and forth like an ensnared hare— her face crestfallen.

—

Clarice felt a primal surge of panic shoot up from her solar plexus as she tried to make sense of where she was and who was in the room. Her body grew cold. Consumed by unrelenting exhaustion, she had no energy to assume a mask of bravado. Fear seeped into her very soul and smothered her spirit into hopeless silence. All she wanted to do was to lie down and never get up again.

Brusquely tossing the ladle back into its rotting receptacle, the surgeon spoke. "It's so good of you to join us at our little gathering, *ma chérie*. I hope your stay here has not inconvenienced you too much. I bring good news. Today, we put an end to your suffering." Reveling in his self-appointed role as spokesman, he continued. "If you would, *ma petite*, I would like you to familiarize yourself with your surroundings." His big-knuckled, blue-veined lump of a hand waved to the left and behind. "Over there, you will see some tools used to extract the truth."

Clarice licked the dryness of her cracked lips and croaked, "I have done no wrong."

"Ah, but that is not how the authorities see it. You are accused and, therefore, presumed guilty of witchcraft and heresy. We have the full and lawful right to extract and record your confession."

Accart feigned concern as he continued, "Of course, it would be much easier on you if you would confess your sins in front of us and God. That would negate the need for any further suffering to be inflicted," he said, directing a meaningful gaze toward the oafs towering over her.

Clarice turned and shifted her gaze to Sister Bernadette, who stood in front of the rusted iron of the cell's opening.

"Sister, please, I beg you, with all that is holy, do not let them do this to me. I have done nothing but assist the weak and the sick." With her energy spent, she slumped against one of her captors.

"With all that is holy, you say! You would not know what being holy is about. Your total lack of concern for following the holy rules of our order has sickened me. Instead, you think you are above such things. You have flaunted your unfettered spirit in my face, and I am tired of your flagrant disregard for my authority, for the authority of others, and the rules of the Church. Child, you represent everything that disgusts me, and I hope to God that you do not confess so that we can rid the world of your evil ways. You will have no help from me!" Sister Bernadette said.

Clarice's head hung so that her hair scraped the filth of the ground as she pleaded to no one in particular. "It was my desire only to help people in need. Souls no one else seemed to care about. I—"

Accart shouted, "Enough. Tie her!" The guards pounced into action.

Consumed with pain that knew no bounds, Clarice screamed when they ripped the abrasive rope from blood-soaked ruts in her wrists. They forced her arms behind her back, retying her hands with the rope's dirt-encrusted strands. Blood trickled anew into the palms of her hands and over her fingers.

Eyes, damp with tears, glazed over like a frozen wasteland. Her body convulsed in reaction to the brutal agony searing through her wrists, arms, and the rest of her body. She writhed with pain until, at last, the welcome relief of darkness consumed her.

~

"Cut her down this instant!" Papa yelled, bursting into the cell, followed by two of the abbey's guards.

Accart came face-to-face with the fate he now knew awaited him. He turned around, his eyes bulging with indignation and hatred, as he shouted to the oafs to add weights to the postulant's feet. They had already suspended the limpness of her body into the air with a crudely tied rope, one end attached to her wrists, the other end to a pulley. This mechanism pulled her arms up and back. The priest could see that her left shoulder was pulled from its socket.

Accart ordered, "Do not listen to him! He has no authority here. Do as I have instructed, or there will be hell to pay."

Papa lunged forward and sent the shrieking Sister Bernadette headlong into the wall. "You will make the only payment to hell. Cut her down now."

On his signal, the two guards from the abbey dealt blows to the sniffling oafs who let go of his ward's limp body to protect themselves, leaving her suspended in the air.

Clarice's terror-filled shriek ricocheted off the hostile cell walls.

Papa rushed to cradle Clarice's battered body in his outstretched arms as they lowered her to the ground. Sweeping her close, the priest brushed aside the matted and scraggly bits of hair plastered to her dirt-streaked face. Rocking her back and forth as if she were an infant in need of comfort and solace, he looked up at the surgeon confined within the brutal grasp of the abbey's guards.

"You have been like a snake, lying in wait until the moment was right to strike, but no more. Your narcissistic, evil heartlessness will never again go unnoticed or unpunished. I am sure the abbot is waiting to hear why you believed you had his blessing to inflict such brutality on this innocent child of God!" He turned to the abbey's guards and commanded, "Take this worthless piece of existence out of here."

As they dragged Accart away, Papa said, "May God have mercy on your poor demented soul!"

CHAPTER FIFTY-TWO

A FLASH OF PAIN seared through Tara's left shoulder as she shuddered back into consciousness. She grasped for the warm hand that disappeared as she woke up. She was wrong. Although Accart couldn't assault her, she had felt every bit of Clarice's pain as if it were being inflicted on her.

Tara cringed to ease the throbbing, which had overtaken her entire body, as she used her right arm and hand to push herself into a semi-upright position. One thought reverberated across her mind: Thank God for Papa.

Lying back against the undulating earth beneath the hawthorn, she shivered and wrapped her cotton cardigan around her. The thin veneer that stretched over her "I-can-handle-this" approach to life showed signs of cracking.

She had no one, no one in the world she could turn to. No one to listen to her doubts and fears without judgment and to tell her it would all be okay. There was no one to tell her she just needed to rest without trying to figure everything out on her own and all at once. The phrase, "It is time for you to know your worth, your value. That knowing, my child, will never come from anyone but you," infiltrated her sadness.

Once more, years of dammed-up raw, angry tears burst, erupting down her face. Muscles in her chin trembled like a small child. A woolly static clung to every nuance of her brain.

Tara pummeled the earth with her hand in a vicious attack until blood trickled into the soil. What could she do to quell the incendiary flames of fury that devoured her? She heard a soft, familiar voice whisper, "My child, it is not so much a question of what you will do about your rage but what you will do with it."

Her eyes darted from left to right, scanning the terrain. As she examined her blood-stained, aching hand, she realized it was futile to think the old woman would be anywhere in sight. The only thought that took center stage then was, enough is enough! And with that, she rose and left the hawthorn's disturbed and disturbing peace.

Later that night, sitting in bed, a cold cup of tea in her hand, she looked down at her vibrating phone to see the last of several texts she'd ignored.

Where the fuck are you? How dare you ignore me? I demand to know where you are with the writing! Stop screwing with me.

"Who the hell do you think you are?" Tara screamed down at the inanimate object in her hand. "I am so fucking tired of your bloody audacity, you moron! Get out of my face."

With meteoric intensity, her decision to confront Guy for the second time in as many days ripped through her lifelong resolve to always take the path of least resistance. And with that firm intent in place, she dialed his number.

"It's about—"

"Guy, as I told you yesterday, I have decided not to write the crap you want me to produce. I am going in another direction to write about the lives of women. I will entitle it *The Extraordinary Lives of Ordinary Women Across the Ages*. You will not change my mind. I am determined."

"How dare you cut me off! You will do as I want, or I will bury you and your sniveling determination. Of that, you can be sure."

"You can no longer bully me with your idle threats. I will not cave. I am capable of so much more than what you ask."

"Oh, trust me, my threats are not even close to idle."

He disconnected. Tara stood staring down at the black screen of her phone. Her body tingled with exhilaration, laced with a whopping dose of fear. She had opened the lid of a box filled with consequences but somehow didn't care. Well, at the moment, anyway. Up to now, her life had been like a house buffeted by a gale raging outside. She had chosen fragile safety rooted in rotting fear, but she was over it. New determination drove her to meet her fear head-on with tenacity, as resolute as a rock in a windstorm. She prayed her newfound courage would endure.

As the stars lit the sky with radiant fire, a startling desire crept into Tara's awareness.

More than anything, she wanted to know what was happening, or was it "what had happened," to both Clarice and Ama. No longer afraid or needing an answer to her "why me" question, she went to bed to see what came. It didn't take long!

CHAPTER FIFTY-THREE

PAPA WAS FIDGETING on a white-slab seat in the austerity of a stone-cold passageway while Clarice received medical attention from the abbot's personal physician.

As he bent his head, he acknowledged that there was still a threat to Clarice's health, as well as to her safety.

His second interview with the abbot did not garner dissolution of the charges or a full pardon. What the man agreed to was her transfer to a cell in his private tower where the Inquisitor, Guiot Acquitart, would investigate the charges.

Even though he had moved Marie and her family, Papa knew the swine of a surgeon had more than enough resources to buy false witness statements. Slumping back against the hard, whitewashed stone wall, he realized he must come up with a plan that would extricate his beloved ward from harm's way.

Even with all his petitioning, the abbot had told him it was not within his power to ignore the charges against Clarice, but he would ensure they gave her a just and fair hearing.

"At least, my son, the Inquisitor's role is not predicated on the desire to oppress the innocent. The procedure stops their unjust execution. It is the Holy See's way of saving souls and members of his flock from unwarranted death."

"But holiness, Clarice has almost certainly undergone undue torture and God knows what else."

"That is unfortunate. There are certain procedural methods used to determine the guilt or innocence of the accused. I am powerless to abort the established and natural flow of inquisition. I pray that your ward comes away from this experience with absolute exoneration. There is nothing else I can do."

Although they both knew this was a ploy to cleanse both his hands and conscience of the matter, Papa offered a solemn bow before the abbot and thanked him for his kind assistance.

Under his breath, Papa swore that as long as he took a breath in this lifetime, Clarice would never again suffer in such a manner!

He strode from the darkness of the tower into the warm sunlight of the day, moving toward one particular alleyway just north of the harbor. He knew what he needed to do to free his precious ward once and for all. There was no time to waste!

From experience, he knew the mild internal chatter of annoyance he felt would soon flare into full-blown anxiety, and, in that state of mind, he would not be of benefit to anyone. He attempted to slow his pace and glanced back at the imprint of his steps in the grime that gathered whenever humanity attempted to conquer and confine the natural flow of life.

Like sunlight illuminating a dark alleyway, a warm glow of knowing thawed the apprehension that only moments ago threatened to consume him. Papa smiled, his decelerated steps shifted to a slow, fluid motion. He chuckled at the insidious nature of the concept of time, to which he had momentarily given in. Had he not learned that humankind was never so much attempting to escape from their past and present as when they desired to escape into their future? And from his experience of life, he knew beyond any doubt that the concept of past, present, and future was a fallacy. At least it was in the way humanity continued to think of it.

He realized he had allowed himself to be consumed by the notion that time was a way of measuring the daily grind of earthly existence. It was a rut he had often fallen into while on his own journeys through life on Earth. In the moments when he could calm himself enough to separate his eternal self from the experience that living wrought, he would remember that this temporal view of life and time had nothing to do with its true nature.

He could now acknowledge that his own experiences of life had taught him the true nature of time more than once. Life and time were not a neat, compartmented sequence created by laziness and ignorance. They were dynamic and boundless.

"In the presence of this moment, that is something worth remembering," he whispered to himself.

He concentrated on the rate of each breath, controlling each inhalation and exhalation. The tension in his shoulders, which had taken up residence since Clarice was seized, relaxed. All would be well. Everything would turn out the way it turned out. Hurrying did nothing but fuel time's illusion.

As he refocused on the here and now and where his footsteps were taking him, he knew his contemplation on the notion of time would keep until…. Chortling out loud, he realized that— being part of humankind—he had no other way of saying it. His contemplation would have to wait for another time.

⁓

Meanwhile, in her cell in the tower of the abbey, a debilitating agony that coursed through her entire being overwhelmed Clarice. Lying in pain, she breathed in short, shallow bursts. A fiery spike shot through her body as she inhaled and exhaled as deep as her broken ribs would allow.

A black mist swirled around her mind, lulling her into the sweet oblivion of a realm far beyond any physical existence. She drifted, as though floating in an amniotic sac, to another world or astral plane. It was as if she were being enveloped in the warm, unconditional love of a well-intentioned hug.

The main thought illuminating Clarice's mind concerned the banality of time and space and the limitations of the rational mind. As her breathing lost its shallowness, she swam in a fluid pool of knowing beyond all knowing. She relinquished all earthly desires as these thoughts whisked her away, like a solitary leaf in an autumnal breeze, to another place in time.

Papa arrived at his destination.

A narrow, crooked alleyway, robbed of the sun's warmth, led to an ill-built wooden complex and a sign that proclaimed this was where one Yosef ha-Kohen plied his trade. Papa smiled. Even if he had been unsure of Yosef's whereabouts, his nose would have told him he was in the right place. A pungent cornucopia of sweet and acrid smells saturated both the exterior and interior of the shop, rendering fresh air nonexistent.

Crammed between similar abodes, the premises of ha-Kohen had remained unaltered for at least four centuries. Wooden roof gables tilted at precarious angles toward the other side of the street. The cracked and fading façade was adorned with carvings whose details, along with their meanings, had faded to the naked eye. The darkened penthouse, where Yosef and generations of his family had and still lived, overhung the mercantile shop beneath. He walked toward Yosef, who appeared from behind a well-worn patterned curtain.

Papa scoffed at the belief of uninformed members of the diocese who swore they could distinguish Jews from non-Jews by their physical appearance and demeanor. These ignorant individuals stated, without hesitation, that anyone who possessed sallow oily skin, a hooked nose, puffy lips, thick eyebrows, dark curly hair, and short stature with an exaggerated, flat-footed gait must, in fact, be Jewish. Yosef defied the logic of this belief. Although well into his fifth decade, he still sported blond hair and was almost as tall as the priest. He strode erect without the stoop ascribed to his tribe by the uneducated. He had a long, graceful nose and a supple mouth that often spread into a wide smile. There was no evidence of effeminacy in his countenance. Except for his address, one would be hard-pressed to place a yellow star on this man's chest and call him "other."

Yosef greeted the priest with a perfunctory bow. "Shalom, Father Philippe."

"Shalom to you, my friend."

"How is that lovely ward of yours? I have not had the pleasure of her company for some time. She must be busy with her duties at the convent. I know how she loves to spend time among the herbs, spices, and concoctions in my establishment. You must implore her to come and visit me soon. I miss her questions and inquisitions." Yosef then asked, "What brings you to my humble establishment on this blessed day?

"Yosef, my friend, I am in desperate need of your help. It regards the future well-being of Clarice. Accart has accused her of witchcraft and heresy, and I am in fear for her life. After being brutalized by his louts, she lingers between life and death in a cell at Abbey Saint Victor. I fear there is little time before the Inquisitor, Guiot Acquitart, arrives. Even from his enforced confinement, the surgeon will abuse some and coerce others to stand witness against her. He will not rest until he sees her hanged. Of this, I am sure!"

"That is indeed terrible news! How may I assist you?"

The last vestige of tension drained from Papa's countenance. "Bless you! But what I am about to suggest is dangerous to all those who choose to be involved, and failure will be especially hazardous to my dear sweet Clarice. Time is of the essence."

The shopkeeper's response was instantaneous and firm. "You can count on me!"

Papa bent close and spoke in hushed tones to Yosef so no one could hear what passed between them. When he straightened, the priest looked into Yosef's hazel eyes and asked, "Can you obtain that which I seek?"

Yosef's face relaxed into one of utmost confidence. Reaching out, he clasped Papa's hand and said, "Of course! My cousin, who lives in Kochi on the Malabar Coast, does trade in such things. As luck would have it, I have a small supply on hand."

The smile vanished from the corners of Yosef's lips as he whispered, "You know the danger of administering the wrong dosage. Even a minuscule *goutte* over the prescribed amount will herald the quick and speedy demise of the recipient! You must be diligent, or we risk losing our dear Clarice forever!"

Papa shuddered, nodding his weary head in agreement. This action was Yosef's cue. He turned and was devoured by the dark, cavernous confines of the room behind the curtain.

Moments later, Yosef returned with two small vials of liquid. One was clear and the other a soft shade of green. His time-worn hands had a slight tremor as he handed them over and said, "*Mon ami*, I implore you, give Clarice only one-eighth of a *petit cuillère* of the clear liquid. You must instruct her to keep her eyes closed at all times after she takes it. The Arothron meleagris will do the rest." The urgency in his voice was palpable as he continued. "Once the potion has done its work, you must hasten to administer the green liquid no more than two hours later. I cannot emphasize the need to expedite this second stage in all haste!"

Yosef produced a pouch of coins from his tunic. "You will need this for assurance," he said, proffering the purse to Papa. "Some monetary means of garnering success."

Papa clasped his hands together as if in prayer, then took both the pouch and vials and placed them in a secret pocket within the deep folds of his robes.

"Thank you, my friend. I am forever grateful for your help.

However, if I might trespass on your goodness further, I have one last favor to ask." He whispered again in Yosef's ear.

Papa retraced the steps he had taken less than sixty minutes earlier. His long stride resounded with determination and purpose. Back inside the cell where Clarice lay, Papa looked at the ashen, swollen face of his beloved ward. He recoiled as his warm hand reached to caress her skin as cold as a cadaver.

He recovered long enough to notice that the balm of marigold petals, olive oil, and comfrey leaf had helped relieve the bruising on her face. However, it had done little to dispel the grotesque welts of brutality that covered the entirety of her body. The purple-blackness just above her left eyebrow had slid into the socket of her eye, darkening it as well.

Scanning the entirety of her frame, he was thankful her dislocated shoulder had been fixed with callous proficiency by the abbot's personal physician, but through the thin fabric of her shift, the raised ridges of angered skin covering the cracks in her ribs were visible.

Papa raised his eyes to the God in whom it was becoming harder and harder for him to believe. He reminded himself that the image of the divine created by humanity for its own purposes of control in no way resembled what he knew to be true. He understood, as Meister Eckhart, a Dominican priest born almost two centuries before him had, that all of creation resided in God and God resided in all.

Flinching back to the present, Papa looked down at his only priority, praying she was strong enough to endure what was to come. The lives they had known were ending. Accart's lies and money, combined with the political disinterest of both the abbot and abbess to intervene on her behalf, was a recipe for fatal disaster.

He reminded himself that what persisted beneath the shadows of lies was an unenlightened truth. As he trembled with nervous anticipation, he knew that although this might be very true, right now, the only thing that would dispel those shadows was the swift execution of his plan.

Meister Eckhart had taught him that every deed, however puny, that resulted in justice gladdened God. In those moments, the Godhead danced for joy.

His focus returned to his only mission in life, soothing her fitful slumber by stroking the one spot on her arm not swollen with ugly wounds. With his gentle touch, the postulant opened her eyes and saw him. Papa bent close to whisper into her pulverized ear. The screech of the wind outside, which had whipped itself into a frenzy, blocked all traces of what transpired between them.

Chapter Fifty-Four

TARA SWIPED AT blood she felt sure clogged the corners of her mouth and cheeks. Her eyes darted first to the left, then the right, then straight ahead. She realized she was still in bed. The dregs of her teacup had spilled onto the sheets.

She grabbed her cell phone and saw it was nearing midnight. Was she insane? Her daily wandering into realms unknown was feeling more real than her own life.

Her heart flip-flopped with violent beats as she imagined being chained to an asylum bed, her face and mind wiped clean by medication, her cell adorned with the smooth gray metal of a door devoid of a handle. Forced to lie on the filth of a paper-thin mattress, an illusion of warmth and comfort offered by a threadbare blanket, her only companions the screams of unseen others who'd wrestled with the intense isolation of the place and lost the battle. She saw her mother, father, and Guy standing on the other side of a one-way mirror, wearing hyena masks and cackling as she plunged further and further into a chasm of oblivion, incapacitated and alone.

"Serves you right," they shouted in unison. "If you'd only done what you were told and been who we wanted you to be. We tried to warn you, you ungrateful cow. We tried to warn you, but you were too stupid to listen!"

Like Ama, Tara wanted—no, needed—to claw the smirks from the faces of those who had tormented her. She lusted after the sound of their terrified primeval screams as she severed their carotid arteries with glee. She craved the pleasure of eradicating the paltry remains of whatever soul they might possess from the eternal cycle of life.

With the viciousness of those images rampaging across her mind, she slumped against the calloused bark of the hawthorn, willing the nail-bomb agony exploding in her gut to subside.

Well, at least she told Guy where the hell to get off, she acknowledged to herself, as she struggled to calm the thunder in her chest with slow, purposeful breaths. Her mind stung with the realization that obliterating all of her nemeses would never bring the peaceful solace she so craved.

She hobbled to her feet, picked up the drained teacup, and made her way to the kitchen. "Oh, for the love of all that's holy," she hissed upon hearing the familiar lyrical softness of Mamó's voice, inviting her into the garden.

Mustering one last ounce of energy and civility, she opened the kitchen door and called out, "Not tonight. I am far too exhausted. What I need is the warmth of a bath and my bed."

But her reply did not deter her guest. "Come, keep an old woman company for a short while. Cado is a wonderful companion, but right now, I would love to share the gift of time with you."

As Tara breathed into the inevitable outcome of this dialogue, she knew who would be the victor. "All right. Just for a short while. But please, no talk about the possibility of me creating a different life than the one I've got. I am in no mood for such a conversation."

The waxing moonlight shone around the old woman, illuminating the lush waves of hair cascading freely over the slender curve of her ancient back. Mamó responded with an amused undertone, "Well, my child, it would seem that you are most definitely in some sort of mood."

Tara flopped to the ground, inches away. Without hesitation, Mamó took her hand and asked, "What troubles you so?"

Her usual response was "Nothing," laced with animated, false bravado. But tonight, she was beyond pretending. Feigning a modicum of forced cheer was a lost cause. She searched the beautiful, lined face of her visitor and saw nothing but an authentic desire to help. An expression of loving concern was etched across Mamó's face. It reignited a flame of yearning that Tara had doused long ago.

Plunging into the murky waters of the lonely darkness that overshadowed every moment of her life, she revealed her concerns about her most recent adventures in the land of crazy. As the night sky greeted the dawn of a new day, Tara realized her head was resting in the crook of Mamó's arms. Too tired to care, she lay there as the woman stroked wisps of hair from her face.

Tara was unsure how long they had stayed as they were until dawn washed the land with the beauty of silent promise. Neither one had the desire to break the sanctity of their connection. The old woman was the first to speak.

"My dear child, it is time to rise. The sky has transformed the darkness of night into the glorious hues of a ripe mango. The sleeping Earth is once again brightened by the sun's rays. Let us stand and feel the vibrant energy of Mother Earth as she greets the newness of this day."

Not wanting to extract herself from the safety of Mamó's arms or the sense that the future felt a little less bleak, Tara was in no hurry to comply.

"Come, dear one. It is time!"

Reluctantly, Tara lifted her head and rubbed her eyes. With the fluidity of that simple motion, her resolve to tell Guy and the others to go to hell seemed to evaporate like the dew. "But Mamó, what will happen if it turns out I am just an ungrateful crazy with a long history of illusive and delusional visions and dreams?"

"First, my dear, know this. You have legions of beings willing and able to support you as you allow yourself to transition and transform throughout your current life adventure!"

"Pray tell, where is this legion? Up till now, I have seen no one willing to assist me as I journey through my so-called 'life adventure.'"

"Maybe, just maybe, dear one, you have been looking in the wrong place. And from my perspective, you missed the essence of what I just said. These beings are more than willing to support you as you allow yourself to transition and transform. In no way did I mean to suggest they would wave a magic wand and allow you to live a cosseted, tranquil life. We all come to this world to experience, learn, and grow to our fullest potential while here!"

"But time is running out. My future depends on—"

"Long ago, I learned that none of us on this earthly plane are so much attempting to escape our past and present as we are trying to escape into our future. Our concept of past, present, and future is a fallacy. Humankind uses time as a measurement for what they often see as the daily grind of their existence."

Shocked into momentary silence, Tara at last blurted, "Pardon? I can't believe you just said that. Why—"

Without skipping a beat, Mamó went on. "Maybe you are looking in the wrong places for those who care enough to show up and support you while you traverse the rocky road of life. In addition, might I suggest you ask the wrong questions?"

"But how will I know what—"

As if she hadn't heard, the old woman walked toward the corner of the cottage. Turning the radiance of her face toward Tara, so consumed with pain and wondering, standing in the center of the labyrinth, she offered, "Instead of searching for the cause of your current experiences, ask why they are occurring. You might also look at how these episodes, as you call them, are attempting to assist as you navigate toward the best version of yourself."

"But I need to know what—"

"My child, part of the answer may just be that you are waking up to the gifts you brought into your current reality! We are all given gifts of insight. Our job is to explore why we are being presented with them. We show our gratitude for them by asking how we might use those experiences to enhance or express our lives, moment by moment. Such learning is our gift back to the universe! Every moment, every experience brings with it both the joy and responsibility of choice."

The old woman vanished around the corner. Tara ran to catch up. She still had so many questions. Rounding the corner, she surveyed the periphery of the cottage and its grounds, frantic to find her confessor-advisor, but she was nowhere to be seen.

Tara knew there was no hope of finding Mamó. She turned and walked to the cottage door without caring enough to slam it shut behind her. She wilted, fully clothed, into the recesses of the mattress, like a flower exposed too long to the chill of autumnal air.

The last thing she contemplated before the darkness of sleep subdued all the questions begging answers was the thought that maybe, just maybe, the visits from Dana and Mamó—as well as everyone in the lives of Ama and Clarice—held valuable nuggets of wisdom she might apply to her own life.

Before giving into sleep, she could have sworn she heard the old woman say, "Dear one, this line of questioning has the greatest potential for extraordinary self-enhancement. Well done!"

Tara was beginning to realize there was no point searching externally for the source of this voice. She knew she wouldn't find it.

Chapter Fifty-Five

I N THE SOLITUDE of pre-dawn quiet, Papa allowed weariness to consume him as he shut his eyes. His rest was shattered by the sound of breaking underbrush in the thick forest flanking the other side of the meadow. Eyes wide and alert, he scanned every shadow in the distant woodland. He felt the sharp knife of fear twist in his gut and a hammer pounded in his brain.

Satisfied the sound came from an overzealous wolf returning late from a nocturnal forage, he allowed his broad shoulders to relax. A smile tugged at his lips as he reached over to grab a bundle of dried twigs. Snapping them in half, he lowered them to the subdued flames and stared as the fire sprang to life.

Across the meadow's multi-colored expanse, a hare sprang to full height as it surveyed the adjacent land through ever-vigilant black eyes. Sensing no immediate threat, the creature hopped off to parts unknown.

Glancing over to reassure himself that Clarice still slumbered under the protective boughs of the grandfather oak to his left, he allowed his eyes to flutter into repose.

But sleep would not come. Images of the most recent past filled the weary landscape of his mind. Adrenaline coursed through his veins. The jagged sharpness of those memories shredded any desire he might have to let them go.

—

As she watched Papa, Tara's heart ached with compassion. She wanted to lean forward and hug away the man's sadness. Instead, she whispered, "You are an amazing being, and Clarice is so very fortunate to have you in her corner as a protector, teacher, and guide."

She was stunned into silence when he looked straight into her eyes and whispered, "It is not the student that is fortunate, but the teacher. For we are there when the souls we have the privilege of guiding at last recognize and realize their own potential for the world. Your time is coming, dear one!"

Shocked that he had both heard and responded to her, Tara was becoming less and less surprised by her nocturnal adventures. Letting go of all thought, she was once again swept away as Papa relived what had transpired in Clarice's cell.

CHAPTER FIFTY-SIX

CLARICE LAY IN fitful rest. Papa dared not tarry. Time was of the essence. He could not and would not fail, even if it meant his current life would end. He would find other ways to protect and guide her throughout the rest of her life.

Watching wisps of silver-gray smoke from the fire curl and dance their way into oblivion, he replayed the images of his ward, closing her eyes in innocent, faithful trust after he administered the potion.

From what Yosef said, he knew the concoction would take less than thirty minutes to do its job. He waited only half that time before leaving Clarice's side to walk to the austere sterility of the room occupied by the abbot's personal physician. There he pleaded with the man to visit her bedside, telling him she was not responding to his touch.

Papa had known his request to visit Clarice would go unheeded, so—God forgive him— he lied, saying the abbot had granted permission for the visit.

Once he had informed the surgeon, he waited in the cold recesses of a vaulted archway, just along the dank passageway from where Clarice's limp, motionless body lay. Besides the thundering beat of his heart, he did not dare move a muscle for fear of being detected. After what seemed an eternity, he heard the heavy footsteps of the man thundering against the cold, battered stones of the corridor. Thanks be to God it had not taken too long.

Counting on the callous disinterest of the physician, Papa trusted that Clarice's frozen face, slackness of mouth, rigidity of body, and lack of discernible pulse would be interpreted as signs of death. And he was right. In his impatient desire to free himself of the encumbrance of caring for an insignificant wench, who was, in his pious mind, guilty of heresy and witchcraft, the surgeon was quick to act. After a perfunctory examination, he stormed out of the room and yelled at the guard, who lounged on the slab floor at the opposite end of the thoroughfare.

"Guard, come at once. Rid this holy place of the vile creature's body. I have wasted enough of my valuable time on her."

"But Monsieur, what should I do with her?"

"I couldn't care less if you feed this wench's body to the wolves in the forest. At least then her pitiful life will have served some purpose! Now make haste and get rid of her. I will inform the abbot."

This command had been Papa's call to action. There was no way the abbot would allow Clarice's body to be taken from the abbey without his own personal assurance of her death.

The priest counted on the fact that the physician would not hurry to inform the abbot of what had just transpired. He waited for the guard to disappear into the room where Clarice's paralyzed body lay. Leaving the darkness of his cramped confines, he strode toward the next harrowing leg of their journey.

Papa entered the cell to find the depraved oaf licking his lips in anticipation. Sweat beaded on his filthy forehead as he raised the postulant's soiled tunic.

The image ripped away the last vestige of Papa's patience. Blinded with bitter fury, he lunged forward. His hands curled, pressed hard, closing tightly against the throat of the guard. All his pent-up rage

leaped, wolflike, gripping and strangling the life force from the
bugged-eyed guard who gasped for air. It took all Papa's willpower to
release the fierceness of his hatred into the fatal grasp he had around
the vermin's neck.

Wheezing for air, the man slumped to the ground as he feigned
the audacity of authority. "How dare you attack a guard of the abbot?
I will see you hang for this." The wet, soiled mark in the crotch of his
breaches belied the bravado of his declaration.

Papa allowed his breathing to stabilize before he said, "Well, perhaps we should both wait here and see how the abbot feels about
someone who planned to defile the sanctity of death. What do you
think of that idea, you worthless speck of humanity?"

Not waiting for the reply, Papa reached into the folds of his tunic
and threw a sack of coins to the floor beside the man. "Or you can
help me get her body as far away from this place as possible so I can
prepare it for a proper burial. Your choice."

It did not take long for the lustful gaze of the guard to shift from
Clarice to the pouch of coins. Still, he uttered one last jibe, "They will
never allow you to bury the witch's body in holy ground."

"That is not your concern. Now, are you agreeable or are you not?
For I will see she has a proper burial, and I would much prefer it not
be over your dead body!"

The thug moved to sweep his newfound treasure into the grime of
his greedy hands, but Papa beat him to it.

"When we are successful, you will have your ill-gotten bounty
and not a moment before!"

The guard shuffled to his feet, massaging the visible impression of
hands on his neck. "It won't be easy." He was scowling.

Jingling the coins in the man's face, Papa said, "Well then, it
behooves you to make it happen, for all our sakes!"

As Papa attempted to wipe the harrowing memories from his
mind, he offered a silent prayer of grateful thanks for the underbelly
of greed and corruption, which had seeped into every fiber of Abbey

Saint Victor, except, of course, for the pious man at its helm. He switched his focus to what happened after he and the lout had managed to extract Clarice's limp body from the abbey.

Yosef, true to his word, had left a cart near the north-facing exit of Saint Victor. After placing Clarice's body onto its fresh straw, the guard shuffled off, eager to cover up any part he might have played in her disappearance.

Papa found a safe place to administer the antidote to his precious charge. Realizing he could not risk waiting for the fluid to do its work, he hastened the mule forward, leaving the city and all they had known behind forever.

Chapter Fifty-Seven

THE TOUCH OF a hand caressing the inside of her thigh and a heaviness of breath that wasn't her own catapulted Tara into wakefulness faster than a cat dunked in ice water. Every nerve urged her to claw her way to safety. Eyes wide with fear, she jumped to the opposite side of the bed and smashed her head against the wall. Frantic to understand what was going on, she wondered how long she'd been out and who the hell was touching her in the most intimate of ways.

"Well, my dear. Not that long ago, you enjoyed a bit of slap and tickle while waking up."

Clutching her cardigan around her upper body, she looked down and realized Guy had removed the jeans she'd been wearing the day before. Even from several feet away, she could smell the stale alcohol on his breath. "What? Get the fuck away from me, you pervert. How the hell did you even get in here?"

Without hurrying, Guy stood up. A look of condescending boredom replaced lecherous desire. "Tara, if you don't want late afternoon amorous trysts, I recommend you close your front door. Passersby might take it as an invitation to rut you in your sleep."

"Shut up and get the hell out of here. Now!"

Before she could do anything, he lunged across the distance between them, grabbed hold of her throat, and began strangling her air supply, his eyes ablaze with hatred.

Without releasing his grip, he yelled, "How dare you speak to me in that way? Who the hell do you think you are?" Her chest heaved as she tried to suck a scrap of air into her lungs.

As he pressed harder, she felt urine warm the inside of her thighs. He silenced the hoarseness of her plea as his fingers crushed against her larynx. Her body went limp. Before the world went black, Guy forced her hard against the wall. She spluttered for air as he released his grasp.

As if nothing of importance had transpired, he said, "Darling, why do you make me do these things? Do you have some tablets? You have given me the worst of headaches."

With all the strength she could muster, she sprang from the bed to run to freedom just beyond the cottage walls. She made it to the kitchen before Guy tackled her. She fell to the ground, slashing her forehead on the edge of the table. Blood spurted from her brow.

He yelled, "You ungrateful bitch! Don't flatter yourself by thinking I have the slightest desire to fuck you or sully your worthless body in any way! That ship sailed long ago. To be honest, the ship of desire was never portside, anyhow. No, bedding you was just part of the plan."

"Oh, sure!"

"Why not? Your willingness to work so hard on my behalf was touching. I knew I could make money off your writing. Why not a little something extra on the side? And if you believed I loved you, so much the better. It would make you easier to control. Now, be a good little girl, and open up that bleeding laptop and start writing what I want."

Struggling to her feet, Tara grabbed a clean dish towel from the side table and wiped the blood from her head. Her brain kicked into high gear to devise a plan to get Guy out and far away from her. The futility of her situation sank in as she said, "Okay, you win. I'll do whatever you want. But please leave me in peace to get it done. I won't be able to write with you hovering over me every moment."

"Nice try, buttercup. But I'm not going anywhere until you produce what you owe me. *Comprenda*? Nowhere!"

To her disbelief, before she could utter any response, he whipped out a single cable tie from his pocket and dragged her to one of the kitchen chairs. In quick succession, he secured the plastic tie tight around her left calf, as well as above and around the crossbars of the leg of the chair. He took another tie and fastened the chair to the table leg.

"Guy, for the sake of God, what the hell are you doing? You can't just keep me prisoner! There are laws! This is forced confinement!"

"My dear, write what they have paid you to write, and I'll let you go. You'll never have to see me again. Besides, I have friends in very high places and an impeccable reputation. Who the hell would believe such a fanciful tale? Now, get to work before I finish what I started in the bedroom!"

"You're insane!"

Guy stood with his arms folded across his chest, looking self-satisfied. "Again, who would believe you? Besides, you're not the only one with problems, you inconsiderate cow. I need you to honor the commitment I've made to BBC4 on your behalf. I need the money!"

"Look, Guy, if it's money you need, I'll give it to you. No questions asked. Just let me go, and I won't say anything to anyone about your visit here. You have my word."

"It's not your word I need. I need a lot of words. I need the damn manuscript. Now tap away before I give you what you deserve."

And with that, he turned to leave. At the door, he stopped and said, "Oh, and by the way, just so that you know, I've spent most of your money. You were too stupid to know that one document you signed in the throes of infatuation was a power of attorney."

Her mouth dropped open. There were no words.

His parting shot was, "Don't worry, my lovely. I'll be right back. I just need to bring my things from the car into our little love nest!"

The quiet that followed was like the rawness of ice, solidifying her current reality. She'd always known Guy to be a self-serving narcissist, but not for one moment had she dreamed he was unencumbered by even a smattering of conscience.

Her senses strained for a sign of his return. She tensed her calf to test how tight the tie was fastened. Pain seared her skin as it bit into flesh. A muffled scream tore through her. Jerking her head toward the door, fearful that Guy heard her cry, it relieved her to hear no pounding feet.

Think, Tara, think. Squeezing her mind for a solution, she racked up nothing but an all-consuming rage, overwhelmed by a sense of desperate futility. No one could or would save her. She might as well admit defeat and give the bastard what he wanted. After all, she thought, being alive was better than being dead. And at that moment, she was very sure that dead she would be, if she didn't do everything that Guy asked.

As if on cue, with all the gaiety of someone embarking on a week-long vacation, the man she'd never known at all came waltzing back into the kitchen and dropped his Louis Vuitton overnight satchel on the floor. He wandered over and opened the ancient fridge door. Peering inside, he turned and asked what there was to eat.

"For God's sake, Guy, let me at least wash and get a clean pair of underwear."

"No time for that. Just sit there and create some magic, like a good little girl."

Well past midnight, Guy finished reading the twenty-odd pages she'd written while fused to the leg of the wooden chair and table. "Now this is more like it. Why couldn't you have written this before and saved us both a lot of bother?"

The heaviness of her heart, head, and limbs made any sort of retort, sarcastic or otherwise, impossible. He turned the laptop back to face her and flicked his hand with the silent command for her to carry on.

She risked unleashing his wrath once more and said, "Guy, I can't. I'm exhausted! Anything else I write will just be a load of gibberish. Do what you must to me, but I need to rest."

Seeing a flash of anger streak across the contour of his face, she tried to fend off further outbursts by adding, "Just give me a few hours of sleep. Chain me if you must. I'm begging you. Let me lie down and close my eyes." Her gamble paid off. Guy couldn't resist a woman so diminished that she resorted to pleading.

His face lit with a brilliant smile of victory as he agreed. "Fine. I never could resist being a knight in shining armor. But I have plenty of ties where those came from. And I will make sure you don't bolt in the night." He rose, took out his Swiss Army knife, and hacked the tie from her calf, nicking her skin.

As Tara rose from the confines of her prison, she stumbled from stinging pain as blood and oxygen rushed into the veins in her calf. The dreary darkness of her predicament threatened to swallow her whole as she limped toward the bathroom.

Slumped forward on the lid of the toilet, she turned her aching head sideways and glanced up at the small window above the bathtub. She wondered whether it might be a portal through which she could escape.

"Don't even think about it! Besides, your ass wouldn't permit. It would be like a camel trying to get through the eye of a needle. Now, be a good girl, do your business, and I'll tuck you in, all nice and cozy."

She stood, flipped open the toilet seat, yanked down her underwear, and relieved herself.

She was past caring about anything. Even before she'd a chance to wipe herself, Guy grabbed her by the arm and led her toward the bedroom. Without ceremony, he threw her onto the bed. Extracting yet another tie from his pants pocket, he lashed her left wrist to the metal frame.

As he leered down at her half-naked torso, Tara bent her knees and clamped her legs together.

In a split second, he jumped onto the bed. As both hands wrapped around her neck, her eyes widened in horror. He forced her legs wide open with his knee until she lay spread-eagled, gasping for air. Flailing from left to right, she saw a glint of violent delight in his eyes. He was getting off on her frantic struggle. She heard him unzip his pants. With renewed panic, her free hand clawed at his face, which only seemed to arouse him further.

He ripped the flimsy protection of her panties to shreds and thrust into her. As his pleasure increased, so did the grip on her throat. The last thing she heard before losing consciousness was a screech of animal lust as his semen exploded inside her.

Chapter Fifty-Eight

Mamó sat in the garden, silent, every muscle in her face contorted by angry pain.

"Patience, Cado, my friend," she whispered, stroking the mottled fur of her companion as he strained to be released from her grasp. "Above all, we must practice patience. We cannot intervene until she breaks free from the binds that tie her and takes responsibility for her own salvation."

And there they sat, in complicit silence, waiting as the moon illuminated the night sky and terrors below.

CHAPTER FIFTY-NINE

AMA FELT HATRED erupt like fire throughout her entire being. "Why in the name of Neito did you let me live, old woman? It would have been much better if you allowed that beast to kill me in the arms of my mother. Who were you to decide my fate?"

Leaving a pot to sway gently over the fire pit, Baba rose from squatting and turned to face the child of her only child.

Ama's eyes were heavy with the tears she refused to shed—her face livid with emotion.

"Dear one—"

"Do not 'dear one' me. I am not your dear one! I am no one's dear one. And I never want to be a dear one!"

"Very well then, Ama. I will tell you. The fight to spare your life was not my choice but your mother's. She knew what that beast, as you call him, would do upon your birth, so she pleaded with me to ensure her unborn child was safe. Would you have me ignore my daughter's dying wish?"

"You cannot convince me that my mother's last wish was for me to live a life that has resulted in me being shamed in front of my fellow warriors and ridiculed as I sucked the dirt of the earth into my lungs. Is that the life my dear mother sought for me? I am now the butt of sneering jokes. How can I stand tall when everyone diminishes me? How can I show my strength when everyone sees me as weak?"

The old woman sighed as her granddaughter slapped away the hand she had extended to caress the young woman's face.

"Ama, how many times have I told you that strength is not a show of brute force? A willingness to stand alone, to have the courage to be who you came to this world to be, is strength. It is about being brave enough to shed light on the darkness within oneself and choose the path of love and compassion. I beg you to choose love over hate before you are lost forever."

Ama grabbed for the sword she no longer possessed as she exploded with a desire to end the ceaseless babble of this old woman. Forever! "You are most fortunate, you crazy old woman, that I do not have my weapon, or your head would now lie gaping in the dirt. From this day forward, you no longer exist to me. Do you understand that? My sword is my strength! There is no other."

Lingering within the hut, Baba whispered, "My child, when did you learn to run from what your soul craves?"

As Baba stroked the mottled mane of her trusted four-legged companion, she sighed, saying, "Patience, my friend. Above all, we must be patient."

At dawn the next day, every sinew of Ama's body stretched tight with nervous anticipation. She and the others stood, looking out from the tower embedded in the walls of Numantia. As the mist licked at every surface of the forested hillside, the would-be warrior brushed the hair out of her eyes and scanned the landscape for any signs of advance by the Roman dogs. Her hand went to the sword at her side, which she had taken from a comrade who would not know it was missing until he woke from his drunken stupor.

Scouts had arrived under cover of night with news that the

beleaguered forces of Quintus Fabius Nobilitor had set up camp a quick march away. He had chosen the site where the swine Marcus Porcius Cato established a Roman presence in her grandmother's father's time. During his ruthless plunder of tribal lands to the south and east, Cato had no compunction about slaughtering victims, even those who surrendered. Some said he boasted of destroying more towns than he had spent days in her homeland. Where was the honor in such actions? Many captured warriors had chosen to kill themselves rather than submit to the brutality of this usurper.

Thumping her fist into the wooden support of the tower until the rough-hewn edge drew blood, Ama cursed, "At least taking one's life is a sign of bravery, unlike the actions of those Roman pigs."

At once, she flinched into alertness. As her eyes scrutinized the landscape across the adjacent plateau, she caught a glimmer of movement at the edge of the woodland, a distance to the east. Blinking to clear her eyes, she was now sure she could see a solid mass moving across the raised ground, like a well-organized swarm of ants.

Without hesitation, she jumped, clearing the eight wooden steps leading down to the wall's rampart, and raced across it with the agility of a starving wolf closing in on its prey. The rhythm of her feet kept perfect time with the pounding beat of her heart.

With no thought as to the impudence of her actions, she ran to the tent where Ambon and Leukon, the recently appointed leaders of the combined forces, had set up their command post. A host of burly warriors assigned to protect the duo barred her way. They yanked her left arm with such force that she was sure they had pulled it from its socket.

On her knees, sucking in the earth's dust in front of her captors, full of rage, Ama spat, "For the love of Neito, I must speak to Ambon and Leukon at once, you brutes. It is a matter of life and death! Now, out of the way before I cut down your worthless bodies."

The guards were so caught up in the waif's hysterics they did not realize Leukon had emerged from the tent behind them. "Silence, all of you! Tell me why I am being disturbed at such an early hour. I am in the mood to strike without delay at the instigator of this commotion."

The guards parted ranks, allowing Leukon to witness the young warrior on all fours, spitting dirt from her mouth. "You there. Are you the reason for this ungodly interruption? Answer me. Are you?"

Ama scrambled to her feet. She straightened her back and stood as tall as her failing nerves would allow. "Yes, Commander, I am. I believe I have glimpsed Roman dogs heading our way."

Leukon strode over to her and grabbed the scruff of her tunic and commanded, "Well then, let us see if your vision is better than that of my seasoned sentinels."

He dragged and pulled her toward the spot on the tower where she had stood a moment before. Attempting to recover both her breath and dignity, she pointed in the direction she had seen the approaching forces.

Leukon peered into the distance, then back at her, and then into the distance once more. Without apology, he pivoted to the guards gathered behind him and shouted, "Sound the alarm. The Roman swine are on their way. If they are looking for a fight, they will have one this very day." He lunged down the steps, running toward the command post, and disappeared in a cloud of his own dust.

Hours later, as the scorching sun glared down from the cloudless sky, Ama's skin felt seared like a wild boar over an open fire. The only shade was the shadow that pooled at the feet of each warrior. She gave thanks to Neito that the heat-soaked sun was not lower in the sky, or she and her fellow warriors-in-arms would have been blinded by its rays and at a distinct disadvantage.

The Romans stood a field-length away from Ama and her comrades, who protected the walls of their hilltop stronghold. Every muscle in her body and mind tightened as she viewed the enemy formation, attempting to second-guess what Ambon and Leukon's strategy would be to cull this pack of dogs.

In the foreground were six small groups of infantries with shields and swords much shorter than the ones used by her army. The groups formed a wedge, with one soldier at the front, behind which was a line of two soldiers, then a line of three, then four, each line increasing until twenty men stood abreast of one another. A short distance behind this formation, a line thick with infantry stood, with numerous lines of foot soldiers at equal distances behind them, all waiting for Nobilitor's orders.

Hundreds of men on horseback flanked the right and left of these columns. The physical appearance of these men was nothing like their fellow Roman soldiers. As they sat mounted, she guessed they were at least a head taller than the men on foot. The darkness of their skin and hair gleamed in the bright sun.

Rivulets of sweat cascaded like a waterfall down Ama's back, pooling at the top of her buttocks, as she calculated the warriors from her confederation were outnumbered by at least two to one. Pulling herself up into a proud, defiant stance, fueled by razor-sharp nerves, hatred, and resolve, she whispered, "I will defend my tribe to the last of my days…to victory or death."

The Roman army marched forward as one.

A mixture of delight and dread rose within the young warrior as she drew her sword and waited for the onslaught. But to her amazement, as the enemy came within a stone's throw, half their ranks moved left while the other half maneuvered right, creating a cavern between them. Ama and her comrades only had a split second to revel in the stupidity of their enemy before the hairs on her neck shot straight up.

A herd of strange beasts taller than two warriors and massive in girth with wizened, thick, slate-colored hides charged from the rear. Their mammoth, stocky feet crushed all life in their wake. Massive, sharp teeth curved upward, well beyond their mouths, and their snouts hung almost to the ground, turning up at the end.

Ama could feel the demon of fear devour her senses. Calming

herself as much as she was able, she remembered the elders' tales of such beasts from a time when they fought as mercenaries for tribes far to the south. Her comrades broke rank, turned, and ran toward the town gates behind them, pushing and shoving everyone in their way.

She bellowed, "Do not run, you cowards! We must stand and fight to the death if need be. Do not let these beasts be our downfall. To victory or…"

A few deserters had turned into a flood. A wave of fellow warriors ran, stepping on and over those who had fallen. As others attempted to escape the stampeding herd, she heard screams and groans as bodies were crushed and bones were broken.

Leukon's voice rose above the din, commanding them to retreat. With a saddened heart, she turned and joined the fleeing throng of her tribe. As the gates closed behind them, they climbed up the ramparts to the towers. Looking over and down, she saw the bodies of dozens of fellow warriors strewn like straw below. The Roman dogs and their beasts refused to stop. She guessed they were going to use the enormous beasts to demolish the gates and walls. Not without a fight, she thought.

Ama picked up whatever she could find and began raining it down on anything that moved below. Before long, others followed suit, and soon there was a continuous volley of javelins, slingstones, and rocks careening down.

Picking up the largest rock she could find, she aimed to slash open the skull of a beast below. With crushing accuracy, it hit the creature square on the head. The savage beast reeled from the blunt force of full impact, but instead of buckling to the ground, it uttered a loud and ferocious cry, wheeled around and rushed against the tight ranks of the Roman infantry. In quick succession, the other beasts rallied and joined him in the carnage, trampling anyone who got in their way with their enormous feet while tossing others high in the air as if they were feathers.

Uproarious laughter and whoops of victory leaped from the lips of the warriors peering over the ramparts as they watched the beasts destroy the integrity and discipline, not only of the Roman central battle formation but also its flanks, as the soldiers took flight to escape the rampage.

Amid wails of laughter, Leukon issued the command to pursue the fleeing enemy and cut them down. With renewed spirits, heightened vigor, and the promise of bloody victory, Ama and the other warriors stormed out of the town, swords waving high in the air.

Chapter Sixty

TARA WOKE WITH a start.

The stickiness between her thighs and the smell of Guy's sweat and stale semen were more than enough to remind her of her current situation. The cool chill of morning air raised goose bumps along her outstretched legs.

Twisting sideways, she could see Guy's sleeping hulk snoring inches away. Staring at the slackness of his jaw and the thinness of his lips, she knew one thing for sure. He would not defeat her, no matter what he did to her body. She would not allow him or anyone else to get the better of her ever again.

It was at that moment that he snorted awake and stretched the length of his frame.

Through the fog of almost-closed eyes, she saw him reach over to shake her awake. "Come on, sleepyhead. Rise and shine. Another full day of writing lies in wait."

He propped himself up onto his elbow, and she felt his eyes sweeping back and forth across her naked flesh. She repressed a shudder as he whisked his index finger across her pubic hair.

"You know, my dear, fucking you was always so predictable,

pedestrian, and, well, just downright dull. But last night, we turned a corner, my sweet. It left me wanting more."

She saw him, as if in slow motion, rise and straddle her legs. Images of the faces of her parents, contorted with hate, now glared down at her, expecting—no, demanding—her absolute passive acceptance of the pain they felt was their right to inflict.

A fury as cold as frozen wastelands burned like frostbite throughout her being. Before he could pry her legs apart, she brought her knees up in one swift movement, with a strength she didn't know she possessed, and caught him square in the groin.

As he curled into a fetal ball, writhing in pain, sputtering obscenities, she shrieked, "If you want me to write one more word, you poor fucking excuse for humanity, you'll not touch me again. Do you hear me? Never again! If you do, I swear to God, I'll kill you, you fucking bastard!"

He was silenced. Tears streaked down his contorted face as he retched dry heaves and grabbed at his balls. She watched, uncaring, as he rolled off the bed. He tried to stand but fell to the coldness of the stone floor, hitting his head on the night table on his way down.

Fear of reprisal now obliterated her fury. As if plugged into an electrical socket, her free hand jolted upward and over her head in a maniacal attempt to be free from the biting grip of the restraint before he came around.

Where the hell were Dana or Mamó and Cado when she needed them?

Her desperate desire to have someone, anyone, come to her aid was replaced with paralyzing fear as she heard groaning from the other side of the bed.

The muscles of her arms and legs cramped with terror as she attempted to disappear into the sweat-soaked sheets of her prison. Her eyes widened in anticipation, expecting him to deliver a blow that would end her existence.

Grabbing onto the night table and then the bed frame, Guy rose, wincing as he raised his hand to the cut. With a deliberate, unhurried movement, he lifted it to the cut over his left eye while raking his gaze over her body.

The silence between them was venomous. The cracked dryness of her mouth would not permit even a croak of a scream. She was, once again, at his mercy.

When he spoke, the coldness of his tone sent shards of ice coursing through her veins, hacking away at any hope of escape.

"Right now, I don't just want to kill you, you fucking piece of shit. I want to drag you outside and club you until you are close to death. I want to use that same shovel to dig a hole in the earth and toss your still-breathing, worthless carcass into it. I want to end whatever bit of pathetic life you still cling to and rain muck down on you, filling every life-giving orifice with dirt."

"Guy, I am sorry, I just —"

"I don't give a goddamn if you're sorry or not. We are way beyond sorry."

He staggered across the bed until he was once more on top of her, pulling the Swiss Army knife from his pocket.

Inhaling, Tara shut her eyes, and her nails dug deep into her palms as she curled her fingers into a fist. All she could do was wait for the knife to hack deep into her heart or belly, cutting off her life. She felt the swish of the knife as it came down over her head. But instead of it sending her into the endless cold that was death, the knife severed the plastic tie from the metal of the bed frame.

Grabbing at the ache in her wrist, she dared to unclench the tautness of her eyes to stare up into a face awash with cruelty and hatred.

"Make no mistake. I have no qualms about ending your life. My need to preserve myself is the only thing keeping you alive. If you don't do as I say, I'll see you dead and buried without shedding one goddamn tear. Do I make myself clear? Now get the fuck up and start writing. Right now, your willingness to produce what I want is the only assurance of a prolonged life that you have."

CHAPTER SIXTY-ONE

WITH HER EYES blurred by sleep deprivation, Tara scanned the top of the rustic oak table to her left to see what time it was.

Four-thirty! It had been less than twenty hours since Guy's depraved assurance that he would end her existence if she didn't do as he wanted.

As the numbness of sleep left her, she realized she'd slept for three hours. While most people in the northern hemisphere were still chasing their white rabbits down imaginary burrows, she lay shackled by the choices she'd made in her life.

Those precious three hours of sleep were spent with Ama and her comrades as they ran and screamed from the hill fort, wielding merciless swords. She'd felt the bloodlust as it rose from the pit of the young warrior's gut until it choked all but a raging desire to see every Roman head adorn her belt.

Once the clangor of swords subsided and the slaughterous shouts were hushed, she lay within the ravaged body of Ama as her eyes fluttered open to see the shadows of black vultures circling above, waiting to pluck the eyes and strip the flesh of the departed. A mist of pain soaked every fiber of the young warrior's body, extinguishing the ferocious hatred that had burned within. Tara knew Ama was on the brink of death.

Squirming to ease higher into the bed to ease the pain shooting through her wrist, courtesy of the plastic ties, Tara understood death to be a great leveler. It didn't discriminate. It took what and who it liked, when it liked. Sighing, she felt an enormous sense of pity for this young woman who'd never allowed the loving warmth of her grandmother to touch and defrost her ice-encased heart.

Guy stirred as she reached with her free hand, repositioning her pillow in order to stop the metal of the bedstead from digging into the flesh of her back. With beleaguered eyes, she relived her most recent nocturnal escapade.

Chapter Sixty-Two

AMA COULD SEE the scavengers circling high above the wounded and dead spread over the scarlet-tainted earth. The blinding pain, as the connection between her wrist and arm had been severed, had faded to a dull ache. A short Roman sword had slashed Ama's side as she'd twisted away from its impact. In his frenzied state to kill as many of the enemy as possible, the soldier had left her for dead.

As blood oozed from the gash in her side, she offered feverish thanks to Neito for the drowsiness that assailed her. It had overcome her urge to vomit. Even the pounding in her head had subsided to a tolerable level. She knew it would all be over soon.

Amid the cesspool of decomposing life, her thoughts no longer focused on an embittered lust to kill or the glories of an honorable death. Instead, the desire to be embraced once more, before she died, in the warmth of Baba's loving arms consumed her. She was once again a little girl on her grandmother's knee, being rocked in front of the flickering embers of a fire until her demons were banished.

Lulled by these images, she awaited the hooded figure of death to take her. She did not fear death. She feared not knowing what would become of her once she left the Earth. In bittersweet delirium, she wondered where the darkness might take her.

She heard a familiar sound. Weakness rendered her unable to lift her aching head to see if it was illusion or reality. She heard it again and thought it was getting closer. But it could not be, she told herself. What would Baba be doing so close to the killing field?

Moments later, she felt the warmth of her grandmother's arms around her. So this was what death felt like, she thought, no longer afraid. In the gentle haze of letting go, she swore that something or someone was lifting her aching body into the caring warmth of a caress.

Ama felt Baba kneel beside her blood-soaked body, stroke her head, and soothe her. "I am here, dear one. Dear one, I am here. My sweet child, open your eyes. On all that is sacred, dear girl, do not tell me I am too late!" Ama's lips twitched while her eyes, dimmed by pain, attempted to flicker open.

"Thanks be to Cernunnos!" Baba said.

Gentle hands lowered Ama's limp body to the ground once more. The old woman stood and shouted, "Sisters, she is over here. She is alive. My blessed granddaughter is alive, but barely. Quick as you can, we must hasten to the safety of the sacred grove. Sisters, do not dally. Help me! We must save her. She needs time to heal."

Half a dozen aged women from the hill fort ran to where Baba stood. With a strength that belied their age, they lifted Ama's battered body onto a crude litter and dragged their precious cargo away from the putrid smell of death.

"Make haste, my friends. We have much to teach her. She has much to learn."

CHAPTER SIXTY-THREE

WONDERING WHERE BABA and the others had taken Ama and what had become of her, Tara was glad at least that the young woman had a chance to begin life anew. Unlike Ama, her own state of affairs seemed to offer no relief.

It had been two days since Guy had stormed into her bedroom, demanding she do his bidding. Resistance was futile, and she felt there was nothing to be done but comply. She was thankful the hateful bully hadn't attempted to rape her again.

Parched from thirst, she looked over at the table where a water glass stood. If she were ever so quiet, she might reach it without waking the man snoring beside her. Lying flat on her back, her free hand shaking, she reached for the glass.

"Fuck," she swore as the glass slipped from her grasp and crashed to the stone floor, shattering any chance of satisfying her thirst.

"What the hell?" Guy bolted up as if someone had shot him with a large dose of methamphetamine. "For Christ's sake, you bitch, what the fuck are you trying to pull?"

Feeling the cold numbness in both her right arm and her deadened heart, she responded in a tone that was matter-of-fact. "I was thirsty and tried to reach for the water glass. That, as you say, is all I was attempting to pull." As she braced herself for the deluge of his onslaught, every muscle in her body tensed as his bare upper torso uncoiled like a snake.

"Just because you've been such a good girl and written over a hundred pages so far," he said, propping himself up on his left elbow, "doesn't mean I won't beat you senseless for my abrupt awakening. Tell you what, I'll bring you coffee in bed. Now, don't say I never do anything for you."

He bounded to his feet and out of sight. She heard water being poured into the kettle and the slamming of cupboard doors. She struggled, without success, to wrangle her way out of the restraint binding her to the bedstead.

A litany of expletives spewed from the kitchen. Doubting she'd ever be able to disentangle herself from her prison, Tara stopped any further attempts at escape.

"You're out of coffee, not to mention any form of edible food," he accused her from the doorway.

"Well, I am sorry," she shot back, not worrying about recrimination.

A look of pure hatred burning in his eyes withered any further response.

"Not a very good wifey, are we? Now, I shall have to go into Dunsany and buy some sustenance. If you're good and make the revisions we talked about while I'm away, I might bring you some sort of treat. We can't have you go weak in the fingers, now, can we?"

The anger she had let simmer for far too long erupted like a volcano, blowing all caution to the wind. At that moment, she didn't care one iota about the consequences of her words. "You can't be serious. Do you think you can get away with this! What will the BBC say when I tell everyone that you used brutal force to make me write? That you raped me! What will happen to your precious reputation then? You won't be able to brutalize me or anyone else from a prison cell."

"How dare you try to intimidate me? Do you think anyone will pay the slightest attention to your sniffling accusations? You'll have no proof. It will be a matter of, 'he said, she said.' Who do you think they'll believe? A jilted lover with no connections or an upright citizen with a pedigree? You're a moron if you think anyone will believe you! Now shut up."

He loomed over her, knife in hand, and sliced the plastic tie in half. She rubbed the flow of life back into her hand and arm.

The hatred that raged in his eyes morphed into icy disdain as he said, "I wouldn't get used to being free, my dear. I'll be taking your phone and laptop with me. Can't have you calling for help, now, can we? There's no escape, not until you give me what I want. Now hurry and go to the little girl's room and pee so I can go get breakfast. I'm famished."

True to his word, he had allowed her to not only pee but to brush her teeth and wash before leaving her tied to the bed once more, her feet bound with the nylon belt from her dressing gown. Giving her a printout of the chapters in question and a pencil, he made sure she was free enough to do the revisions in relative comfort.

She waited for a few minutes to make sure he was gone. She had about forty-five minutes before he returned. Frantic about finding something, anything, to release her from her current predicament, she searched the room but could see nothing.

"Think, Tara. Think!" her rant ricocheted off the coldness of the stone walls, and cold despair boomeranged back at her. "For the love of God, think!"

Nada. She expelled both an excess of air and any hope of escape as she took up her pen to edit the manuscript. "How nice of him," she hissed, "to leave the restraint loose enough that I'm able to write. What a fucking hero!"

CHAPTER SIXTY-FOUR

I T TOOK ALL Mamó's strength to hold Cado in check as she and Dana watched Guy drive at a leisurely speed up the dirt track.

"We must act now," Dana implored.

"No, my child. We must have faith in Tara. We can do little to free her from her visible restraints until she realizes she is the only one who has the power to release herself from everything that binds her to the life she has lived until this present moment."

"But grandmother, what if she doesn't have the strength to break free?"

"Have faith, dear one. We must have faith that she remembers she has more than what it takes to do just that."

Chapter Sixty-Five

IT HAD BEEN about half an hour since Guy left her trussed up like a turkey waiting to be strangled, plucked, and stuffed. Frightened and frustrated, she threw her pen down on the bed. No matter how hard she tried, she couldn't bring herself to deliver the drivel he wanted.

"This is a load of crap." She sighed, moving higher on the bed to relieve the pressure on her aching wrist.

The softness of a whisper came. "This is your story. Find the courage to write it as you see fit, dear one. Release yourself from the shackles that bind."

"Easier said than done," she seethed.

"Remember, my child, you are not alone. You have never been. We are here, waiting just beyond the veil, to assist you, but you must take the initial steps. You can do this!"

"I can do this," she said, not really believing it. But she had to do it. Her life depended on it. She began with renewed vigor to release her wrist from the tie binding her to the bedstead.

As she twisted around, using the fingers of her free hand to weaken the plastic tie, Tara could smell her distinct brand of body odor. One minute, then two, then three, and then five minutes passed. The hysteria of laughter followed bemused confusion as she wriggled her right hand free of the restraint. Tears of relief swelled and poured down her cheek.

The hands on the clock told her she had to act fast. With both hands, she unknotted the belt, binding her feet together, and hopped from the bed. She grabbed her car keys, flung open the door, and ran barefoot toward her car.

"Oh, for the love of—" she said. Guy had punctured the car's front tires.

CHAPTER SIXTY-SIX

MAMÓ CROUCHED WITH her trusted four-legged companion in the bushes, just out of sight.

She smiled as Tara flung open the door and ran toward her car.

"Patience, my friend," she whispered, keeping a tight hold on the scruff of Cado's neck. "We must wait just a little longer before we act."

CHAPTER SIXTY-SEVEN

"S HIT," WAS THE only word that escaped Tara's lips as Guy's car raced toward her, spewing dust and grit. Distance, she needed to put distance between them and fast. The maniac sure as hell wasn't easing up on the accelerator. Turning, she realized that scaling the boulder wall to her right and running for the safety of the woods a short distance across the open field was her best bet. With newfound strength, she clambered over, slipping as the speed of her ascent dislodged some of the wall's unmortared rocks. Even though she felt the warmth of blood trickle down her leg, she didn't stop to determine the damage.

As she picked up speed, her feet slipped on the grass, still wet with dew. Her heart was pounding in her ears, but it wasn't enough to drown out the sound of Guy's car as it came to a screeching halt.

Tara didn't look back. There was no need. She'd heard the car door open and Guy's running feet as he sought to lessen the gap between them. Her breath came in short, nervous spurts as she curled her fingers into sweaty fists as if that simple action would propel her faster.

Behind her, she heard Guy's jeering laughter as he yelled, "Really?

You think you can outrun me? There is no way out. You will do as I bid, or it will be the death of you."

Sweat dripped from her matted hair. Her lungs and heart pumped faster. As Tara lunged wildly forward, she prayed aloud. "Please, God, let me be free. Let me leave all this behind once and for all. I need your help!"

Expletives erupted behind her. Glancing over her shoulder, she saw Guy had fallen but was hastily righting himself. That was when she saw the glint of a knife in his hand.

Holy shit! This was no time to do a swan dive, she thought, as her feet slipped on the wet earth.

Frantic, she scanned the horizon, hoping to hell she could make the woodland before he caught up with her. There, at least, she might find a place to hide.

She was so close.

"Give it up, Tara, and save us both a waste of time! We both know who will be the victor here."

A determined voice raged, and she knew, beyond all doubt, that this was no one else's voice but her own. "No one will butcher me. When I get myself out of this, I swear no one will ever again determine how I live my life." In that instant, arms flailing and mouth agape with fear, Tara slipped on the greased slickness of the grass and crashed to the ground. Her temple connected with the blunt force of a rock.

In the dull grayness, just before total blackness overshadowed all fear, she swore she heard three things. The first was Mamó shouting, "Now, Cado, now!" The second was the menacing growl of an animal. The third was the thundering vibration of hastily retreating steps.

Then, all went black.

Chapter Sixty-Eight

THE CORNERS OF Guy's mouth rose as he watched Tara take a nosedive to the earth up ahead. He had won! His glee was short-lived, replaced by an innate sense that danger was fast approaching. His fingers clenched as he saw the massive, brindled hulk of a wolf as it streaked, ears erect and snarling, straight at him.

Guy's breath came in short, sharp spurts as he turned and catapulted himself into frantic flight. He heard the baying growls of his predator getting closer as he slid out of control on a sodden patch of clay and spiraled downward at such a speed that left him devoid of breath.

Before he could stand up, a snarling mass of mottled fur knocked him onto his back.

Urine stained the front of his trousers as the beast's lips curled upward and back, displaying sharp incisors, while the hairs on its back stood erect.

Time seemed suspended as Guy cried, "Get off me, you filthy beast."

When his creature showed no signs of capitulation, he said, "Oh, for the love of God, let me live."

"You, my friend, have not the faintest concept of the word *love*," Mamó declared, now standing over him.

"Get your mongrel off me now!"

A chill ripped through Guy's body as he stared up into eyes dark with cold resolve. The curl of her upper lip left him in no doubt that the old woman would have no compunction about leaving his entrails as bird fodder.

"Oh, do not worry. Cado will do you no harm. Not unless I command him to. Now let us discuss the terms of your freedom."

"If it's money you want, old woman, I can get it for you."

"How sad is it you think the world revolves around money?"

Cado snarled, reminding Guy that he was there at the old woman's mercy. "Then what is it you want?"

"I want nothing for myself. But if you value your life today and for all the days that follow, you will leave our young friend alone. Forever, do you understand? And if you think Cado and I will not hunt you down if you renege on the promise you are about to make, then you are mistaken."

At that moment, Guy knew two things. One was that he had lost. The other was that he was under no illusion that these two were only bluffing.

Chapter Sixty-Nine

CLARICE AWOKE TO find her view consumed by the lines of loving concern etched on Papa's face. Within the gentle murmur of dancing leaves waving in a soft breeze, she heard the deep, vibrating purring of nearby turtle doves. Seeing the reassuring gaze of her beloved Papa and hearing the sounds of winged friends, she relaxed.

Clarice licked bloody residue from her cracked, parched lips while she struggled to raise herself into a sitting position against the bark of a tree. The sky was post-dawn, the temperature still cool.

She looked upward through weary eyes. For the briefest of seconds, she was lured into a false sense of well-being while she observed the twisted, curling gleam of the boughs above, clothed in shades of green, as they fluttered in the soft breeze.

As she scanned the near horizon, she deduced they must be at the edge of a dense forest that she did not recognize.

A cacophony of color colonized the meadow, which spanned out in all directions, choreographed by no other means save the wind. Dark-purple, veined aphyllanthes danced amid the pale amethyst of peacock anemone, the shadowy yellow of broom, the bright sky-blue and leafy branched spikes of chicory, and the playful, innocent pink-ness of the catchfly.

A bolt of pain shot through her shoulder and arm, smashing any sense of calm. Papa wrenched a vial of willow bark from his burlap sack and holding her head in the crook of his arm, bade Clarice to drink. Wiping her mouth with the hem of her disheveled tunic, she glanced up at the strained lines etched into her protector's face.

"Papa," she managed through a rasp she did not recognize as her own voice.

"Rest, my child. You must rest! We still have many more days of travel before we're out of immediate danger."

Grasping for the hands that had been her only genuine source of love and security for many years, she attempted to clear the grate in her speech, which brought its own unique pain as she implored him.

"But Papa, I do not understand. How do we come to be in this place? I remember you telling me to keep my eyes closed, at all costs, and to utter no sound as you gave me some potion to drink."

Sucking in her breath, she continued, "Papa, I was so afraid! First, I couldn't catch my breath. Then my lips and tongue tingled, prick-led, and burned. After a short while, I could not move. In the end, I remember thinking I was dying and then darkness descended." A mute shake of her head was her feeble attempt to bring clarity to her present circumstance.

Was it only a short while ago she had a clear view of her destiny? The innocent belief that her life's purpose was to ease the suffering of others now felt as bruised as her body. In the throes of confused exasperation, she looked through tear-stained eyes and cried, "Papa, what is to become of us?"

Papa bent over his ward, stroked her dirt-streaked hair, and whis-pered the story well overdue in its telling.

Chapter Seventy

THE CRUSTY-SKINNED WOMAN allowed a glimmer of a
smile to invade the puckered austerity of her features. She had won!
Sister Bernadette was reclining, basking in the glow of her victory,
within the sanctity of the convent's cloisters. Gossip had it that the vile
little creature's body had been taken to the woods north of the city and
fed to the wolves.

There was much to celebrate. The surgeon Accart had been sentenced to a period in prison for abusing a nonexistent relationship with
the abbot, and the postulant had been cleared of all charges. And none
of Sister Bernadette's actions had come back to haunt her.

As she struggled to straighten the hunch in her back that refused to
comply, she rejoiced that never again would someone as irreverent and
willful as that little snippet darken the doors of the place she had called
home for the last four decades.

Closing her eyes to shut out the bright sun, she did not hear the
approaching footsteps of the person who now acted as a blessed screen
from its rays. With no further need to shield her eyes, she opened them.
Her breath stuttered in her lungs. Standing before her was a chained
and gaunt Accart, the Abbess, and guards from Abbey Saint Victor.

Chapter Seventy-One

A FIERCE PAIN SHOT through her skull. The moon was high in the sky as Tara jolted into consciousness. Her head was no longer pitted against the hardness of rock but shielded in the warm softness of Mamó's lap. She attempted to bolt up into a sitting position but slumped back down. Her head hurt way too much, as did the rest of her body. Weak and confused, she raised her grass-smeared hand to the left side of her temple. The oozing blood had long since ceased, but it had left a thick, congealed crust in its wake. The left side of her body felt like someone had hammered it with a ball-peen hammer.

"What? How?"

"Shush, dear one. Rest. Cado and I are here, and you are safe. That is all you need to know at this moment. My solemn promise is that piece of vermin will never, ever hurt you again."

Chilled by the night air, she said, "But how can you promise such a thing? You don't know him. He has connections, and I'm afraid he has the power to make me do what he wants."

"You are stronger than you think, and you are not alone, for we will always be with you, my child, even when you most doubt our presence."

"But how can you promise—"

"It is not about a promise from me. It is about you waking up to realize that our presence is a given," the old woman said and smiled. "Besides, from now on, you are going to make our job a lot easier, are you not?"

"I'm not sure why you—"

"Let me remind you what you swore moments before you fell. You said, 'No one will butcher me. When I get myself out of this, I swear no one will ever again determine how I live my life.'"

"But I didn't get myself out, did I? It was you—"

"Oh, but you did. Your plea for help from forces you have never seen or believed in was the kindling. And you expressed your desire to live a life directed by yourself and not others with such passion; it was the match that lit the flame."

"But how will I ever be able to live such a life? I'm just not—"

"You have had the courage and strength, through many lifetimes, to overcome countless moments of adversity. Moments that were, may I add, created by you as you journeyed toward becoming the best physical version of your divine, authentic self here on Earth. Dear one, you have come to the Earth with many past and present talents and gifts. For too long, you have taken the simple route and allowed the desires of others to be your compass. Now, you are waking up to the joyful responsibility of plotting your own course. Write your book, live your life in a way that makes your heart sing. When you follow that path, life will unfold in ways you never knew possible."

"What do I do when shit happens? It's hard to make my heart sing when things occur that I have no control over."

"No, but this shit, as you call it, is the fertilizer. If you allow it, it becomes the fertile breeding ground for new learning, perspectives, and opportunities. How you view yourself, others, and life is, and has always been, up to you!"

The old woman then took Tara's hand and asked, "Would you permit me to tell you a story?"

Tara offered an almost imperceptible nod, which was a more than adequate sign for Mamó to bend ever closer and whisper a story she knew was well overdue in its telling. At the end of her story, Mamó stood up, and she and Cado walked away.

"Wait. I'm still not sure how——"

The old woman turned, an impish expression on her ancient face. "Oh, do not worry, my child. There will always be a legion of us poking and prodding you to be all that you are!"

She vanished as the last word left her lips.

Chapter Seventy-Two

TARA BREATHED IN the aromatic and soothing concoction of pine, spicy herbs, the sweetness of flowers, and sea air as she sat in the shade of an orange-canopied table at the Beach Café on Quaidu Port, waiting for the first course of Marseille's most famous, two-course bouillabaisse dish.

Massaging her protruding belly, she was glad that fish still agreed with her.

Before the doctor shared the results of the ultrasound, she knew she'd deliver a healthy baby girl into the world. Abortion had never been a consideration. Despite being conceived in the violent hatred of rape, her daughter would be born into all the love Tara could offer.

Amarice was the name she created for her baby girl. Tara would ensure her child never doubted herself, the expansiveness of life, or anything logic couldn't explain away. She would teach her to embrace it all, not by telling her what to do, but by showing her with her own actions. Teaching her daughter to embrace life to explore how all interactions, wherever they came from, might apply to the immediacy of her own experience.

Her lips curved upward, blazing into a full-blown smile, which surged from the uninhibited depth of her soul, warming places within her the sun could never reach. These days, her heartbeat was so strong she sometimes thought her chest would burst. It no longer pounded from uncontrollable fear but from the exquisite beauty of unconditional love.

Sighing with a contentment that had eluded her for most of her life, she raised her fingers to her lips. Kissing them, she then lowered them to her belly.

It was at that moment the squawking ha-ha-ha-ha of flocks of gulls out in the bay, foraging for food, took her back to a time long since passed.

She had just come from Fort Saint-Jean, where she'd stood on the terrace of its tower looking out across the bay to L'archipel du Frioul, wondering if it was the same scene Clarice had witnessed all those years ago while searching for the cause of the outbreak she'd been so sure wasn't leprosy.

Of course, she realized Clarice wouldn't have had the same advantage of height from which to view the archipelago. They built the fort over two hundred years after the young healer had walked the streets of Marseille. But Tara had still indulged in the feeling that she wasn't the only one looking through her eyes from that vantage point.

In that instance, she heard the familiar softness of a whisper, "Ah, but my dear one, linear time is an illusion, as you now well know."

Glancing up, she saw a brisk young server place a steaming dish of fish broth on the table and point at her belly. "*Quand votre bébé est-il dû?*"

Although she knew little French, she was sure she understood the question. Smiling up at the young woman, she replied, "*Février.*" Satisfied, the server hustled back to answer an impatient bell ringing from deep within the recesses of the restaurant.

Before she picked up her soup spoon, Tara looked across the street to the sailboats anchored in the bay, their naked masts piercing the blue October sky. Twirling the necklace her mother had thrown at her so long ago, saying it was the only piece of junk her crazy grandmother had left behind, she mused about time. Had it only been five months since she left Ireland?

After her escape from Guy, she'd chosen to stay in Ireland for a while to recharge her batteries and contemplate her new life. She had decided not to go to the police with accusations about Guy, knowing at some point his lifestyle would catch up with him, and she'd been right.

A month after his spinning car tires made their hasty retreat, the authorities notified her that his body was found in an alley beside one of the more famous sleaze-grinding brothels in Soho, drenched in whisky, with Hoyo de Monterrey Epicure No. 2 cigars shoved up his nostrils. His throat had been slit. Guy hadn't changed his details, and Tara was listed as his emergency contact.

Not surprised, glad, or saddened by the news, she understood the piper collected his due from the person Guy had become. And for her, that was the end.

Spoon now in hand, she blew on the savory richness of the fish stew, thinking about the events that had led her to be sitting in this very spot.

When she left Ireland, she flew back to London and met with the producers at BBC4. Their excited response to her proposal, which replaced Guy's, was surreal. She presented a detailed outline of her vision, entitled *The Extraordinary Lives of Ordinary Women Across the Ages,* and they loved it. The only change they wanted to make was to replace "Across the Ages" with "Down Through the Ages." She had been adamant, however, that the title should remain intact because she now knew that the linear concept of time was both an illusion and a delusion.

Months later, she was in Marseille, eager to retrace the steps Clarice had taken so long ago. Smiling, she mused out loud, "Was it so long ago?"

The rich aroma wafting up from the dish in front of her cajoled her back to the present, begging her to take a mouthful.

When the bowl was half-consumed, she laid the spoon on the plate beneath it and picked up a still-warm slice of bread. She pushed her chair back from the table to savor for a moment what she had just consumed and what remained to devour, and her thoughts turned to Dana, Mamó, and the ever-present Cado.

Tara still didn't understand everything that had occurred in her life, nor did she understand everything Mamó had told her. But one thing she understood now was this: She not only had the joyful right but the responsibility to live her life in any way she chose. She would no longer allow others to dictate who she was becoming.

The conscious choice of her path through this lifetime was her vocation. The gifts she brought into this world with her were only gifts if she shared them with others.

Nibbling on the fresh bread, she thought about what had occurred just before leaving Dunsany. She'd seen nothing of Dana after Guy's forceful intrusion and, in the week before she left Ireland, Mamó and Cado were nowhere to be seen, either.

She scoured the countryside for any sign of the trio, but in her heart, she knew she wouldn't see them again, a conclusion that was confirmed just before her retreat from the cottage two days after Guy's departure. She had wandered over to the garden with a steaming cup of coffee in hand to see if the old woman and her trusted companion were sitting at its center. When she rounded the corner of the cottage, the garden was once again a neglected pile of stone rubble and weeds.

Taking another sip of her broth, Tara recalled her last day at the cottage.

She drove slowly down the dirt track, the replacement tires of her rental car gripping well. As she glanced in her rearview mirror to catch one last glimpse of the cottage, she saw no sign of it. Panic and fear subsided to calm relief as a loving voice echoed from deep within her. "Remember, dear one, you can never go back to what used to be. Your joyful job is to be open and aware of the fresh possibilities of each new instance." With those words whispering in her head, Tara sat higher in her seat, readjusted the rearview mirror, and focused on where she was going.

Notes

- Fairy Lullaby. "The Shamrock." (1871)
- The references to intuition in this novel were greatly enhanced by the information contained within the Hrund Gunnsteinsdóttir documentary, entitled *Innsaei*, which explores the subject.

  https://www.imdb.com/title/tt4924624/